THE TOMORROW BOYS

Patrick Denton Mackay

JAKE BOOKS • 2015

Printed in the USA.
ISBN 978-0--69253010-8

Cover art (Glock Angel) by Brendan Murdock
Book design by Sasha Newborn

To purchase The Tomorrow Boys, please order from
Amazon Books under the author's full name

JAKE BOOKS

Titles by Patrick Denton Mackay

Your Majesties
The Crystal Set
Perfect Entropy
Deadpan
Experimental Music
The Book of Jake
The No Theater
A-Metrical Techniques of a Schizophrenic (novel)
Flux Kingdom
Homage to Charlie Koshi
Circuitry
Graffiti Download
Ink Lift (CD)
Below The Frequency of Light (CD)
Graffiti Download (CD)

CONTENTS

to Aaron

THE TOMORROW BOYS

"A paranoid is someone who knows a little of what's going on. A psychotic is a guy who's just found out what's going on."

— *William S. Burroughs*

EMPATHY RESULTS

Edward sat across from the two formula suited men in a drably decorated, dimly lit office at Tellcore Services. They regarded each other in a crisp professional silence. Edward tried to maintain the essential stiff-jaw seriousness for this meeting. He did not know if he would be passed or dropped from his desired C1 psychiatrist position.

"Edward M. Wells?" One man said.

"Yes."

The man coughed, stubbing a cigarette out in a company labeled ashtray.

"774 Slope Drive, Los Angeles, CA. 90292?"

"Yes." Edward flinched as the other man unslit the blinds.

"State Imagination Test 4452?" The man looked at the tape on the table that whirred in analog sensitivity. Edward knew they used the analog and not digital because it could pick up spatial emotions better. Something to do with the relationship with the varying signal of the body. It crackled a little and resonated a lisping circuitry in the room.

Edward looked at both of them. Professional Board Status. Called Checkers by the class, yet were Door Men to the Academy. He looked at the neural film display on the wall where they had watched his reactions. The room was air-conditioned and a fan turned overhead, clicking every once in a while.

"Test subject 654," one man said to the other. The other man nodded and wrote something down on a pad of paper. The office was void of computers. Similar to the analog it was said to get in the way of the human qualities that empathy levels needed in observation. Then the man, who had written on the paper, put his arms on his desk and gazed at Edward point blank.

"You did rather well, Edward, for your C1 position. Rather well..." he trailed off as if deep in thought. "Yet...we were disturbed by your final analysis of the empathy regard for Officer Aremac." He paused and shuffled some papers, looking for something. "They say you were top of your class?" The question passed through Edward coldly. He knew he was being searched.

"Yes," Edward nodded from his chair.

"And your psychological analysis of bi-polar persons was very nice...very nice. Did you mean to insinuate that if you depress from too much dopamine then your dopamine levels should be reduced before the fall?"

"No, sir."

"What did you mean?"

"I meant that if you are bi-polar then you should not take twice the amount of medicine you are taking to mirror the illness."

"Not take?"

"Yes," Edward straightened up in his chair. "I suggested creating a placebo vacuum of the kind that reflects the semantic of bi-polar..."

"I see," the man said, interrupting. He thumbed through some papers in his lap, and leaned back in his chair. "Signed on to experimental practice at the age of 18?"

"I thought I would be more experimental then, sir." Edward

knew they were just winding up...little Skinnerian prompts, Freudian symbols, Jungian synchronicity, Maslowian graphs, Perlsian exaggerations. The man turned and looked at the other.

"Well," the other man said... "your empathy exams were highly unusual." He paused and cocked his head to the right. "You shot the monitor twice."

Edward looked at the man who looked at him. The air between them was curiously relaxed. The fan ticked overhead.

"Yes, sir."

"You shot the synth-officer as a student and as a partner in law..." The man emphasized law. "You shot Officer Aremac once at the top of the stairs and once at the bottom..." The man looked matter of fact at Edward. "Do you think that's proper psychiatric conduct?" The man chipped the suffix of conduct at him, like a German.

"No, sir."

"And the student was..."

"Frank Spec."

"Patient or counselor status?"

"Counselor."

The man's eyebrow rose as he wrote on a piece of paper.

"So you get in a police vehicle, you intervene in a robbery, you get caught by a criminal, you accidentally shoot your ride, you become a student to hide from the error and then shoot the officer again?"

Edward paused. They were prompting him to elucidate upon the scene he could not fully understand himself. He looked at them and replied.

"Yes, sir, the Operation A Gel Tab might have been stronger than the dos..."

"...Sage," the man cut him off, "was perfectly normal, Mr. Wells. Can you tell us why you shot the monitor two times?"

Edward fumbled in his chair. "I, ah, didn't understand how I shot him as a cop or as a student, but..."

"And there was a third shot..." the man looked at his papers... "a woman shot your criminal behind you. You dropped your gun to second level. Officer Aremac picked up your gun and was going to shoot the woman..." he trailed off.... looking at Edward firmly.

"Yes," Edward said. "The woman shot the criminal, I lost my gun, Officer Aremac was going to kill the innocent subject who had saved me...yet it was wrong."

The two men looked at Edward curiously. One of them pulled out another cigarette and lit up. "So, tell me Mr. Wells...empathically...why did you shoot your own partner...twice?"

Edward watched the smoke plume into the fan and dissipate and then settled his eyes upon the two. He took a deep breath. In his mind he still could not believe that the test had even given him this error. He knew it relied upon very fine lines of thought, fine lines of feeling. He knew that his empathic response that he had figured was untenable. Edward looked fixedly at the Door Men and then spoke.

"I shot Sergeant Aremac for love."

The room was dead silent save for the fan. The two men looked at him as if living somewhere else in their heads. A cold distance in which they analyzed facts of emotional significance.

"You mean you killed the law monitor for..." he paused, "love?"

"Yes, sir."

"Did you even know the woman?"

"No, sir."

"How can you kill someone for love if you don't know the subject in question? Love? You cannot love your patients, Mr. Wells."

The question was absolutely absurd. Were they playing him to see how insane he might be?

"No," Edward composed himself. "I shot the officer as both student and partner in law to save an innocent woman."

"But that is against the law," one man said. He turned to the other. "It is against the law to kill, for one, and it is against the law to kill for love, for two."

"But it was a program."

"Yes, but your empathy level was acute. You had high neural stats. You did everything perfectly."

"Yes, sir."

"But you felt joy?"

"The excitement, sir...I felt joy because," Edward paused... "the thrill."

"So how can you, at an empathic level of superior statistic, shoot your synth-officer as both his partner and a student and tell us that your empathy for love is so strong with a woman whom you don't even know that you kill the test monitor...for joy?"

"I don't know, sir."

"You are supposed to know. You, as a C1 certified psychiatrist, are supposed to know." The man flicked his ash in the ashtray. "What if your patients come in with a similar conundrum and you cannot properly sort it out?"

"Patients aren't programs."

"So it's the program's fault?"

Edward stopped. These men, he thought, were clinically insane. But that could be part and parcel for the tests...put the medicine in the most compromised of places and people and see what occurs. He could not deny that the program had a fault, however. And that he was at fault for virtual homicide was telling of the overall insidious nature of the whole State Test process. Nevertheless he had to pass. He looked straight at the two officers.

"I shot the synth-officer because he was going to kill an innocent woman. That I shot him mistakenly or on purpose I do not know. What I do know is that I felt empathy for all subjects yet the greater empathy..." he paused "...was for the innocent woman. I felt happiness."

"We think you were trying to get out of the exam like so many others, Mr. Wells. We think you are trying to flunk intentionally to hide from the test emotion. We..." the man stopped and adjusted the hair on his brow... "we think you killed your test driver two times to do away with the entire C1 processing and get a job freelancing at counselor status in downgraded schools. And you felt...joy, you say?"

"Yes, sir. I felt the joy of love."

"So you think it appropriate if your love interest is being threatened that you save her at all costs? This makes you happy?"

"Yes, sir."

"So you think that if an upstanding, noble, law abiding, innocent person is going to be shot by another upstanding, noble, law abiding, innocent person that you discriminate at a level so particularly refined that you know who to...ah, eliminate?"

Edward followed the man's eyes as he looked at his partner, the language for death becoming sterile.

The man continued. "You think that if my friend here were to try and kill my ephemeral love that I could just shoot him in the head and that would not be contrary to the law?"

"No, sir," Edward shifted in his seat, "I think that if there is a higher value than life it is love and if that love is jeopardized by another value that is just as high yet is faulted by an act, even by mistake, of homicide, then it is the higher value's right to protect itself."

The men looked at Edward in silence.

"How do you know the higher value, Mr. Wells?"

Edward gazed back at them. He could see the tech creases in their faces from years of looking into translucent screens. He could see their formula thoughts percolating and settling behind their expressionless eyes. There really was not a more correct answer than what he had given. To save life, even if it meant a greater good—you must protect it.

"Love is not a higher value, Mr. Wells," the man said. "Love is an irrational reason to hope. Love is a feeling separate from the intellect. Love is the sanguine essence of mutual agreement to live, but it is not a higher value than The State."

Edward knew he had been defeated. Who, after all, would kill someone for love? Whether the medicine was to blame or whether his analysis was faulty, Edward knew that he had fallen. He looked up and watched the men file their papers. Then one of the men looked at Edward and smiled.

"You have passed your empathy exam...low marks. You will be certified C1 psychiatrist. But please remember, Mr. Wells, when love decides to rule the conscience chaos often rules the heart. How can you, after all, shoot someone for love? Your patients will shoot someone for love. Their minds will tyrannically take over their bodies and they will pull the trigger, not you. You must remember the State Codes. Logic and emotion balanced make a better doctor. Emotion in a doctor can be a very dangerous thing, Dr. Wells. We will be watching your progress."

EMPATHY LEVELS

Wells had read one controversy where an identity shot itself in hyperspace mid segue into the translation and the study didn't pass. Pass, he thought...a smart candidate in that fritz...the study had overridden the chemical semantic and got out of the test as a reject. He did not "pass on" was a crack way to look at it. Something about the synapse relay as the neural film gapped. They say this candidate tripped through the micro-environment at the point where the bullet fired...just fell through a "hole" in the program that was supposed to be his head. Then he was booted from the Academy. That nobody could locate his response indicators on the tests after caused a stir. Where had he gone in his head that allowed for a blank? How did he fall out of the hyper drive chemical format that was supposed to issue his empathy levels for classification C1 psychiatrist position? But that was in the early tests. This study was supposedly foolproof. The Net required flawless medicine. You would be dropped from the rehabilitation standards list if you botched it. Edward quivered as the Operation A Gel Tab hit his bloodstream. He began to tremble. Then his eyes shut.

Edward packs into the black and white with his virtual partner, Sergeant Aremac. Aremac is the dub of the synth-officer who drives all the tests, a standard procedure that is, like old DMV exams, supposed to be in the mental seat just incase something goes wrong. Edward's eyes twitch into quick REM.

Aremac puts the shotgun in the rack. Edward tells him it's going to be hot. Aremac takes his coffee and affirms let's roll. They turn out of the police station on a tip that something's going on downtown at Borders Book Store. Edward's Glock feels impressive on his hip. He is aware and sensually heroic in his Kevlar bullet-proof vest. In his mind he conceives that the creed of a cop is to protect and serve the community. Behind the creed he recognizes that there is a lot of other physical nature, substance that young children know when they play cop, substratum like total mass slaughter in mock form where the entire collection of friends who have been invited over to play participate. Like the Pre Post Vital movie, *Lord of the Flies*. Stuff most people don't really think about after seven.

Sergeant Aremac yells as they pull up to Borders and Edward sees a man thieving a woman's purse. They both fall out of the vehicle in a run. Sergeant Aremac has pulled his Thirty-Eight. Edward has, requisite to responsibility levels, the radio on for back up. The man who is stealing the woman's purse runs inside Borders. Aremac stumbles and falls in front of the woman. The woman recovers and steps onto his back and picks up Aremac's Thirty-Eight. Edward misses this glitch and sprints after the man in Borders. He yells Down, Down, Down! to everybody in the bookstore. Every shopper body falls down. The man with the purse runs upstairs. He discharges a weapon at Edward and Edward dives to the ground. He does not notice the victim woman moving behind him. Edward sprints up the stairs without backup. At the top of the stairs in the music section of Borders he discerns no one. He begins to comb the aisles. So intense is the quick of pursuit, Edward forgets about

Aremac. Then, at the end of the aisle as he turns the corner, with his Glock in hand, the purse-snatcher disarms him and puts him in a vise-grip. The snatcher staggers him to the stairwell and runs into the woman whose purse he stole. She is possessed of Sergeant Aremac's Thirty-Eight. The man witnesses the woman with trapped eyes. Edward has become a human shield. The woman is pointing the gun unswerving at Edward. He looks fiercely into her eyes in complete Operation A awe and disbelief. He knows her, but cannot place how he knows her. A familiarity strain in the chemical to force a trust issue perhaps. She closes her eyes tight. He does not know why she is closing her eyes. The gun wavers in her hand like a leaf in the wind. Then she pulls the trigger and he hears the shot pop off into what he thinks is his body. The accent of the shot is deafening. The purse-snatcher behind him, who is holding him in a vise-grip, falls to the ground. As he falls, the purse drops from his hand over the railing and downstairs. The woman turns and runs downstairs. Edward's Glock has fallen to the first level. Sergeant Aremac has recovered, runs in and picks up Edward's gun. The woman, who is running down stairs to get her purse, passes Sergeant Aremac. Sergeant Aremac, thinking the woman has shot Edward, raises his pistol. He aims carefully. A shot fires. Sergeant Aremac drops his gun and falls to the ground. Edward's eyes flinch in chemical override...this wasn't supposed to happen he heard himself think in the depth of his trance. Edward sees Aremac fade into digital death and his body seizes. The responsibility mechanisms in the meds must be upgrades Edward thinks. A test of what? How could the program continue without a monitor? Edward stabilizes and looks down at the woman who has retrieved her purse. He looks to Sergeant Aremac who is motionless on the floor. The Operation A pill is quirking his muscles. He looks in his hands and, in disbelief, finds he is holding the gun of the purse-snatcher. The barrel is hot. When he looks up the woman is gone.

Edward's heart is beating fast. The program will re-loop he thinks! There must be something wrong with the pill! I couldn't have shot Aremac! Aremac is not supposed to die, surely! He looks at the gun in his hand. The barrel is hot.

Then the other empathy identity begins to bleed through. Natural, so they say, at this part of the test...I am supposed to distinguish between right and wrong amongst chaos, the trial for every psychiatrist under fire. I am supposed to do the right thing. Edward's eyes are closed tight. He catches up to the difference of empathy for Officer Aremac and something new, then focuses.

He imagines himself in the role of teacher. He imagines himself walking into a classroom filled with the seething beauty of inexperienced young adults. When he walks in they become silent. Although he is in love with all of them in the most Platonic way, he realizes he must temper them to the multiple difficulties of the world. This is a job he doesn't really desire, but nevertheless imagines. He assigns a project in which all the students have to go out into the world and find an experience that means something to them. They are to go out into the community so that they might learn.

The glitch with Aremac is still pounding in Edward's language center. He fans out in his mind, feeling the edge of what he thinks is going to be disaster. The program...he thinks...must have just skipped or something. Edward realigns his conscience as teacher, eyes fluttering in space-time reflex, awaiting the empathy value.

One of his worst students, Frank, who never listens, goes to Borders Book Store. Not thinking of the assignment, he is just about to boost a CD and finds himself in the midst of a shootout with two policemen running to apprehend a man with a purse. Witnessing the gun battle in which a woman shoots a man holding a cop and the man drops the purse and the other cop runs in and picks up his partner's Glock, Frank pauses as if all of time had been stilled. Frank, who is downstairs, sees the woman, who has shot the criminal, now running downstairs to get the purse. The purse falls next to Frank who picks it up and, trying to help, gives the purse to the woman. In fright Frank drops the CD into her purse as well. She turns away quickly, dropping the gun on the floor next to the student. As the woman runs away, Frank, trying to give her back the gun, pulls the trigger. The woman runs up the stairs and out the front door. Aremac at the top of the stairs crumples to the ground. Frank looks as Aremac falls and, dropping the gun, runs up the stairs and out of Borders.

Yes. This is the innocence role, Edward thinks...shift the empathy from my own mistake to a student's. Who is to blame? Have I, as cop, the responsibility for taking the life of Aremac? Or is it the student's? Whose bullet was it, an innocent student's or mine? Edward shifts in hyperspace in his brain, the trial outing a most important kernel of feeling. Am I supposed to have the proper empathy for my student for killing an officer who is going to kill a woman? Or, rather, am I to drown in doubt that I actually pulled the trigger myself? Am I supposed to now have empathy for the woman who saved me from the purse-snatcher? Edward pauses in disbelief. I can't stop the program, he thinks. It will run right through me to every ounce of psychological irony in my brain. He can feel his jaw vibrating chemical strain. Edward relaxes back into the exam without an answer.

Frank hands in his assignment the next day. This is the story he has produced. Edward reads the story to his imagined self, the teacher he now wants to be, in a classroom with a bunch of wonderful students. The character in the story that was written by his student he realizes is the identity he would prefer to have. He passes the empathy level from cop to teacher, but the decision is critical. What responsibility does he have and what empathy does he feel for the law, for the student? Then, suddenly, Edward begins to shake. The Operation A Tab seems to explode inside of him. This is it, he says to himself. This is when they overlap...if I fail this part I will not be certified. Light blankets him and then he falls into a scintillating, almost out of control plummet of value...

Edward as student has bolted after the woman and he is scared because in Borders there is one dead cop and one dead criminal. Everything is convoluted. When he writes his story he is the teacher reading the story as much as he is the student writing it. What he imagines as a student is that he wants to be the woman who shot the criminal. He wants to be her because she saves the cop whom he doesn't want to be. More than this he wants to be her because she, delivered from Borders, is innocent, as innocent as the shot that felled the criminal, as innocent as her desire to keep her purse, as innocent as himself standing at the bottom of the stairs with her purse. When he tried to give to her the gun, the gun exploded and the policeman at the top of the stairs fell. This is why he runs. When the officer at the stairs is shot, he is shot because a gun went off. Outside of Borders he watches in the crowd with the woman, he and the woman, both of them together as much as apart. As the ambulance comes and Sergeant Aremac is wheeled away, he watches his identity as policeman at the top of the stairs who was preserved by the woman. He watches as he talks to the other policemen. In his hand he sees that he is holding the criminal's gun, his own Glock, and Sergeant Aremac's Thirty-Eight. He talks to the other officers about the weapons. We can hear the story from where we are in the crowd. The chemical pause is to let you know your study is being watched. He is informing the other officers that there was a woman's purse stolen. He and Sergeant Aremac took pursuit. The man with the woman's purse went into Borders. Sergeant Aremac fell in front of the woman. Edward pursued the criminal inside the store. He did not know that the woman was behind him. The criminal went upstairs where Edward followed. In the music aisle the criminal with the purse disabled him and held him with his gun to his head. Making his way to the stairs, with Edward as a human shield, the criminal ran into the woman whose purse he had stolen. The woman, holding onto Sergeant Aremac's Thirty-Eight, closed her eyes. A shot fired and then the criminal fell, dropping the purse over the rail. Edward tried to see through to her face, something inside his guts demanding her presence. The medicine flickered film light of a silhouette. The student picked up the gun, the criminal's gun on the floor. The woman ran downstairs to get her purse. Edward looked up and saw Sergeant Aremac holding Edward's Glock. As Aremac took aim at the woman he thought had shot Edward, the criminal's gun in the student's hand misfired. At that moment Edward saw Sergeant Aremac fall to the ground. He was not aware of anybody else with a firearm save for himself. After Edward shifted to Sergeant

Aremac and assessed the wound, he did not witness the woman. All he could see was Sergeant Aremac who, in the stroke of time in which he administered CPR, was failing to breathe. He continued administering CPR until Sergeant Aremac's pulse stopped. Edward looked at his closed eyes. This is not to be happening he thought. The test driver should not have been hurt. Edward fluxes in chemical relay and continues involuntarily...he was my partner. He was... When he looks up nobody is in Borders. When he looks for the woman downstairs all Edward sees is the Thirty-Eight, which is Sergeant Aremac's weapon. When he realizes that Sergeant Aremac is dead and there is nothing else he can do he walks outside with the weapons you now see before you. As you can see, all the weapons have been discharged. This is all I know.

Edward heaved up from the sentient patches on his body. The isolation chamber was deafening silent. His heart was beating fast. Sweat dripped from his brow. It wasn't supposed to happen that way he thought. The synth-officer was not to be killed. There was no way he was going to end up rejected from the assimilation process. His responsibility had been acute, his awareness had been sharp, and even his empathy was...no, it was questionable...what was it? Edward reached deep into his brain to find his reactions recovering in shock. Three shots had fired, the woman's, the student's, and his own. Did The State Test seek to split the empathy of an individual candidate to see their reaction? Choose between innocence killing Officer Aremac, or responsibility saving a woman...who had saved him? He focused intensely. He had pulled the trigger that killed Aremac, his synth-partner, and he had pulled the trigger as the student, both mistakenly. Edward's eyes went wide as he found, deep inside his head, an intellectual emotion that wasn't supposed to be there. It was joy. Joy and something else...just a small flicker channeled through his mind in swift imagery. The woman or Officer Aremac...that was it...that was what The State wanted. The State wanted for him to discern the miscalculation of Officer Aremac as law and that of the most forbidden homicide of a policeman in order to save an innocent woman.

He closed his eyes to recall fully what the test *could not* want of its takers. But he knew it could not want what he was thinking. It could not desire that he, Edward Wells, candidate for C1 psychiatrist, kill Officer Aremac. Everything for Edward suddenly hung in peculiar balance. He thought—amazed by the drugs' powers—I must choose *the reason* why I would have shot Officer Aremac, as both his partner and innocent student. A great space crushed into his guts. He reeled out of the State Exam echo and back into himself. What was the best answer? Then, somewhere in his very core a word appeared. The word was Love. He perceived it in his brain flux like a beautiful and terrifying jellyfish, the word that had for so many years been eroded by the horror of State Controls. For love, he thought, innocently. He knew the test would not take this emotional answer. He understood that the logical solution would forbid these results. His body shook in post pixel pill withdrawal. Love...love could be the only reasonable emotion why he irrationally pulled the trigger. And that is what The State wanted. It wanted him to find the most vulnerable emotion inside of him to expose him to the most profound irrational necessity. With the deepest empathy that he could fathom in the post quick terror of a virtual crime, Edward could not deny that he shot Officer Aremac to save the woman in his head...because he loved her.

THE EMOTION GARDENS

Cleo slid her I.D. card into the female check system and walked down a hall with softly lit advertisements fluxing from pixel plasma boards. The advertisements blipped out a seductive rhythmic generation. "Ride your elevator to the top of this experience." "Creep into the visceral jack and pass through." "Flow into a circuitry with friends." "Take kick back to your fondest memories." "Buy jazz and beat through to the node." "Download truth and see for yourself what reality is better." The ads promised a variety of things, she knew. Elevator was the name of a joy packet you could get to uplift your emotions. Creep was the common name for the visceral depression of sadness. Flow was another name off the street for a trust option. Kick was what the industry called a surprise sale. Jazz was another word for kindness. And Truth was exactly what a majority of buyers wanted in order to see reality. Cleo opened the door at the end of the hall and stepped into the cache room, passing the tear vats.

Her position as librarian was not easily won. Many people wanted to work in the Emotional Library Gardens, some for illicit reasons, others for reasons of self-service. Cleo had luckily persuaded the State run facility officers to higher her. She had a clean record. Her work at St. Mary's, another governmental institution, was good. Her ability at organization was adept.

The room possessed a running fountain in the center of an array of shelves with chip-stored emotions from many times and many places. The market for emotions had begun at the turn of the century in The Big Dry when one entrepreneur found, like the bottle water industry, a public desire for the deficit of feeling, which had become noticeable as a progressive problem after the third Depression. The public was in a political and economic flux that called for radical creation. People from depressed to ecstatic states, which were said to be dangerous, were beginning to act in unification. Sadness, joy, hate, trust, anticipation, surprise, kindness, pity, indignation, envy, fear, anger, disgust, and love grew into a market both on street and off. Some said to balance. Others said to record. And still others said that it was the new industry to replace the drug market. Visceral emotions and emotions that were pure, or raw, were high in demand, the experience of something close to depth feelings. At first popular in the media industries, like film, and news, the emotion market spread out and into all substrata of society. The effect on the public of everything from hate to love was seen as liberation.

As librarian Cleo was responsible for finding the right emotion for the right person and then checking out the emotion for however long it would last. The mind's memory in most of the interactions was augmented so that there would be not only a visceral response, but also a visual. The longest lasting emotion oddly was not hate, or love, or anger, or joy. The longest lasting emotion was sadness, sometimes shame. Anticipation burned off very quickly, as did fear, and disgust. The medium ones that most people would use, such as kindness and joy—although joy tended to crash quickly— were common amongst the elite. The strangest one, trust, tended to last only a few minutes and then was said to fall to skepticism or despair, which was also valuable. People had a choice: you could choose between synthetic and raw classifications. The synth-emotions were much cheaper than the unadulterated caches. They had a median shelf life. But when it came to the highest demand, a demand that was, outside the library and in, the purity of emotion was the most valuable. They had to lock purity up behind special sense security after a thief cracked the library and hiked the chip vials. That was all the thief stole. He didn't even touch happiness or ecstasies. On the market a pure sadness, or a pure joy, that lasted for one half hour, would go for thousands of dollars. Pure trust was, at its highest, a million. Pure hate, in its raw state, had also become a very high commodity. It was said that countries had stockpiled emotion like tea and oil, but nobody could ever verify it. The binge centers for emotional markets were often in cities where there was some form of interactive industry of media like in Hollywood. If you went out on the street you could find emotion in the rawest, broken down for the best dollar. Jazz, Kick, Circuit, Flow, Jake, Emphatic, Creep, White, Sleep, and others. Elevator rooms had become common, places where joy and happiness were sold and you could sit and drink smart drinks while being moved emotionally by chips. Yet that was mostly synth and the true sales of visceral emotions would, on the average, take place privately.

Cleo knew secretly why she had desired this job. She desired it because her curiosity about the mentally ill could be investigated. She was at the node of the greatest question: how does a human feel to life? Although not common knowledge to most individuals, the mentally ill were considered closer to raw experience and emotion than normal people. She had read a study where it was reported that The State actually valued its millions of mentally ill people because they represented an imaginative and physical force. What that force was they did not say. This did not prevent discrimination. Many still thought the mentally ill to be a problem. Yet The State kept them very well, like possessions or artifacts, well groomed as they say. There was research that she had found that informed her of a most salient point: mentally ill people were considered valuable because they were broken. Broken, she thought. What is the value of being broken? Wasn't everyone broken in a way? As she read on, however, she discovered that "the constant state of difference in a schizophrenic person creates an emotional falling and then rebuilding of the body." So that's it she thought. The mentally ill are valuable because they feel. They not only feel, but they feel deeper than most people due to the fact that their emotional centers have been crushed.

She looked into the tear bottles. She could remember reports of violence as people of the past fought over happiness. People had actually died. For every emotion there was established a different value. People had crunched the numbers and if you were capable of laughter and you were not aware of the price of sadness you were considered a fool. She looked at the tear bottles. They had become an art every since The Big Dry, a one year vacuum, much like a dessert, where people were in complete automatic state due to the change over. Then a random creative, a young mentally ill man, had sold his tears in a bottle and a craze erupted. Capture your sadness physically and sell it on high. He had gone on to some great emotional resonances.

There were a lot of bottles, mostly of famous people. In the refined section the salt had been extracted leaving crystalline matrixes upon slides. Those would be infused with some ecstatic legal drug agent. People would drink, sniff, shoot, smoke, and insert chips to get a feel, mostly moneyed people, with means to support this expensive habit. On the outside, the street, of course, would do different things.

On a political level Cleo had heard that the Emotion Gardens, of which there were several per city, were used to map the fluxing topography of past present and future. How they did it she did not know. Something to do with satellite grid readings that picked up the emotional resonance of persons. Like a picture taken of feeling in the early Empathy Tests for loyalty, balance, and what they said was brotherly love. When they put it together after the Tech Revolution you see where the sadness conglomerates, where happiness collects, where the feelings of hate, and disgust act out, where love and shame commingle. She had heard that they are called Sym Maps, for The State to see agitation and reactionary movement. One customer at the high level had come in for Trust, a very high paying customer, and had told her, after he took the mix, that one could read the cityscape from space like the surface of a pond for its emotional future. He had said something about an electronic Braille Project where empathy was lifted from the streets and neighborhoods so that The State could register the emotional levels of a textural visceral alphabet. But this was never confirmed.

The bell at the entrance rang. The fountain masked a form hobbling toward her. Cleo could see that he wore a hat, had a cane and was unsteady on his feet. She watched him approach and place a bag on the counter. He was breathing heavily. His face was bulbous and red.

"May I help you?" Cleo asked.

He coughed once. "Yes, I am here to pick up the collective emotional array I called in."

Cleo looked down on her data board. "Dr. Bessingham?"

"Yes." He smiled a great smile. "Nothing like a good elevator on a smoggy day."

Cleo smiled at him. She noticed that next to his name was the order. A full vat of emotional array for Official State Party.

"We are dry," Bessingham said.

"Of course," said Cleo. She reached into the back of a vault and pulled out a briefcase. "You want the entire Circuit?"

"Yes."

She looked at him shaking in front of her...probably deficit post emotional. She placed the case on the counter.

He smiled and pulled out a check. "I don't want this to be, ah, known," he said looking carefully at Cleo. He winked. Known, she thought, a check would make it indelible.

Cleo nodded. There were many private accounts she knew. But why a check?

He wrote out the amount and then smiled at her. "Nice

fountain in here. Is it alive?"

"Yes," Cleo said. "You can talk to it if you want. It is a divining."

Bessingham looked at the fountain and said, "Am I going to live past sixty?"

The fountain gushed and then responded. "No."

Bessingham looked at Cleo askance.

"It's not obviously capable of real prediction." She looked at him kindly.

Bessingham's eyes had slitted. "I'll try again..."

"It only gives yes and no answers," Cleo said.

Bessingham looked at her and then back to the fountain.

"Are we capable of knowing the truth?"

The fountain bubbled and then responded. "Yes."

"Will I," he continued, "be capable of telling the truth?"

Silence. Then the fountain gushed, "yes."

"Well that's good enough," he said, taking the case from Cleo.

"Did you put love in here?" he asked, almost nervously.

"Yes," said Cleo. "Every emotion is in the case, and there are doubles. Call when it runs out. I'll send someone to pick up the empties."

"You are very kind."

Cleo watched Bessingham walk out the door. She looked down at the check. Her eyes flinched and then focused. Ten million dollars...

She had taken, when she arrived, a retroactive Ginkgo pill to quiet her head. Headaches had come and gone frequently now for about a year. The pill had begun to resolve. She went to check the emotions for love. There were liquid essences, chip storage electricals, chalk substance, and powder. How they had managed to sort it all out she was still learning. At first they had hooked people up to trauma machines and read their mental relay and were able to store it in the sense data reactors. But that was old. Now they simply lifted you via an interaction of cerebral magnetism that augmented feelings of all sorts. She looked at the love vials.

She was recalling her childhood as she worked, the retroactive a way for her to avoid her brain pain. How long had it been since she had felt love? She looked at the vial and then accidentally knocked it over. The liquid essence of love spilled out into a truth chip. Suddenly she recalled her first relationship. Had it soaked through her finger? She closed her eyes while shaking her hand. Edward was his name. What a strange occurrence in our school she thought. The liquid sizzled on the chip. "Damn it," she said out loud, "the truth is going to be ruined." What irony. Love ruining truth. What irony this surround of stored emotions that are imbibed by the wealthy to save their souls. She could see an image of Edward in her mind. Love and truth burning together, destroying each other in minute chip circuitry.

SPIRITUAL ZONES

Edward Wells withdrew an American Spirit from a pack of cigarettes and looked at the sign. Lorretos. Seattle Company of superior coffee manufacture. Purveyor of fine beverages. Multiple cafes wed to the concept of good taste, and air-conditioned stores with knick-knacks for the comfort of professional clientele. He took a deep hit off his cigarette, flicked it into the street and tried to get his hand to stop shaking.

He had just secured the High Standing award for a psychosis study that crisscrossed manic episodes with psychosis and proved that if you are mentally ill you can do special things that will knock the disease out. His paper stated "that a counter 'fritzkrieg' of the nature of symbolic undulation supplanted the neural synapse with a 'docking' symbolic harbor effect that usurped the power of delusions by surrounding the enigma with the best place to weather the storm." Hence 'docking'. He perceived Lorretos again and walked in, aware of the reflection of himself in the dark glass. In his mind he wasn't feeling the satisfaction of having won a professional trophy.

He had imparted his paper at the conference. He had illustrated it in the most professional manner. Yet he could not help an alien occurrence, which, by page ten, had undressed him. Edward, absorbed in his study, had become psychologically powerless. All those years after he had passed the empathy levels...he had crawled to the top. His practice had been given "liberal" status. Indeed, he had done something that was most contrary to The State: he had been allowed the C3 level of social interaction that would afford his patients and him experimental practice. And he had only broken down once, a write-off he had claimed was an inside psych trauma study that the authorities shrugged at, letting him proceed to C3.

That he was suddenly confronted with an intense frailty in his paper hadn't stopped him. He had read on, casually, tossing off the concept as if he were a great orator. Slowly, however, as he advanced his ideas, he had become what he thought of now as 'overly' present. No one had noticed save for himself. He had upheld the greatest thoughts he had penned. But each word that he uttered began to strip from him his....he thought of shells...calcium, eggs, psychological carapace, his Reichian body armor. Yes, he reasoned as he looked into his reflection, I stripped myself down to the bare quick, the minimum, my tender inner softness. So he trembled. He could not stop the trembling. He trembled and almost folded in the glass of Lorretos feeling more naked than an anemone touched by a stick in a tide pool. Buckled, he thought. Sheer buckling. The door opened. He walked to the cashier and asked for a coffee. His hand on the counter fumbled and he could barely hold his wallet. Withdrawing a couple of ones he handed the cashier his money and gazed at the paraphernalia surrounding him. His look took on the material intensely. The coffee pots became a deluge of information he could not process, the baubles and candies struck him as liquid and squirmy, animated in their material to something other. He thought of a thunderstorm and the tumult of rain that erodes hillsides. He thought of worms. Then, as if struck by a bolt of lightning, Edward fell sideways and almost knocked over his drink. Scrutinizing the room for privacy, his eyes found the restroom and he staggered to the door. His hand on the handle felt like a noodle, slippery around the knob. Managing to find his grip he turned the handle and flung himself inside.

Jesus Christ he blurted to the emptiness. His eyes focused in and out and settled upon the Georgia Pacific towel dispenser. Then, hand still on the knob, Edward took in his surrounds: Kohler toilet, Sentry mirror, anonymous sink. Tissue littered the floor and the trashcan was full of used paper towels. He stumbled to the sink and turned on the tap. The water was cold and the sound that emitted from the on position was a high running-water sound that somehow comforted him. Having washed his face he hovered to the toilet and sat down. As if with all the clarity in the world he experienced his insides grumble and then emit. LIFE! He thought. What kind of life is this! His hands smushed against his face. He had heard that people had epiphanies in toilets, shit that makes even the Dalai Lama simple. Profound moments on the throne of release. Sick, he thought, I am a sick professional scientist; I should not ruminate about life over the stink hole! But he did. He couldn't stop the out-welling, perhaps from the previous jitters. With his hands upon his face and in his most disgusting and yet pleasurable moment, he suddenly was struck with the irony. He spoke it out loud. "This is the most profoundly private place on the planet." His hands slid from his eyes. Utter shock riveted him. This is the most private place on the planet, he repeated. The information froze him somehow outside of every gigabyte that had ever stored fake solace. He realized that he had just understood the entire problem. The entire problem of Post Vital life...He had had no privacy since The Techno Revolution...

Upon rising from the Kohler toilet, Edward Wells felt all the shit in the world that was stopped here, but free. Here, in the most disgusting of places, the figurative pile of excrement in the world faded into actual truth. He rose into his newfound realization and pushed the toilet flush. This is it, he thought, looking into the abyss, this is the whole solution. In the trial of human existence, the same way inoculants eradicate disease; the only remaining

31

peaceful place was this vital room. And how much would anyone pay for such realization, for such peace? Millions. Indeed, what Edward perceived was that this hole, this sanctum sanctorum where all must come to empty themselves, to clean, to become washed of the vileness of their inner and outer selves—in this place there was no camera, no mic, no problems, no essence of the big, over-crowded world. It was like another unknown and unknowingly over-used world that had justice in it. He looked around. The white tile walls were pure. The Kohler had taken from him his product of digestion. The wash from the sink was without the "mix" of everyday technological dissonance. He splashed his face with cold water, water that could very well have been from any desert well upon earth, granted the coalesce of this molecular necessity. He saw it in all of its H2Oness as a vital poem. Suddenly rejuvenated, Edward stepped to the door and turned the handle. The knob was cold and reassuring. Thrusting open the door he put himself in motion and into the phenomenal recognition that his paper, a paper that he had been working on since he passed the empathy exams, which he had loosely titled, *The Harbor*, created literally to save people, was exactly this space. It was this very theory of toilet that he had been trying to separate from the complex medical world. Had it somehow, *coup de plume*, created this "place"? Was this part of his addendum address...a sort of freak continuation of the answer of his thesis? This room. These amenities. All were far superior to the meds, he felt. He mused about the new-found reservoir. Nobody noticed his face relaxing into the room, his jaw unwinding, his eyes without the fragmented zip effect of pixel screen, un-crashed into by the tech barrage. Then he walked out of Lorretos, out and into the understanding of his profound thought. Passing the window, he looked into his silhouette in the glass and recalled his experimental patients.

Mark Nichols. Paranoid schizophrenic with bi-polar symptoms. Terrified of machines. Prone to sporadic hallucination. Uses hallucination to cause reality to change. Subject to major dissonance with authorities. Shaky in public settings. Classified unstable.

Jack Spillain. Classic case bi-polar schizoaffective depressive. Five four pressure cooker. Cleft palate. Difficulty speaking. Expresses his words in gesture. Fighter. Fights everything. Thinks pugilism is art. Will, if insulted or talked to the wrong way, act out violently. Yet insecure and oddly tender.

E.L. (Edmund Little) Diagnosed mixture paranoid bi-polar kleptomaniac. Nice young man. Came to him through the parole board. Chatty. Almost high wired with manic joy. He is a specialty booster. Leave your smile next to him and he'll boost your teeth. Tendency to test limits of thievery upon the system by direct confrontation. Goes manic, then crashes, then goes on thievery kicks to save himself. First class liar. Tries to get out of everything.

Frank Spec. High-class paranoid schizophrenic. Enjoys attention. Tendency to exaggerate doom. Likes oration. A test subject addressee for The Psychiatric Board. Professed professional pre-mortem obituary scribe. Paranormal hackwork. Possible prescience. Said to be able to predict death.

Norbert Cherry. An extreme empath. Feels everything. Classification schizoaffective. Prone to hallucination. Mumbler. Chants his way through society. Highly sensitive to space and time. Can intuit anything…location, feeling, emotion, danger, yet cannot feel love.

They had been with him since he made C3. He thought of his patients fondly. They were mostly disheveled, lost, disability-struck, fritz kings. All of them had fallen hard, a requisite for experimental. All had quirks so beyond they fluttered like manic butterflies between total floral dissolution and pollination brilliance. Yes, there were heroes. My fallen angels, he thought. They had all looked into the abyss and the abyss had looked back. What they had become, involuntarily, in their adaptation, was something quite profound he thought. Profound enough to have him constantly in awe at what their perception would do next. Crushed by medicine, resurrected by medicine, taken down by society, compartmentalized into this disease name and that, shuffled like a madhouse deck of cards in some great gamble between society, God, and fragmentation of reality pitching from their desperate mouths. He could not fathom half the stuff they came up with. You just had to look the right way, they said. But what were they looking at really? They had given Edward glimpses of other worlds so private he had felt like he was trespassing on the divine. The currents they had to swim in, the cold electric world interfaces, separation, shallow visions, conformity, status-quo responses. Who lived more? His patients or regular people? Edward could not really compare them, so unusual was his discourse and socializing with his experimental group. And then, in the moments where they connected and became alive in their own ways, moments when the world in them seemed to collide like some Big Bang and they gave birth to the truth of their souls, the unfathomable truths that were to be unwritten, hardly noticed fields of profoundly deep perception—*these* lost worlds were precious. Universes that no one would understand unless they listened. Unless they felt.

He paused and looked in the glass through his body and into something either vacant in him or simply lost. The depths of space had been charted, the human had been cloned, the world had global government, water ran all electrical systems...but the mind, the fallen mind...where had it gone, what did it see, how did it return, and what did it return with? These minds still remained largely uncharted. All topography would be hard pressed, he thought, to define the difference between the charted space systems and that of my patients' minds.

Edward passed the glass and his body shifted unusually in the reflection, like a shiver or a ghost in flow with the very melting sand that made the pane reflect, the very pain of his patients who reflected through him. Farther, he thought, than the edges of our Milky Way man had reached out. How far would they reach out to another person? His eyes turned away from the glass he was looking in. How far would the mind go?

MARK NICHOLS

Edward's first patient was Mark Nichols. Mark who had broken down after downloading every ounce of information he conceived into the Net. The same Mark who, after this engagement, could not tell whether the past was the future, the future the present, or now was elsewhere.

And in a manic continuum Mark could not stop. He had purchased a ticket on line to get his body back and now, still freaking out on the plane, soared over the LA basin. It was enough that he had made it through customs, let alone onto a commercial airline that was showing a pre-21st century *Matrix*. His mind—what he thought was another mind, a mind in a psychosis, a mind that he was going to save—replayed at hyper cut-up speed his entire trial in the airport.

There he stood in LAX with a backpack, as alone as he would ever be amongst the hundreds of flyers. The security was heavy, like intelligent molasses, sticky with the urgency of the

times. Every eyeball from every individual violated his sacred being. More importantly, he did not know if they knew that their
existence was a fabrication of a group mind, a Ubiquitous Mind
that might deter him from his mission. As he ambled through the
crowd he thought-blocked as best as he could, head bowed as he
shuffled along. His thought-blocking worked so well that he forgot
whom he was when asked for his passport at the ticket counter.

"Hello. Mr. Nichols?"

He stared at the polite, windup-doll ticket lady with make-
up and nametag. I am not Mr. Nichols he thought to himself. Who
the hell is Mr. Nichols? In the background slur of his neuron landscape, fritzing at hyper speed, he could see Billy the hamster, his
little Bill, running around madly on the wheel. Trying with all its
might to go somewhere. Somewhere desired. Like the billions of
people in the world. Billy kept his brain brewing with every turn.
A minute later the address of the ticket lady reverbed through the
thin skin of their thin space. She repeated.

"Mr. Nichols, are you carrying..."

"Bill."

She stopped short and looked at him quizzically not knowing what to make of this difference, what he just said; the announcement out of line. Just as suspicion was popping into her
eyes, Mark managed reentry into the real world.

"What is the Bill?" he said, cryptically.

"What?"

"For the ticket?" He mused, then, of his hamster, the existence of the hamster, and the existential existence of his hamster.
Indeed, he considered what Bill was and how in the hell his Bill
could be a "Bill for the ticket." A ticket to what. To eating? A circus? Mark tried to conduct the digression but could not.

"You have already paid, Mr. Nichols." Her face turned into a
surprised here-is-your-prize smile. Then she continued.

But Mark was slipping back and forth through visions, auditory sound bytes and paranoid schizophrenia. The blender word-
salad hyper-paranoia of perception overwhelmed:

Are you carrying any bombs, guns, knives, or any sort of

explosive paraphernalia that you would like to declare, anything
dangerous, anything we should put you in jail for, torture you for,
lock you up in Guantanamo for, disappear you for, essentially ruin
your life for...

The messages in Mark's brain ad-libbed her fundamental
question. He knew it had something to do with airplane etiquette,
but still his mind rebelliously filled in the blanks.

Has anyone given you a nuclear device that you plan to det-
onate on the plane, has anyone exposed you to small pox or given
you any anthrax or have you contracted the Ebola virus or any...

Mark stood, terrified and amazed, looking at his creativity
effusively beating through her. He could not imagine in the entire
world how he could be so creative since the accident that landed
him in St. Mary's Institute for the healing of the insane, with his
life support, Dr. Wells. How, in all the phenomenal world, had his
mind changed from the stable, stand-in-line-obsequious man, to
the radical, hyper-paranoid, shatter-glass reflective somewhat be-
yond-all-reason human? How?

The ticket lady persisted.

Would you like to declare your soul before you go into the
heavens and possibly crash into a mountain at five hundred miles
per hour, liquidate in a ball of jet fuel, get shot out of the sky by
friendly fire, die of a poisoned microwave fish selection, choke on
ice during air turbulence, trip and fall down the stairs upon land-
ing, get sucked through a bullet hole made by a man posing as a
nun in first class?

"Yes, Nichols, that's it." Mark could barely contain himself.
If she had said all those things then they could happen, which
meant that...

"Here's your ticket. Boarding in forty minutes at gate six."
The ticket lady smiled.

Mark looked, trying not to think of gate six as the gate to
hell, looked at her in complete disbelief and then hurried away
to a corner of the rotating restaurant upstairs where he ordered
a very large Long Island and drank it as if he had not had water in
ten days. He shook.

But it was worse at the metal detector.

After thoroughly searching his pockets for all metal objects, which amounted to one dollar and fifty-one cents worth of change, his keys, a miniature key chain with a metal frame picture of Billy, he felt confident and calmed into the line. Yet the eyes—the eyes of everyone that judged, that held him as if holding Satan himself—were metaphysical frisks that wounded him to the Nth degree. Head cast down to avoid such stares, he put his bag on the X-ray rampart and then put his metal belongings into the tray, glanced at the green light of the portal and stepped through. Right at the middle of the portal the light flashed red and the machine whizzed. Upon hearing the report, ten guards with big Kevlar laden chests and black uniforms looked at him with suspicion.

"Could you step back through, sir," the portal security said in what sounded like a voice from an automated answering service.

Mark was trying not to be paranoid. He began thinking of Heaven and if Heaven had customs like this. What if? He shuddered involuntarily. He decided that he did not want to go there.

"Empty your pockets," the security said blankly.

A message played through the back of his mind. "The woman, holding onto Sergeant Aremac's Thirty-Eight, closed her eyes. A shot fired…" What the message was he did not know. He had become porous, he thought. The diaspora of the universe somehow invading him easier than regular people.

Mark turned out his pockets and went through again. The buzzer sounded off another time and five of the big guards looking at the spectacle shifted in their seats, hands dropping to gun level.

"Please step aside, sir," the portal frisker said.

He closed his eyes… "the criminal's gun in my hand misfired. At that moment I saw Sergeant Aremac fall…"

Mark stepped aside, but he was bewildered. Had they said, "please step outside, sir?" Obediently, he moved for the door, mentally allowing for the message to pass through…could they see?…this action incited yelling.

Mark stopped and turned back to the fury in their eyes,

angry at the translation that he had mishandled, angry that he was an anomaly, excited by the action. He returned to the metal detecting portal and they took a device to him and began sweeping him like a rag doll, prostrate in front of an audience of now very nervous but fascinated travelers. When the detector got to his shoe it beeped.

"What do you got in your shoe, huh?" said the guard who had motioned for the others to come over. They surrounded him, hands now on the butts of their Glocks.

"When I tried to give her the gun the gun fired and the policeman at the top of the stairs fell." Mark listened in his head. This must be the other airport security, he thought. The physical symbiotic echo effect of the paranoia of the public that has coalesced over the years into the foci of fear. A patchwork of messages overlain somehow. The reality of the situation was becoming terrifying.

"Take off your shoe, Mr.," said one guard, who now had enough professional distance to draw his gun and blow Mark away if it was a bomb.

"I can explain, I, you see I put it in there, so I don't have to remember and forget that it is in there and... 'as the woman runs away, Frank, trying to give her back the gun, pulls the trigger...'"

Mark considered the message. He knew a Frank, Frank Spec in his experimental group with Wells...professional schizophrenic. He translated...This must be a contiguous paranoia, he thought...I must be hearing a virus of the overall system under attack by a rogue media! He turned back to the officer.

"Slowly," said the security, "take off the penny loafers very slowly."

Mark was now hopping on one foot trying to get his loafer off, hopping like a pogo, very awkwardly, in the hand of a child who is just learning.

"Stop moving, stop moving," the security said.

"Everything is convoluted...the policeman at the top of the stairs crumples to the ground..."

"But I am just, I mean I just the shoe, it has a..." Mark's shoe ejected along with its contents. One toenail clipper ricocheted off the cop's bulletproof vest. Instantly the five other cops watching drew their guns and started yelling. "DOWN! DOWN!"

Suddenly in Mark's head a spool of action reeled out into the space around him, like some kind of resonant living text that blanketed his surrounds. He squinted, reading it.

"Every shopper body falls down. The man with the purse runs upstairs. He discharges a weapon at me and I dive to the ground. I do not notice the victim woman running behind me. I sprint up the stairs without backup. At the top of the stairs in the music section of Borders I see no one. I begin to comb the aisles. So intense is the feeling of pursuit I forget about Aremac. Then, at the end of the aisle, as I turn the corner with my Glock in hand, the purse-snatcher disarms me and puts my identity in a vise grip. He drags me to the stairwell and runs into the woman whose purse he stole. She is holding Sergeant Aremac's Thirty-Eight. The man looks at the woman with trapped eyes. I have become a human shield. The woman is pointing the gun directly at me. I look fiercely into her eyes in complete awe and disbelief. She closes her eyes tight. I do not know why she is closing her eyes. The gun wavers in her hand like a leaf in the wind..."

"But," Mark said, completely diminished and becoming terrified, the situation plugging him into a million television channels of response. However, a big hand grabbed him and threw him to the ground silencing his protest. A boot stomped on his back.

"It's all right everyone, it's all right. Just a nail clipper. Just a nail clipper. Louie, let him up."

Mark, from his spread-eagle position, rose slowly. "I have run after the woman and am scared because in Borders there is one dead cop and one dead criminal..."

The transmission did not seem to broadcast through the officers, Mark noticed.

"Now," the guy who told Louie to let him up said, "Why do you have a nail clipper in your shoe?"

"To remember to cut my nails."

"Likely story," Louie chipped to the other. "Were you going

to use the file to do something on the plane?"

"I don't use the file, I am not on the file, I use only the clip-per," replied Mark, now looking at the cop, looking, as he stammered, a total wreck of vitally strange cop curiosity. The cop iced him back with a metal I-can-fucking-kill-you-and-get-off stare.

"She closes her eyes tight. The gun wavers in her hand like a leaf in the wind. Then she pulls the trigger…" Mark watched in horror as a bullet blew through the head of officer Louie. Then, in some kind of noir effect the cop's head recomposed.

"Sure. Sure. Why was it in your shoe, you can tell us? You know it is illegal, under the new laws, to keep any metal objects that have lethal potential concealed."

"But, it is a toenail clipper," whined Mark, becoming scared of the field interaction, as if he were being effected by an unknown dosage he and all psychotics must interpret as they feel from para-noia to different states of arduous chaos. "It is not a lethal weapon. I would never clip someone to death, you can't do that because…" But the physics was lost on security.

"Yeah sure. Tell that to the inmates in San Quentin. You are going to have to come with us."

Mark was shuffled away, beset by a group of ten guards in Homeland Security black. They brought him to a room and bolted the door. The room was white, much like the special room for hard cases at St. Mary's. The room the doctors there called Sanctuary or The White House on their funny days. In a minute the door without a handle opened and two men with suits entered.

"Ok. We know who you are. We know where you are go-ing. We know what you ate for breakfast in the morning. We know what got you interned in St. Mary's in 2015. We know that you take meds and that you are barely stable on meds. We know that your doctor is one Edward Wells. And we know you were given an Operation A rather than Amadine this morning by your doctor. What are you seeing?"

Mark shivered in his seat. An Empathy Exam pill? Dr. Wells had given him this! He looked up at the security.

"Nothing."

"Why the nail clipper?"

Mark looked at both of them. Did they know that they were under psychical attack? Did they know?

"A shot fires. Sergeant Aremac drops my gun and falls to the ground. I look to Sergeant Aremac who is motionless on the floor. I look in my hands and find I am holding the gun of the purse-snatcher. The barrel is hot…"

Mark looked at one of the security's head split open as a nine-millimeter dum dum popped through. He looked at his hands. A Browning fluxed apparent and then disappeared. He looked up at the man he had shot. His face recomposed into a smile. Mark wondered if they were in Ubiquitous with him or if they were rogue agents outside the group mind. The bullet must have been virtual, Mark thought. His eyes widened and tried to see the damage his hallucination had done…if it was hallucination, but he could see only a blank face. Some chemical was acting out he considered, a chemical violence in a virtual or real format he could not tell. The Operation must be acting as an empty drug vortex and is convincing my neural messages into enhanced agitation. The officers didn't seem to know that he had just blasted a hole through the questioner's skull. Yet Mark was oddly pacified by the virtual violence…like a movie, the mesh making him less frightened of the law, the attack comforting, like danger in media.

Mark found composure. If he revealed his visions off meds he would be taken away for life. "I don't want to forget to cut my nails," he said sheepishly.

"Sure. And I am the Queen's mother. Were you going to use it to disable the pilots and crash the plane? You can tell us. Other people have manipulated clippers with that very intent."

"I don't even know how to use it to do anything like that. I barely know how to cut all my nails."

"All right. So you cut your nails with it and that's all?"

"Yeah."

"Don't you know anything about airports? DON'T you know that we are in war and in war everything, even a nail clipper, is lethal potential? Do you know that the taxpayers are paying for your interrogation and our time as we speak and that they would be pissed to know that some imbecile like a nail clipper toting schitz is wasting their valuable money? I bet you didn't know that did you."

"No," Mark acquiesced. But he knew the general public was paying for this.

"Ok. What we are going to do is let you go on your flight. But if you so much as show up on our radar in the near or far future you are going to be either cuffed, snuffed, or rebuffed so bad that you wished you never were potz. GOT IT!"

"Yes, sir."

The flashback in Mark's head slipped away like a receding tide on some electric shoreline. The stewardess rolled up and asked him if he would like a headphone for *The Matrix*.

"Is it free?" he asked in relapsed contortion, hoping that she would say yes, yes to confirm that *The Matrix* was actually free. As he looked at her holding the headphone he could not deny a very important observation of the entirety of this debacle. With an Operation A his mind had seen the movie before it was shown to him. Indeed, *The Matrix*, or something like the movie, had played out in his head. Had he seen the future off Amadine? Had he somehow become prescient in the portal where his mind was agitated to a point of foresight by drug change? He looked at the stewardess.

"Ten dollars, but you get a ticket for a free movie next flight. It's a good deal, you know. Courtesy of the Warner Brothers."

The plane began to shake as it hit turbulence. Mark's eyes were jettisoned into wide, I-can't-stand-this terror. A child was screaming in the front of business class. Warner he thought. Warner. They're watching Warner and they don't even know what it is. And I, Mark Nichols, am seeing the future of film before it happens.

Mark's perspective shuffled like a deck of cards until he extracted his feelings. He had made it through. He had to admit, after the virtual destruction, if he was a paranoid schizophrenic in a circuitry of other schizophrenic wire he had manifested his visions in vicissitude and not with the chemical drug he was so used to taking. Was the hallucination then real? He could not, however, properly define why he would think such things? Why was his vision physical to him but not to the environment? Why did he see the security assaulted but the security did not respond? Off his medicine. His mind rose above the city of LA with the plane. He looked out the window and could see the template like a great mind. One gigantic circuit board of tangled buildings, grid streets, skyscraper plugs that plugged into the smog, one giant emission. Would he have created a city that was once an orange orchard into a data bank? He saw vitamin C in wires. Would a society not imitate their external vision with internal? He could see the chaotic data board below no different looking than many people's thoughts. Random juttings, a web work of wires, dissonance, fluxing architecture, despair, a language of slang in the whole thing, a debased crushing miasma of fakeness. He thought of society being the illness that he had to fight as an anti-body, a lone white blood cell defending the imagination against a horrible disease. Were his violent hallucinations responses to the disease of a security actually protecting this horror? He kept rising over LA, the architecture used piping with a life in it that was electrical in a great rusted basin of lostness. The plane shook again and he could see his mission rippling out in his soda cup. At the edges were Frank, Cherry, E.L., Jack, Cleo and Edward. He took a drink and the tonic effervescence barely appeased his trial. Then he shifted into his seat; he had enough story to settle his plan. Warner, he thought... "when I realized Sergeant Aremac was dead and there was nothing else I could do I walked outside with the weapons you now see before you. As you can see, all the weapons have been discharged. This is all I know."

JACK SPILLAIN

Jack fell back against the alley fence and dropped like a puppet snipped from its strings. He wiped his hand across his mouth. The blood tasted like sea salt. A feeling of raw pain flinched out of his cleft lip. It felt like when he was searching for words, how impossibly they wounded him in distortion. He looked up into the sharp sun at the silhouettes of three forms.

"Go on get up you retard!"

A foot kicked him as his hand found the metal of a car pipe. The three forms he knew were the football jocks that had seen him at the bus stop. They must have followed him after his word salad. Did he sound that different? Cleft palate, five-foot-four, features of a stunted baby. They must have thought him fifteen. But he had spoken to the bus driver and the language had come out funny. Like taffy vocabulary that must have stuck in their minds in some crystalline difference that was what? Mentally ill? Inept? Retarded? Dangerous?

The pipe, like the promise of fall weather, felt cold in his hand. As the words of his tormentors chipped through him in staccato hate he felt his guts retract into muscle. His face turned from the sun that shone down upon him. The echo of the fist that felled him he could feel now in his jaw. It had tension in it, like what he thought of virtue, the sacrifice in order that it be pure. He smiled. The light across his face flexed a universe of definition that was absolute. Another foot slammed into him and the multiple violations in his history that were so similar to this mounded up and spread through his form with visceral force. Difference was a ghost that no one wanted to see. Difference was a scourge that made people angry. He knew the word for it was ignorance, but something deeper moved people; a possession of some sort that made them act in fear...a loss of control that was forbidden to the ego.

When the pipe swung up in Jack's hand it felt like a tennis racket putting spin on a ball. It arced up in slow motion like some film noir focus on a kiss the director wanted to be seen for a long time. The emphasis when it hit the jock's jaw was like punctuation in a sentence he had been told to correct in school. Wham! Period...busted for misspelling. Busted for misplacement of a word. Busted for making pictures instead of paragraphs. He felt the jaw condense in the motion of violence like the art with impasto paint Dr. Wells had shown him was the feeling of the guts of the awe of the creator. The particular force of such act in the creation of beauty where previously there was none made him feel happy. The pipe glanced off the chin of the jock. The jaw cracked like a nut. It was lovely and complete. Like a dropped egg yoke with an embryo in it, it splattered red everywhere. As the form crumpled, Jack could see the pipe retract into his clenched fist and then swing up as he turned forward and into the center of the two still standing. Kung Fu played in his brain. The ancient Bruce Lee suddenly within his spring swing into another face. The eyes of the second man went wide with particular shock. Jack felt inside the swing a place where the ultimate depth of justice fit his small muscles. Dense and beautiful. The ironical superior strength of his five-four mass infested him with glee. In the pure nature of its right, he thought, I am vindicated by my disease.

The pipe swung up and into the third young man. It was as if the blood was psychological paint, the fallen bodies were a depiction of tangled figures of the language that hurt him, and his memory of the action the soul of some great portrait of life's horror. The third tormentor dropped as the pipe smashed into his squinting features, connecting with the language center. Jack could see, in noir frames, something that was indecision, indignity, and loss. The pipe clocked off his temple and his entire countenance, jack witnessed, popped like a watermelon into broken silence. The form flopped to the alley dust.

Jack regained his balance and looked at the empty alley. Dropping the pipe, he squinted at the three bodies. Sprawled out around him in various contorted shapes, they lay like an art project, he thought, that just didn't get the subject of gravity quite right. When he turned around he saw Edward Wells smiling at him. Why he was smiling Jack did not know. His mouth opened and words fell out.

"Jack, are you all right?"

"I don't hallucinate when I fight," Jack said.

Dr. Wells' mouth trembled from smile to concern. He handed Jack his handkerchief. Jack whipped his mouth with it.

"You didn't stop it," Jack said.

"I couldn't," said Wells.

"Why not?" Jack said, padding his lip with the white cloth.

Edward flinched. Why didn't he stop it? His mind reeled in a number of impossible answers. Some strange force had paused him on an edge he could not quite comprehend.

"It was beautiful,' Edward said.

Jack looked at Edward and then at the fallen bodies on the ground. Beautiful? Why had he said beautiful?

"There will be more than this," said Jack, handing back the handkerchief.

"More?" said Edward. His eyes, Jack saw, were excited.

"I've got to pick up my son at the high school."

"I'll walk with you," said Edward.

Jack picked up his backpack and they walked away in silence.

Edward recalled the first time they met. Jack wasn't fighting a person. Some time after his Empathy Exams, when Edward had established his practice, he found Jack by the telephone downtown, outside his office, staring at a telephone with a wildness in his eyes that was animalistic. Edward witnessed this from a distance. He watched Jack step back from the phone and then, with all his five-four might, Jack hit the phone so hard the cradle broke. As Edward watched him in awkward amazement, he stepped back and then, in a barrage of blows, he slammed the phone again and again and again until his hand was bloody. Edward put his hands in his pockets nervously and felt his fingers grasp a quarter. Cautiously, as this furious man rained blow after blow onto the phone, Edward moved forward and Jack stopped in mid-swing. Jack looked hard at him, his hands bloody, his nostrils flared, and his chocolate brown eyes innocently wide.

"Here," Edward spoke, handing the quarter to him. Jack looked so severely Edward thought he would turn his rage upon him. However, it was at that instant, Jack's eyes filled with unusual fury, that he, in an unguarded moment, collapsed into a smile. Edward watched his mouth split into an awkward cleft. He held out his bloodied hand and took the quarter.

"Thanks," he said.

That was the first exchange that had founded their relationship, both in and outside the office. With trepidation Edward watched him deposit the quarter, the phone cradled against his ear. "Love, could you please come and pick me up," Jack said. Then, putting the receiver down gently, he turned to Edward, "You want to come over and play with my Legos?" his eyes wide with bright friendliness. Edward nodded.

After this their mutual need had fused them. Jack wanted private psychiatric help for his unusual rage and Edward wanted to watch Jack's expression become what it naturally was. That Edward managed to be at every fight didn't come into question;

Edward counseled and Jack fought. The harder Jack fought, the better Edward advised. And no matter if he lost or won, he was developing what Edward had found to be a unique art and Edward was aware that this art was his own.

That Jack was five-four, had zits on his face, had a pug nose, fat, bulbous lips, could not speak very well due to a cleft palate, was partially deaf, and was inept in a number of very personal ways, might have augmented his internal fury. Yet, Edward found him interesting, and no matter their professional relation, Edward, for Jack, was a loyal supporter of his temper. However, after the phone incident, after Edward knew that Jack's internal combustion was volcanic, and that he was completely committed to fighting everything, Edward began to council him. Not in a way that would impede such expression, but in ways that would help facilitate more flexibility. Indeed, the crude interpretation of Pygmachia Edward knew was deep in this patient.

"Why didn't you stop it?" Jack repeated, as Edward and he found a seat in front of the high school.

"It's who you are," said Edward. "It's your own personal expression." Edward's eyes were wide with natural care. "Why stop something that works for you, that you like, that you are good at?"

Jack looked at him quizzically. He could not remember a psychiatric session ever like the ones Edward gave. Most psychs just listened to you.

"Some people are meant to fight," Edward said. "How many have you had this year?" His eyes were bright with an emphatic, almost maniacal care.

"Twenty-four," Jack said.

"And how did you feel?"

The pause in the air was thick. "Really good," said Jack.

"And did you lose?"

"No."

"There, you see, you are a natural. You never start any of this either. You are at worst just defending yourself. It's what we talked about before. We are not only, as humans, meant to live peaceful, upstanding, noble lives, but live lives that are primal, crude, raw, and natural to our most base senses. If we only lived the way of nobility we would have Eden, but not our most shocking human irony: that imposed order is ultimately a suppressive power that mandates complete rebellion." Edward smiled.

"Yet I get this feeling, as my fist connects with bone and flesh, that it is almost too right a a a fit...."he stammered... "it fee feels like hope."

This was what Edward considered necessary in his *Harbor Paper*, Jack knew. That everything that is born from such oppression—the anger, the lack of privacy, the despair, the horror, the unnatural, law-abiding responses—all of this must be stopped, at whatever the cost. This shone through in his blitzkrieg, and it was this contrary, amoral action that Doctor Wells thought was necessary and true.

Just follow your deepest sense of what's right, he had said, you'll be ok.

When Jack and Edward looked up, a big form of a jock rocked above them. The alley pugilism had traveled. Edward witnessed waves of violation creasing the jock's face. Jack rose slowly on the school stairs and, standing two feet shorter than the behemoth, gazed calmly, like a man against semi.

"Did you really mean that?" The jock said. "Did you really mean to beat up my friends?"

"Look, I don't want any any trouble. I didn't mean to hurt anyone. I am just here to pick up my son."

The jock reached to grab Jack's shirt, pulling him off the ground. He dangled like a noodle for several seconds on his toes.

Then, Edward watched Jack as he, like an unwinding battery wire with electricity in it, cock his right hand, put his left up to grab the neck of the jock and then slam his fist into the chiseled jaw so hard the bully was, like in some action movie, visually sucked back into the school hallway

When the vice-principal appeared and tried to catch Jack's collar, Jack was a continuum of force. Like a trigger spring in some automatic state of fire in a gun, he fell upon the vice-principal and pushed him against the wall, and submitted the interference to pain. Edward watched in mesmerized awe as blow after blow, like some piston in a red-hot engine, fell upon the middle-aged authority. A boom box started up from a passing car, the beat augmenting in pulp rap the situation. A crowd had agitated to the edges.

Witnessing the disaster, the music instructor ran in and grabbed Jack by the neck. Jack shook him off, turned like a windmill and uplifted him back into his classroom upon a snare drum. It split in half like a hissing tide, their bodies musically distorting into chaotic currents on the floor. As the football coach ran in, Jack picked up the cymbals off the broken drum set and smashed the coach in the head until limp. Then, seeing a hole in the crowd, Edward watched him dive through to disappear from the school-yard.

It was sometime later when Edward found him at his house. Jack was punching his punching bag, as if in meditation. "They're going to arrest me," he said.

Edward nodded and took in his face. "I can write you a convincing note. You were only protecting yourself." Edward looked at Jack. His countenance was raw and puffy as if he had been crying. His lip was split and his hands were red and bloody.

"Gotta keep moving," Jack said.

"Where?" Edward said.

"Downtown."

They made the Museum of Art within five minutes. As they both arrived at the steps to the entrance, Jack and Edward looked up and saw the rest of the football team on the other side of the road with chains and bats. They fluxed in group muscle, a tribe of confused youth on the adrenaline of the moment. Edward turned to Jack and saw his right cheek caked in dry blood crack into a faint smile.

"There's too many," Jack said, coolly. "Get up on the museum stairs, Ed!"

Edward backed up and quickly made the top of the stairs and turned around. Jack, finding a homeless man on the bench, took his cane and backed up the stairs to where Edward stood.

The team of footballers rolled across the street as giant automatons, swinging their chains and brandishing sticks, rude words and curses emitting in the fall air like the smog in the LA basin. Jack looked at Edward and yelled at him to run. Knowing that Jack would fight, knowing that he wouldn't stop fighting until he won, Edward looked around for help. His ideas of pugilism as art began to take on knew gravity. Edward found a u-shaped Kryptonite bike lock on the top of the steps. When the footballers made the stairs, Edward watched Jack crack the head of the first with his cane, then, in the most ferocious, merciless way, he flung himself into the chain-swinging jocks. As he sank within the sea of jerseys, maniacally swinging his cane, punching and kicking and spitting and yelling, Edward watched the jocks break and a few football bodies crumple as the cane found the heads of those in its way. Then Edward saw Jack sink, buckling at the knees, as a great linebacker pummeled him with huge fists. As Jack went down, a fury Edward had never felt before seethed through his veins. He jumped in and started swinging the lock. He caught the jaw of the linebacker and he went down. He swung out every which way and the jerseys scattered. Then, as he thought he had cleared them from the stairs, a big hand grabbed him and threw him to the ground. On the ground Edward rolled over and the giant linebacker brought his stick down. Yelling at the top of his lungs, Edward put his arms up to block the blow. When he opened his eyes, a hand came before his and took the force of the stick. Edward witnessed Jack standing over him and fighting in raw, animalistic form. He saw him like a deformed jaguar in the center of the horror of an evil jungle. He fought like he fought with his coded language and impeded speech, in a fury of misshapen dyslexia, professionally deft. His arms flailed around and Edward saw him pull an eye out of a football player's head. Edward could hear him yelling with a rage so primal he transcended all morality. He saw him split a young man's face and in the swing he was so pure his fist was lightning. Then Jack flung himself into the sea of jerseys and Edward watched him drop beneath two big linebackers and then rise from the din in a mania so violent it was, to Edward, almost like God. Gaining his breath, Edward heaved himself up and with the lock in his hands stumbled forth.

Jack was yelling that he'd decapitate them all. He had managed to get a chain and wrap it around the throat of one of the players. With his other hand he crushed the nose of the quarter back, bit through the arm of another, and heaved himself into the running back so hard the man fell against the rail and went unconscious. Edward stood there and watched the tempest unravel like a giant multi-headed monster. It was...he couldn't quite term it...the soul against fate, heaven against hell, awe against the system. His eyes were wide. When there was only one player left, Jack threw the stick at him and it stuck in his mouth. The jock fell over with blood gushing from his face.

Edward looked at Jack at the bottom of the stairs, blood all over, knuckles raw, a black eye swelling up like a giant plum. Jack looked at Edward and smiled and then fell to his knees, balancing for a brief moment an idea in Edward's brain of heroism, the sublime, and raw nature of humanity. Then Jack slumped over, unconscious.

Dropping the lock Edward ran to his side. The football players lay around him in a mass of jersey and fallen muscle. It was a Beckman painting, Edward thought, a Picasso Guernica, a refined cubism of bodies. Edward kept playing Jack over and over, on his knees, smiling at him, falling forward and then motionless on the ground. He picked him up and brought him to the stairs. His eyes were puffy and he was bleeding from every conceivable place. He then, mumbled something. Edward strained to hear. "I'm not insane," he said.

When they arrived at the hospital and Jack was wheeled into Emergency, Edward waited in the waiting area overcome with grief. He thumbed through People, Home and Garden, National Geographic, Elle, and other meaningless magazines. When Edward finally fell asleep he found himself in a dream, a dream in which Jack was putting his Legos together with meticulous care. Edward watched him build a tower, a home, a spaceship, and a small city. He watched him as he studied the colors, smiling with the little people he put inside his designs. He watched him as he looked at his city and with a smile, and what seemed to be great relief, Jack turned toward him.

At that moment Edward felt a touch on his shoulder and he awoke to find a doctor standing there. As his eyes adjusted and he took all of him in, the doctor told him that Jack had fallen into a coma, that he was sorry, and asked if he could call Jack's family. Edward got up from the chair in a ghostly state and he walked to the payphone outside the hospital. He reached in his pocket and felt a quarter in his fingers. He looked at his hands and they were trembling. Blood was on them. Edward could see Jack smiling when he gave him a quarter so long ago. His smile, Edward thought, was a smile that anybody might have, save that his smile was poised between the utter violence that raged within him and the innocence of one brief moment of awareness of caring. Out of all the fights that beset him, it was this moment of caring between them at the phone that somehow pulled from the horrific, deeply troubled, violent energy that possessed him, this lasting memory. Edward felt the silver coin in his hand. He thought of where this coin might go, not into a box, but into Jack's indestructible form, to wake him up and return him to their shared relation. Edward flipped it in his hand. He wanted to put it into their past, to a place where they began, where Jack invited him over after calling his family. Seeing him holding the earpiece, Edward handed the coin to Jack, and watched him put the quarter in the slot and wait for communication.

EXPERIMENTAL BOARD

When Edward looked directly into the eyes of the one woman and two men wearing office issue clothes he saw plastic. Like square credit cards, they would file his information and it would go into the system and synchronize with data central. His position he knew was on the rocks. No one called in an experimental, liberal status, unless there was a serious problem.

A desk separated him from the woman whom he assumed was in charge. The other two men sat in easy chairs on either side. The woman's hair was black, cut short in a working bob, somewhat curly and slicked back to augment a china white face with substantially over-made lips and jaw. Both men leaned back in their chairs when she put her hands on a dossier in front of her. She focused her brown eyes upon Edward and spoke.

"Case number 4472, experimental action 447. Do you know why you are here, Dr. Wells?"

Edward conceived space and time folding in front of him, his mind slowly coming out of psychiatric orbit to land upon her pink finger nails.

"Yes."

The woman let the silence do its work on him, a slow spatial trash compacter of authorial force.

"We, ah, are concerned, Dr. Wells, that you are going off the reservation."

Edward's stomach turned and he thought of the impossibility of lying to The Experimental Board, the analog sensors turning on a circuit of truth that could not be tricked. He put his hands upon his lap in a subservient manner.

"I didn't know that I went off the reservation, Mrs..."

"Falk."

"Mrs. Falk."

She turned a report over in her hands and looked up at him.

"High school pugilism, an entire football team destroyed downtown. Young men with multiple lacerations, teachers with smashed noses, the football coach of the school hit with cymbals..."

Edward blinked into the phosphorescent glow-lights above her head and then looked as professionally as he could into Mrs. Falk's face.

"You are speaking of an episode with Jack Spillain."

"Episode is not what we would call it, Dr. Wells."

Edward recalled the beautiful action of his patient, the blows raining down like some cubist fist painting by the Ancient Picasso. He felt himself about to say that it was an art project, but got caught up in the absurdity of that position.

"Jack wasn't acting out...he was attacked by some very large boys, football players..." he stopped abruptly like one of Jack's deadpan punches.

"They say, one substantially insane man along with an older person assaulted four people at the high school, proceeded to go down town on a death rampage where some eight athletes were accosted, resulting in severe damage to their persons." Mrs. Falk spoke crisply and in a managerial manner.

Edward collected himself. "My patient, Jack Spillain, was goaded into a fight at the high school where he tried to escape and then was pursued downtown where I, with him, attempted to avoid an argument with some very fit young men."

"Us, Dr. Wells, are The Psychiatric Health Core." She paused and her nails pulled back on her paper. "There are reports that one Dr. Wells swinging a Kryptonite bike lock broke the jaw of a young lineman who was only eighteen years old. That after this, one Dr. Wells, with his patient, Jack Spillain, annihilated some eight young men on the stairs to the LA Museum."

Edward remembered the joy he had felt in the Empathy Exam, joy that he didn't want to feel but that had happened naturally, beyond his control. He coughed and was just about to speak when one of the men next to Mrs. Falk interjected.

"Dr. Edward Wells, you are e-x-p-e-r-i-m-e-n-t-a-l." He spelled out the letters perfunctorily. "You are not a vigilante. Your job is to protect your patients from harm, from trouble, from abnormal social conditions. Your job is not to encourage your patient's ire so that they commit crimes of violence."

Experimental, Edward thought, what is that? Did they think he was experimenting? He didn't ask for Jack to be assaulted by a football team. He didn't ask for his feelings inside to turn to glee when Jack started fighting. He could not control the sense of wild justice that he thought it was, protection from uncivil people who mocked his patient. He did not, indeed, ask for himself to see, so strangely, the stunning beauty of his patient's expression. He looked back into the face of Mrs. Falk.

"Did you give Mr. Spillain his medicine?"

Edward felt himself plummet inside.

"That was," Edward said, "the experiment…I, ah, wanted to let him go on his own natural biological condition. I switched to placebos."

"Placeblows. Ha ha ha, Dr. Wells. Very funny." The man next to Mrs. Falk reacted dryly. "Do you know that people could have been killed!" His voice rose to almost shrill decibel.

Edward didn't flinch in his chair. He watched the man writhe.

"My cousin was on the football team, if you did not know... broken jaw, multiple bruises, cannot speak to his mother..." The man's face was red.

Mrs. Falk raised a hand. "We shall keep family matters aside." She waved him away.

Edward swallowed. He did not know this piece of information. He looked at the man next to her and smiled.

"Mass violence by a patient may be considered a civil offence. You are lucky he is in a coma. We can't try the unconscious."

Edward suppressed astonishment. He knew that they were actually at this moment trying the unconscious...sleep programs that were to interface with the criminal and eliminate the animal urge mid REM.

"It is experimentally correct," Edward said, "to shift medicinal dosage depending upon the nature of the patient. I am warranted to use placebo. With Jack it was necessary because of his kidney function. The medicines would have caused a reaction increase that might have boosted his creatinine to dangerous levels."

"Yes," Mrs. Falk said. "We do understand patient medicine positions, Dr. Wells." She shuffled the papers in front of her. "You are clear to practice at your level...but...if we see you putting your patients in jeopardy for reasons of sanguine feeling of your own self, we will cut your umbilical and your status will be dropped." She looked at Edward sternly.

"Yes," Edward said.

He then realized his unique position. They needed experimentals. They needed them to broaden the field. They needed their emotion.

"One more question," Edward said, "There was a situation with one of my patients, Mark Nichols, at the airport. He reported...ah...disturbance with a drug field interaction bleed through.

He said the Empathy Exam went rogue...a nuance, he said in the Operation A pills."

"Yes," Mrs. Falk regarded Dr. Wells casually.

"Ah, he said that he experienced what he thought of as an overlay...that he thought was...ah...contagious."

"We wish the exam was contagious, Dr. Wells..." Mrs. Falk looked down... "but unfortunately that is impossible."

"Yes," Edward said.

"Now go do some good, Dr. Wells. We don't want to see you again." Mrs. Falk smiled a uniform smile that was pressed tersely like snake lips and he was dismissed.

As Edward walked down the sterile hallway and back out to his car he thought of Jack. Jack was small, disabled, shy, classified schizoaffective, and lost. That he could not communicate well due to substantial speech problems, a cleft palate, and had a history of fighting seemed to pass the logic of his situation. The greatest thing afflicting Jack was not these solvable dysfunctions. What Edward realized now was that Jack simply needed to express himself. Locked in his small body he had become a pressure cooker. But it wasn't his illness that Edward thought about; it was the art with abandon that Edward realized now was the core issue. Violence as art. How many years had wars been diagnosed in such a way? And in himself...the feeling...for he had witnessed in the multiple blows a feeling of awe, something beyond joy, something that the medicine suppressed...an almost maniacal awe of a superior state. Was this the emotional necessity that The State would pay dearly for? Edward imagined Hitler. It was with that tyrant, too, all tyrants, the ultimate joy of destruction. Although Jack was not a tyrant, it was, Edward felt, an immensely important idea of sublimation that was occurring in his patient, that might even be occurring in the world. Without paint, without palate, without canvas, without paper and pen, without communication, as dyslexic as Jack was, he was acting out in order that his lost speech be sated. Edward summoned the vision of him on the Museum stairs. Jack had saved him. Jack had stepped in against the tyranny of the footballers. Edward would have been dead if Jack hadn't intervened. He watched the fury in his mind, fury in Jack swinging down upon the bodies, over and over and over again until they ceased their corruption. Edward could see this, Jack's fist smashing into the jaw of the young lineman, in slow motion. How it was art was hard to say. It represented the live, unadulterated blow upon the flesh of something maligned. Like a fist pounding clay. In the instant that the fist hit the jaw, the visual crushing force and the solid sound of it, Edward could not deny that in its pugilism was the raw art of suppressed nature. And then his emotions gushed...centuries of suppressed nature. As if it had squeezed out of him or had been squeezed by the wrongness of these youth, a spirit cracked through Jack's body that was justly violent, artistically violent. Yes, a violence that, like jazz, had a tempo, a melody, a beat, and crackled in the fabric of The State's regimentation like illegal but beautiful vinyl with a needle pulsing the flow of the damnation of every single mentally ill patient he had ever seen. He was, indeed, surprised that not every single one of his patients exhibited directly. That they did not explode was truly unimaginable. How much suppressed force could a person take? But they did in their own ways act. Jack just happened to be the more outstanding hammer upon the wall of the institution that kept all of them. Like touching an anemone and it buckles in and the entire family line of emotion squishes back into history and hurts. They would mine that if they could...all the way down the genetic line of pain to the pulsing node of original feeling. All the way back in a historical violation deeper than anyone could think. And what happened when one violated the soul, an entire century of people subject to continual trammeling of the spirit? How long could a person endure such horrendous states before they simply blew? Was this the goal? Minute pressures slowly pressing the human to his limit and then the eruption of an irrational ecstasy?

Edward got into his car and turned the ignition. It started up. The engine would rust he thought, just like us. How long before we simple freeze up in rust and can't move? Jack was motion. Unharnessed and breaking and falling into the very block that stopped him, like an innocent folding up against a tremendous pain. How many times had he buckled inward to an unfathomable place in his history where he had no other choice but to respond?

ST. MARY'S

St. Mary's loomed in the hills of Hollywood, out of reach by most serviceable roads. It was once a seminary for Christian service but the religious practice had faded out like so many others, to reform somewhere else in the fluxing belief systems of State Realignments. That it had been sold and converted into a "place of healing" some twenty years ago was an irony of considerable force. Place of healing could be translated as insane asylum, or as some said, Mental Health Facility. Cleo put her card in the electronic door and entered.

She had found the job randomly, a desire to help in social services a decision not for money or any material reason, although the excellent insurance was attractive. Cleo knew that one in five people would be diagnosed with schizophrenia. She knew that four out of those five people would be submitted to wards and rehabilitation. But she was in invincible support of the mentally ill because she knew that the affliction in these individuals was response against a system that she viewed as sick itself. That she had awoken at the age of four to the massive realization that what was around her could very well be seen as external disease was no insignificant act of consciousness. How could people have a chance if their environments were not a place of salubrious interrelation? And her position of nurse was not the clinical climb most might have pursued. Cleo wanted the lowest position she could get. The lower the position the greater the freedom.

St. Mary's possessed a feel of ancient character that did not apply to the afflicted patients' current problems. Indeed, mental illness to Cleo did not strike her as a past issue, but rather something that blossomed in the present while a future poured into it. Like a metaphorical Niagara Falls, she thought. A huge plunging future that the patients had to stand in the present while it shattered down around them in incredibly imaginative ways. This is what she liked the most. The idea of being ill was not that the idea was ill, but often, if she looked at it critically, which she did every day, it was something environmental. What it was varied from person to person, doctor to doctor, patient to patient. Yet it would strike her as a significantly interesting thing to be mentally ill. Visions. Auditory voices. Massive manic attacks. Horrendous overloads of surreal material. Shocking, even overwhelming distinctions of reality that actually seemed to be part and parcel with the very cityscapes that surrounded. Ideas of hosting other bodies within. Absolute paranoid thoughts of time and space fracturing into this future and that future. She understood a critical point: the crumbling pioneers of worlds no one else had been to saw things. And there was actually many more ways to look at the cases that were subject to institutionalization, up close and human as Cleo could get.

The hall was without lights. There were sounds, like in a zoo, of exuberant struggle, pips and peeps from patients pacing the slick tile floors, some slumped in chairs, a quasi circus like oddity as she met those interned. It smelled of dead things, the mold of time or some sort of unwashed body. She had become used to the smell, the rancid stink of uncared for people floating in the air as if a specialty cheese. It didn't smell bad, but it lay thickly in the air in an oppressive glaze that spoke of unwashed skin. Cleo walked down the hall and was encouraging as she passed her patients recognition with their names. Her responsibility—to administer to each case not simply their room service but to speak with them and to get them to open, to figure out their histories, to do laundry, and to operate in the office where Cleo administered medications—was par for the responsibility of her position. And although the patients were disheveled, she did her best to care for them and keep them clean.

Her job this afternoon would be to engage a multi-personality named Frank who was diagnosed paranoid schizophrenic and had been picked up for somehow appearing at the highest State level conference and orating on the subject of tyranny. That he had even made it passed the security was amazing. He had actually gone through three checkpoints as an Identity Diplomat unnoticed. Then he had commanded an audience for one half hour until his real identity showed up.

She walked in room eight and looked at Frank sitting alone in the corner mumbling to himself. Cleo knew she would not have to coax him out of his privacy. She knew she would not have to invite him somehow to share his thoughts. He was a specialty talker. His chart stated loquacious with cryptic self-regard. She was intimidated that, upon further perusal, she had seen, under his intelligence stats, an off the radar ability. She observed him slumped in the corner with his hand combing back his greasy black hair.

"A flat-line world of shifting voice wherein ghosts pass through, your choice not to fall deep," he said.

Cleo studied him. Frank Spec. The infamous Frank Spec. Word master. Had been admitted in the past for writing pre-mortem obituaries to moneyed people, people who paid for prophecy of death. It was freaky work that had become fad. Nobody believed it possible, like gambling for prescient views into demise. And in one paper on how to disappear in front of an audience of seven hundred authorities nobody saw—unlike his recent act that put him back in the pen—Frank leave the podium. Some said it was one massive incantatory trance, in only an hour. Some said simply the lights went off. But the electricity circuits had not registered a gap. Mr. Spec who had founded a small religious reactionary movement on the idea that if God created everything, including gravity, then God must be, if gravity is a force that undermines free movement, a tyrant. Frank Spec who thought he was only four years old at the age of thirty-five.

"Hello Frank," Cleo said.

His back remained turned to her where he sat in the corner. A large hand kept slicking back hair. He looked like a cat that had gotten wet and was now grooming itself, manically grooming his greasy black hair with paw.

"How are you doing today, Frank?"

His words echoed off the angle of his position in the corner.

"Shut down by meds you deaden through everything false as you fall, too, down steep. An incline of fake picture botch, your head cracking like a ticking watch to somewhere else. Shivers blitz through pity's stare while you do everything to care about your self."

He wasn't going to engage directly she thought. Fine. I'll just listen and see what he has to say. She marked on her slate, "involuntary", and then sat down in a chair. He paused and turned his head toward her with a cocked ear. She had been warned not to fall for his mesmerism, to be cautious when listening and to remain on guard. One orderly had fallen asleep after a brief conversation and Frank had taken the orderly's tag. Almost went through security again. She looked at Frank. Four years old, she thought. He was a big man for having a child inside of him. He continued his soliloquy.

"Yet not well you split in half and turn into some form hated like burden of identity...who you were you're not, you guess who you are has fought...you suss who's in me? So you fall into a drowning state and your lips almost can't relate space or time. You splinter in your crash and blow every neuron you have ever known to place sign. And recovery requires you assess what's not there, nothing on lest you read you. Words of doubt quake in your eyes and you feel your cold shudder rise, bleed anew."

Cleo picked out rhymes from his meander. She smiled. He's doing off rhymes, she thought. She tried again. "Franklin, are you doing well today?"

Frank shifted his position in the corner and then turned slightly, his lips quivering.

"And calling all the gods who've broken, could not ever match your words spoken to the walls. Gravity hits you in the face to disbelief, the temper of some you without relief to match its calls. So you compress into a minute shell and tuck yourself away from hell like a dream. And every terror in your bones shakes through, the masked moans like a team. You flutter insanity upon your tongue and some far off world that is not won dies for you. You light despair on fire, try to leave because this world you cannot believe dies for you. Molecules manifest in moving forms, every person is devil out of norms that cannot relate. So you fall into another part of your very sacred schizoid art, schizoid dates."

Cleo found herself slowly drifting. Her head nodded and then she snapped up in shock. Frank had turned around and she did not even see him turn. He had moved closer to her. His voice was soothing and poetical. He held her gaze.

"Time barely grasped as measurement is hung in front of your pleasure in visceral things. It swings its pendulum about and you see time die, your shout disintegrating. All your friends have given up and you, beyond par, corrupt every thought. I am hated, not loved, left out, done, the words point at you like a gun you have wrought. You pull the trigger and blow off life with a pill while the after life waits patiently. And transcending you fall away into some quiet lay, the pills making me...Cleo..."

Cleo looked fixedly at Frank. He had said her name. His grey eyes were very much like wolf eyes, deep-set, wild, yet soft and yearning. She smiled at him. Her mind seemed to be layering from responsibility to other places. Then she focused upon his stricken face.

"Cleo...you are such a nice person."

The words were imploring, in a theatrical tone.

"Such a nice nice person, Cleo..."

She smiled at him. "Have you eaten today, Frank?"

The pause in the room seemed to collect dust. Ten seconds after her question he responded.

"A flat grey feeling of fury traps you in architectural dislocation, time broken in some dead assault. Your eyes crumble without destination, no light to hold, life's murky facts blurring feelings while awkwardly all you know plummets and you fall flat into a divorced life. Society's fake brain slowly splits you open like a pit, the acidic fruit inside you tying guts, crushes over, is felt like a stake that plants the superficial indefinite."

Cleo watched him begin to pace. His body moved smoothly in the room, hands gesturing philosophically.

"Involuntary, memory's neurons suck into definition, flux umbrella-like, sap your body code and then cast a still-born thought: Are life and death the same whispering voices? Who's in control of whom you are, who suggests other places exist in you, other choice? But you will never know, will panhandles trust, and a whore undresses your language such that you sell out. So you pitch in flux like a fly pitching upon windowsill…"

Like a prop, a fly was pitching upon the windowsill and Frank stopped to watch. He watched it buzz while the room became a strange experiment of focus. Then he continued with his focus upon the fly.

"What speaking is in mania…tap your every movement's twitch until smashed against your mind's reflections…"

The fly stopped. Frank held it in his palm. He then turned around and looked directly at Cleo in shock.

"How you open trust like an eggshell…is how you speak to her, but you are un-being, which like some startled eyelid, cracks back sections of real guesswork as you fall to figures incomprehensible yet alive. You want to save them, you want us to feel them, slow you down to not here…you want to hold them…"

In Frank's eye a tear manifested. Cleo looked into it and imagined a small lake. She knew from her library job that open emotion had become highly marketable over the past twenty years. The first marketable tear that had initially sold for a dollar now sold for ten. All human emotion of visceral quality was up for sale. Love categories, hate categories, depression categories, sad-ness...they had tried to farm them in emotion gardens. The real, unadulterated, pure essence of a visceral sadness was worth more than chemically engineered. But the visceral feelings of despair were sold on high. Hence the new trade in the mentally ill. The market knew they produced more...intensity.

She looked at Frank. She conceived that she saw love in his tear, something so unusual that she opened her mouth to speak. Frank held up a hand that was shaking.

"But the world shakes in you impossible as questions with-out answer: how do you communicate the dead answer to life? How do you communicate your live answer to death? An avalanche of distortion depresses you, strips meaning, you up fall into doubt, and in the current down of information you explode out seemingly other, no glue to hold absence together. And there's no together that can release what it wants to say to hear whether beyond is life believable or un-believed. Reason falls fantastically into your fix, you hold imagination like a child sieved before it's born...is there imagination's child? Where is the innocence that is being killed in me!" He looked desperately at Cleo. He crushed his big fist with the fly in it up against his skull to stop it from shaking.... "You ask, where is life, love, hope, vitality!"

Cleo watched Frank slump to the floor. Her head, suddenly caught in some whorl pool, was spinning. She seemed unable to grasp her location. Her breath was coming in short, heaving move-ments. She got up out of the chair with the intent to leave, took one step and fell to the ground too.

When Cleo's eyes opened she beheld greatly concerned grey cornea with an overly large black iris. She could smell the strong scent of male sweat. Frank held her in his arms and was twitching in what appeared to be fear. She could feel the twitches go through her like Morse Code. His arms felt very strong, as if they could crush her if she moved the wrong way. She felt herself breathing, yet with a great gravity in the room. Frank's eyes, the eyes that she witnessed before her, were wild, sad, and deep.

An orderly entered. "Hey!" he yelled and rushed to Frank.

"She fell," he said, quickly and moved away.

The orderly moved to pick up Cleo.

"I am sorry," Cleo said, "I must have not eaten today."

The orderly helped her up and she regained composure. Frank retreated to a corner with his fist up against his head, a bloodstain from the fly smudged upon his brow. The orderly looked sternly at him.

"It is hot," Frank said.

"Did he try to grapple you?" the orderly quipped authoritatively.

"No," said Cleo flatly. She brushed her dress down. "I better get back to work."

"Yes," Frank said to both of them, "better get back to work." His words trailed off lisping.

Cleo walked out the door, her mind still foggy. Her thoughts as she walked down the hall reeled in an unsteady swim. She remembered the poetic nature of Frank's discourse. Had she been moved by his tear to collapse? How strong was a person's emotional transfer in a society that was as dried up as the Mid West. Had it caused her black out, or was she, as Frank was so famous for, mesmerized?

THE PROGNOSIS OF FRANK SPEC

The question had not yet arisen in the conversation about how Dr. M. Bessingham, one of the most esteemed plastic surgeons in the field, wanted to look after death, a vitally important question—if death may be vitally important—as important to Frank Spec whose specialty was on the line; a question of literal aesthetic that Bessingham, given his years of restructuring faces, tits, ass, and all other personal body parts, now mulled over like a man who was to decide the next greatest feature movie in Hollywood. And the pre-mortem would squeeze out his life's final emotions, Frank knew, in the precarious last moments; an expensive act.

It was always like this, Frank found, especially with people who cared about their cultural impact, their fame, their social connections, their history, their 'appearance', no matter that they would barely be alive to claim the prize of his talents as a professional pre-mortem obituary scribe. And mostly, Frank discovered, families of the to be deceased cared more about how the thing was worded...so the line would emit The Objective Correlative, not simply so just any living emotion of Bessingham would be crushed out of his ancient body, but the virtuous ring of his soul at the last. Of course it could go either way, and this was Frank's technique—he had to juggle the many aspects of the obituary in such a manner that would appease all sides, dead or otherwise. Frank Spec's reputation was indisputably made because he was the most deadly honest and notable poetical wordsmith in the public's eye.

"Well," Frank said to Bessingham, "you do know enough about operations in general to realize how delicate such an operation will be, verbally and financially. And you do understand that my policy requires that the writing be free from all legal restraints—to insure that all my talent goes into it; to insure that you die...properly."

"Of course, I understand," Dr. Bessingham answered, in a voice that had more verve than a normal man who knew that his days were numbered, perhaps because he saw pre-mortem work like his own work: making the line or figure of imagination sparkle in the limelight of the Post Vital. "All I ask is that you write something deep, something visceral enough so that my family sheds a tear."

"Of course, Mr. Bessingham. If you will sign these papers." Frank handed a stack of legalese to the Doctor who sat across from him, hands quivering from Parkinson's, the same hands that were once so steady that they could cut and slice and snip and tuck in such fine precision hardly a client was dissatisfied. In fact, Dr. Bessingham's name in Hollywood was so well known that he was nominated for an Oscar one year, jokingly, for best facelift that enabled a maturing but feeble granddame to continue with notoriety in the State Pictures. Yet it was a time when Tinsel Town possessed more made-over people than the tech facelifts of the 90's, as if by changing their countenances they could change history. The State was very happy with this. The media propagation codes had soared. The grotesque had become attractive.

They shook hands, and Frank wondered if it would happen

again, like the last time, when he wrote an obituary before the person was dead and everything that he wrote about came to pass in a vitally emotional way, even the grim circumstances surrounding the death. How had he predicted it? How could he have possibly known and then penned the disaster that would land him at the top of the obituary writing field, every almost dead person wanting him to perform the miracle again: writing that became real. Frank shivered, feeling suddenly alive with the wonder of his craft as Dr. Bessingham waddled with cane out the door.

It could go many ways, Frank knew, especially with such a case as Bessingham, whose life now lay in a pile of papers upon his desk, diary and all submitted for the specific purpose of prophesy, something that Frank was archeologically expert at, the digging into truth required for the highest aesthetic of foresight into the obituary.

As he read over the Hollywood doctor's life he found that Bessingham had operated on some thirty thousand women over the last ten years, which amounted to eight women a day, all of whom had been made thinner, sleeker, sexier—if sexier was a matter of always risen cheeks, the permanent insect smiles, boobs that were full of silicon, buttocks that had been sucked, cut and tucked into sizes of firm melons, to be, no less, handled by the rich and famous. Of the thirty thousand operations, the success rate over time, given the aging slide of synthetic tits, was about one half, which meant, according to Bessingham's personal notes, that fifteen thousand women had been maladjusted. Nevertheless, a crack team of insurance lawyers acted as phalanx protecting Bessingham from severe penalty, and since the going rate for a boob job was—depending upon desired proportion—between five and twenty thousand dollars, the general income of the office rounded up to sixty million dollars each year before overhead and taxes. Bessingham was flush as the devil.

But things became even more curious as Frank read on. According to, and beginning on page five through page seventy of Bessingham's diary, there was a description of sexual contact with his patients (one woman per page!), affairs and all other manners of lascivious conduct described in detail. And there seemed to be symmetry in the description that became more and more detailed from first to last entry. Where page five proclaimed a tame fondling of the breast, page sixty-nine presented the following:

"Gloria returned today and I can see in her movements that she wants me to operate again. I close the door and ask her to unrobe, only I do not give her anything to cover. She accommodates me, and I can see my work in her like a Hellenic figure: time's corrosion of the body remade into a perfect curve; time's incessant chiseling of the once pure line in pubescence re-chiseled for the sake of preserving the inexplicable Post Vital lust for living beauty. We are tricking evolution and I can't help but shiver as she unfolds. We don't say anything, but I can tell that she wants full consultation. My hand reaches into her and the dew of her flower drips its sugars. She groans and tells me that she wants my cock to press into her…to erase her life for an instant so she will no longer be a star; so there will be a lack of judgment. What deep hatred and addictive denial one learns from acting! There is no emotion in the industry, she says, none. This is better truth than any Empathy Confession Center will ever show you, better even than consummated love. I can only feel that it is my duty, my duty as a doctor to help her in any way I can. Her tongue slides down my neck as she unbuckles my…" The note dribbled off in the diary.

Frank had become excited; an excitation not in the least to do with the sexual passage, but an excitement that struck when he began to see in the diary more passages about Gloria, or at least what he supposed was she, given the enigmatic letter 'G'.

"Again G came in. She said she needed help. Almost desperate. Said her implants were slipping and she could not be in the movie with slipping implants, the public scrutiny of her body so great. Her exact words: "the fucking public has high resolution pause now!" For the first time, I realized that our actions presented a dangerous liaison. She mentioned her husband and how he had found a gray pubic hair post coitus, post going down the slim slide of her body like the multiple movie reels panning her soul for its gold. Damn all so-called distinction! Christ! She mentioned that he had asked her what the hell did she think she was doing and had she been having an affair. She told me that she denied the entire thing, but I know I can't trust a woman I am banging in my office, a woman who gets implants and tucks and fills once a month so she can continue in the industry of mirrors."

And again on page 70, the final page, where every encounter mysteriously stops.

"G and I grappled for a while and I know there will be evidence under her nails. The blood is still on my neck. Should I tell my staff I was shaving? She says she wants me in total, she wants to divorce Rick, her washed up movie mogul dick of a husband. She tells me that if there is to be no more sex then she is going public, like a software company. Doesn't she know I could give her painkillers to erase her angst? Sarvocet, Docodin, Percodial, Shorphine even, an entirely different face so she could drop out of sight. But she doesn't accept. Seven lawyers cannot prevent a scandal like this; a scandal that surely will ruin my respect in the community given it's Venus Fly Trap past. But who has respect in this community? They are all prostitutes of fashion, like myself, like a quick fix infusion of anesthesia before the operation to make beauty dance in a filmy wonderland before your eyes. G said if I do not take her now she is going to the authorities. I decided to take her."

Things became cryptic in Frank's mind. What did he mean by "I took her?" Had he taken her on a Virtual? And why were there no more entries after page seventy? Had this recently happened? Frank opened the diary again to look at the dates, but there were none, nothing like the normal diary dates one would keep track of history with. Frank picked up the phone and dialed. Then, thinking better of making any contact with his client, he hung up and thumbed back through the notebook until he found a tear, or what he thought was a tear, on page forty.

"Do you know what it is like? Do you know after all the years of service to an industry of magic and glitter it is impossible to bear the lie? And that is exactly what it all is, one great big fat lie and I am the greatest lie fixer of all. What would have happened if there were no plastic docs, guys who mold figures to look like emaciated Vogue models so they can go out in their almost skeletal states fully adjusted, smiling plastic smiles that will be as permanent as we are dreamers? I hate myself, and in my hate I erase a decade of wrinkles, like a cut-and-paste computer artist with his synth-playmate machine, giving the world its animation, its jealousy, its design of sublime countenances, its Adobe 1000. But to what end? Fake emotions? This is my profession. And Gloria comes in the first day and I know that she, no matter the fills in her boobs, the altered hairline, the Jazzercise ass, the die in her hair and the make up that makes even Cleopatra's Egyptian eyeliner insignificant—she well knows she is fake, so fake that she is closer to reality than half the bimbos who I prepare, simply because being fake, being virtual, is the abundant fix. This is my confession: the moment Gloria came in I knew for the first time in my life that I, too, was fake and that was the truth."

The teardrop had landed directly on the fresh, ink-scrawled word "truth" making it blur a little as if passionate scribble arising slowly from a coma. An expensive divulgence, Frank thought. He suddenly thought of making a screenplay and delivering it in a champagne bottle to a producer. This would sell! This story would deconstruct the entirety of the Post Vital Age and not just because it was a real depiction of human angst in State Controls. It was a catch twenty-two position...becoming fake to become real...but blackmail, Frank thought, seemed to be a thing of the past. Though Doctor Bessingham was disgustingly human, he was also a vulnerable creature who could not hide; no matter all the hiding he had done for other people's fragile egos in the name of perfect, acceptable, State culture physique. Hence the obituary. Hence airing his soul to the world. Hence, Frank Spec had been brought in for the exacting measure of word like some tailor of future. Bessingham had probably deeper feelings than most in his profession, and it was all here for the finale, to be squeezed out in the crescendo of his now almost passed life. An unusual knot welled up in Frank's throat. He turned the page.

"Gloria now comes in when she doesn't need anything manufactured for her. She is to me my perfect example I give to the human race, of what it means to be in fashion, fame, and lights. I will present her to an audience the same way the still pond presents the perfect, trick-rippling reflection of a cloudy sky. And really, I do not know what else I can do for her physically. She says she wants more alterations, more beauty, but I can only tell her that she is Aphrodite already, in veritas, a Hollywood dame that outclasses all others. She is addicted to the mirror as much as I am addicted to her. She is, like a torrent of need, the flower of my corruption. I imagine even the old, the previous organic her has now forgotten what countenance made her squirm to begin with. Faded in a tuck. And since the hybrid her has bloomed, she, like an innocent child, desires more, my flower, my Gloria wanting more sunlight, more vision, the raw photosynthesis of her plastic aura. Shouldn't she be satisfied? And this may sound totally twisted, but I now know what it would be like to be Frankenstein. I am Shelly on the brink of pronouncing the novel woman. I am a God...and in that I deliver the belief that we may outwit the real world in guises of ephemeral perfection."

All of the passages began to swirl in Frank's mind like a candy cane. He enjoyed, tremendously, the privilege of looking into another's existence, a voyeur who takes pleasure from his lascivious design. But it wasn't always pretty. The last guy who he wrote an obituary for was a stockbroker whose great grandfather had founded the company that made Tear Bottle Drinks. A CEO, no less, who Frank had described as an "emotional brilliance". A man who could give the public its quintessence. When the time came to explain how this great had passed on, he had written one sentence: "James B. Fudd would swallow and choke on his tears while entertaining at a party at the age of 56." And what happened was, Mr. Fudd did throw a party for his 56th, and while trying to show how you could drink your own sorrow, swallowed his stored up tears with a pork loin and choked to death at the party table in front of 101 guests.

The obituary was then printed, and when people heard that

Frank Spec had predicted the death—both device and time—everyone suddenly wanted, no matter the gruesome details, to have their deaths predicted too. The interview was direct.

"Mr. Spec. How could you have possibly known how Mr. Fudd would perish?"

"Sensitive poets choke on their own tears all the time."

"But how can you predict a death?"

Frank looked at the man. He didn't know himself. It was a finesse of chances, voices in his head, social patterns, and, he paused...something beyond a guess where his guts felt...truth.

"Life is an equation," he said. "Death is just a part of the end of the equation."

The news spread as rapidly as the Water Games made to keep children fluent with the future of happiness. The message warped from state to state. The story about the guy who was a famous obituary man. Tears turned to gun. Gun turned to slitting the CEO's throat. Slitting his throat turned to a terrorist bomb that blew up half of the audience. Then Explosive Tear Pops hit the shelves. Trickledown was never so twisted. But the players, those who had the real scoop, were in awe, and Frank received hundreds of calls, finally deciding to settle for special cases, as with Dr. Bessingham, cases that he was highly interested in, odd lives. But as Frank looked at the diary he could not fathom what he would write on the blank page that now lay on his desk. He needed more information, information like what happened to make Bessingham a surgeon to begin with and what were his triumphs, his losses, stuff less personal than the diary, yet just as valuable. He flipped through the stack and came to sheaf of legal papers.

The first page revealed that Bessingham had once been a Neo Mormon and had been indicted on three counts of practicing polygamy in California during the high times of sexual reformation, a religious nuance that hadn't died out. No one had known until one wife, who felt geographically and practically alienated, since she, in her own words, was forced to leave Salt Lake, not to mention her mind, after meeting the Doctor, changed religion from Mormon to Catholic and sued Bessingham for spiritual deceit. The case turned wicked as the fuming divorcee threw in mental rape for spite, something that had hovered in the courts. Neural molestation. Nobody could believe it. But with the one charge against Bessingham, the other wives, although still loyal, were revealed, and Bessingham went to prison for three years (one for each wife), getting off in one on parole. His remaining wives, save for the convert who ended up marrying her crack prosecutor, went back to Salt Lake and disappeared into other harems, never to be seen or heard of again, their devotion to religion stronger than their belief in Bessingham, the man who had screwed up their polygomonial bliss, if it may be called so.

In prison Bessingham became an ink-slinger, something that protected him from the gangs looking to do a little slip and slide in the showers. In fact, his tattoos were so good that he won the attention of all his prison mates, and when they found out that he was a plastic surgeon they asked him to down the system. He had no choice and replaced their fingerprints, for which they named Bessingham Fingers. This alteration screwed up the entire security in the lockdown so much that ten of the inmates were found on the databanks after lift as guards.

Upon release, Bessingham's only alternative was to start over, open his own practice and never mention anything to do with The Big House or Mormons again, despite the fact revealed in an earlier diary that many of his old clink clients came in every now and then to have a job done on their make. His business began to boom and all payment was under the table, enhancing his thoughts about the great human lie in general. Success by averting the law. Going around the hurtles of the system and divining alternate countenances. Alternate bodies, even, as in one particular case, where he performed an entire erasure of a convict's full body tats so the convict could obtain a job working in the court system. The public later found out that the man was out for revenge. The caption still reads in library archives: "I wanted to be a lawyer so I could kill the Judge who clinked me." What a twist, Frank thought. What coup.

But the important thing to know about, for Frank, was how

this man would pass on, an addiction he had since the first success-ful prescience, something that had jettisoned Frank into a sphere of "special ops" reporting, or as he thought of it, 'streamline pre-diction'. For, if he got it wrong now he would be as down and out as the regular obituary writer, reduced to small, insignificant col-umns about what a person had accomplished over their life, how they had contributed, etc. No, Frank, like Dr. Bessingham, who he now felt an odd sympathy for, was a specialist at 'shaping' the events. The body of future was malleable. The exact placement of death, or life coming to death, that was his own special recipe, sick or not, for fame, could sculpt tomorrow. No, not for fame. For the joy of it. For the art of it. For the power. In short, Frank was addicted to his job as cosmetically as Bessingham was tucked into his, and if pre-mortem obituary writing meant killing a person to do it right, then he thought he would do it. His eyes came to a fly madly smashing its body against the closed window. How would Dr. Bessingham die?

There were all the maladjusted patients. There was Rick. There was Gloria. There were all of the prison inmates. There was the super long list of lascivious interactions with his patients. There were his one converted Catholic and two Mormon wives. There was Parkinson's. There was, to say the least, a million differ-ent ways to go considering all of the people who had a motive to knock the Doc off. Even his lawyers whose wives he had banged while they were at trial saving his ass, revealed in an addendum di-ary! The list was a mile long, and surprisingly, it had not happened yet. But why? Why had nobody put a gun to Bessingham's fat head and pulled the trigger? And then, to realize in his diary that he was fake and that being fake was the truth, that oxymoronic confession and hurt and all that was welled up inside the man—all of it would suffocate even the most ardent of living beings. Guilt? The guilt was so thick that you couldn't even fit it in the back row of a church. Moreover, what with the verve in his voice when they met, the irony of excitement that seemed to sparkle in Bes-singham's eyes as he sat across from Frank while they sealed the contract, a contract, no less, in the amount of one million dollars.

Something was up. And Frank now had the road map and he was feeling edgy. The phone rang.

"Hello, Frank Spec?"

"Yes," Frank said, trying not to sound nonplused.

"It's Bessingham. I thought I would call since you now have in your possession my rather outlandish, if not sordid, life and have satisfied yourself. Are you surprised?"

"Nothing is surprising about death. Everyone dies some-time." Frank's voice was cautiously flat.

"Yes, but I bet you have never dealt with such an obituary before, nothing like a life where the candles are lit at both ends, eh. That's why I am calling. Ah...there is something that you don't know."

Frank felt a chill go through his body. "More information?"

"Not really. Just something that will help you understand why I chose you."

Bessingham's voice sounded to Frank like a child playing with words for the first time, slurry words, almost hypnotic, the edges unruffled by some sweet molasses oozing from his mouth. "We need to meet."

"I don't meet with clients when I am working."

"Oh yes, you are a professional, but you will not be able to complete the obituary without this bit of information."

"When and where?" Frank tried to hold up a normal tone, but it wasn't working. There was something extremely unnerving about this obituary, something scary.

"Meet me at the Z Stop."

"The club?"

"Yes, that's it. Ten o'clock this evening."

The Z Stop was famous amongst the stars for its underground raves. A club that had in hand the purse strings of the law so it could oper-ate without being harassed as a high-class den of technotic ill repute. A club that toted the most hip reputation amongst the moneyed people of Hollywood. 'Z' stood for sleep, or what the owners called the magic drug, a new drug manufactured with affects of pristine awareness. You take it and time folds, or so they say.

Before Frank even walked in he could feel the pulse of music beating techno through the walls, a sound that to him felt like the future in the throes of sensuality; a certain plastic, industrial, hedonistic rhythm pumping sound, like a synthetic heart, he thought, the blood jack hammering through the veins of those who decided to take the trip.

He was frisked at the door by a metal detector and then he walked into what appeared to him a cavern full with dry ice, multicolored lights, the entire color spectrum twitching around the dark environs, faces flickering on the dance floor in mesmerizing flux. Around the edges were booths, many full with people drinking smart drinks served up, to think beyond, to think better, to have clarity while the Z kicked in and elevated all senses into a semi somnolent cheer. As Frank skirted the edges of the party, he suddenly became aware that he was in something that he didn't really want to be in. It was only the draw of curiosity about what Bessingham would reveal that brought him here, a draw that was enlivened to a supreme state after gorging himself on the ultra corrupt information of the Doctors' life. His eyes soon came to rest on a booth in the back where two people were seated. A hand gestured him over.

"My dear Mr. Spec, thank you so much for showing."

Doctor Bessingham's large, shaking body shifted in the seat, twitching with the lights. Or was it the lights shifting him in the seat? Frank could not tell. A seductive woman with jet-black hair, manicured nails painted with day-glow red polish, and long, piano player fingers that laid as nonchalantly as a sunbathing cat upon the shoulder of Bessingham, smiled at him.

"Please sit down."

Frank sat down and the Doctor made a motion with his hand, alerting a waitress to their table.

"Drink?" Bessingham asked Frank.

Frank heard "think" and nodded wondering why the Doctor had said that to him. Bessingham leaned over and whispered in the waitress's ear. She slid away into the techno, spinning professionally, like CD on a machine.

"This is Gloria Falk." Bessingham motioned to the dark-haired, riveting, seemingly feline, multiple altered countenance of the lady sitting next to him. He had done a fine job: the cheeks were high and rosy, the smile almost unwrinkled save for two crow's feet lines that appeared perfectly when she shook hands with Frank, enormous cleavage supported by an almost see-through blouse. Bessingham smiled a large, satisfied smile, as if he was presenting his pride and joy; an almost wicked kind of smile that showed he still had a robust ego despite his demise. Frank simply smiled back and wondered what the hell he was doing at a rave with his client, who seemed as casual as ever, almost floating.

"You see Mr. Spec I brought you here, brought you like so many others to see the greatest face lift of all: T-I-M-E. He spelled it out, pronouncing every letter. That's the thing that I'm into now, and since I do not have much more of it, I just wanted to find the person who could do it, naturally."

The waitress came back with a drink for Frank. It glowed neon blue. He didn't touch it. Bessingham laughed a big guffawing laugh and continued.

"You have read about my life and how disgraceful it has been, how I have been a seducer, a manufacturer of countenances, a cheater, a liar, a scam man, a hoax king, even imprisoned for polygamy, and in short, all these things are who I am and now it is time for the greatest scam of all—my cosmetic death and re-birth into immortality. That's why you are here, Frank. We are the same, you and I. You alter the future as I alter people's future expressions. You figure the line and I align the figure. You play with bodies of information and I inform the body of what they may be at the highest corporeal aesthetic. Frank, you must understand that we are conductors of the divine and nobody, absolutely no-body, is as close to God as we both are."

Frank shifted in his seat suddenly feeling different, feeling as though the room was sharp as a pin and all the lights were individually speaking to him, individually perceivable in their rhythmic movement to the music. Even the Doctor's face had become as clear as a glass pond and he could look past the smile, past the bulbous, sanguine cheeks and into a great sorrow underneath. Frank suddenly found himself back in the diary reading the passage with the teardrop on "truth" and how being fake was the truth, at least to this man who had worked in the field of design his entire life. And now, such an artifact, such an unusual being would be taken and Frank was given the chance to place him in the library of immortals simply by divining his death for him. Suddenly the music stopped and all the dancers drew to their table.

"Frank," Dr. Bessingham said, "you do not know the most important piece of information. I am the Head of State for Human Affairs." Dr. Bessingham looked dead into Frank's eyes.

Frank returned his morose stare. It had a desperate, almost vapid look. Frank suddenly realized the position he was in. The Head of State for Human Affairs. He could see a deploring, sad look in Bessingham, as if he were confessing a murder.

"I imagine this..." Bessingham said, pointing to the human press of bodies in front of them... "this stuff, Frank...this state of elated relation."

Frank gazed from the booth and into the techno din.

"I am responsible for the affairs of our contraption here called living." Bessingham bowed his head and then looked up.

"I would like to introduce to you, Mr. Spec, the orchestra of my synthetic world."

Frank looked up in measured disbelief and the Doctor began the introductions.

"Here is Rick, Gloria's husband. Here are a few of the ladies who have been lifetime clients. Here are my lawyers. Here are the un-noted diary dates in the flesh. Here are the prisoners of my profession, all dancing in the room, all folded into this moment. One last party. One last stand against the tyranny of decay."

Frank shifted nervously. What was he saying? What did Bessingham have going here? Was he saying these people were his last ditch social organization that had come to see him alter state?

"That the State was wrong?" Bessingham continued. "That it was working a lie? That I was no better than the cosmetics used to do a job, to make the painting stand out? To make a point. Nothing is as bad when reality breaks us down into what we really are. And when we find out that we are all fabrications of some fantastic, unnatural design we are getting close to realizing that the only way out is its reflective trick. You are my last trick, Frank. This is my last alteration. Falsity. Something, if you don't know, that has been happening to cultures for ages, so much so that the entire money structure of the world today is based upon prescribed drug cultures, as you know." Bessingham stopped suddenly and almost blurted out... "OUR THOUGHTS HAVE BEEN FAKE FOR 2000 YEARS WITHOUT US EVEN KNOWING IT! Look around you. 'Feely Theater's? Synesthaesia? Neural psychotics? Commercial infusion with one million pixels playing the eyes? Who in God's name would make this hell? But we swim in this emulsion daily and when the stoplight turns green we go and when it turns red we stop. Skinnerian labyrinths for the rats that we are. And the cheese? The trick or the trap? It is our desire to feel happy despite the truth. And so we cannot fathom within the walls of societies...unless we are hallucinating. You are here, Frank, to record this fake world. And you, my dear Mr. Spec, will see through...to the very end, I am sure."

Then Dr. Bessingham arose and took Gloria Falk's hand and walked out.

Frank remained at the table, stunned as the many taxonomically preserved museum pieces once in his room, completely undressed by the changes in event, the pathetically loaded harmony of the room and Bessingham's life not the seeming ragged ends of some broken body, but a medical divulgence of a most important State Official.

Frank waited for a second, trying to shake off the oddity, the terror. The terror of mixing his responsibility of scribe with a top official's demise. What the hell had just happened? Was he dreaming? Did he actually meet The Head of State for Human Affairs? He looked around the bar. Nobody was there. Only he, sitting at this table, with the fright of this rude comprehension. Things were echoing. Frank pushed himself up from the table, stumbled and noticed, on the table, a single piece of paper he had given to Bessingham to read, the obituary he had so nervously written. He picked it up and looked at the impression. At the top was the caption: OBITUARY.

"Dr. Miles Bessingham, Head of State to Human Affairs, passed due to a heart attack at 12:00am this morning outside of an LA nightclub. He was an upstanding, caring, and compassionate man who worked in the fashion industry in Hollywood for some years. Yet his main responsibility was in his work in the rigors as Head of State for Human Affairs where he championed changes in the physical and psychical infrastructure so that society could be properly endowed with a better view. In his spare time he enjoyed tinkering in the field of cosmetics, a hobby of his. He will be remembered for his foresight, empathy, and just work."

Frank felt a shiver flash down his spine. He looked at his watch. 12:01 am. He quickly felt his body. His hand met physique. He looked at the once full dance floor, the lights that were still spinning, save without the musical infusion. A shrill silence flooded him. He felt like running, getting out as fast as possible, getting away from his prediction. Yet the more he thought, the more realization sunk in. He had done it again. No, the mirror had been held up to Doctor Bessingham to show his expertise, something horrendously and shiveringly terrifying. Suddenly, realizing the flip, and coldly, with deep ironic clarity even, Bessingham's life passed through his own, the rapture of Franks' early investigations switching to the point of his prediction. FOOL! His mind screamed. The entire State would come down on him. The State would crucify for such a prediction. The diary pages fluttered through his consciousness in an eerie wind. Awkwardly he bolted for the door, an icy feeling in his heart that he must see his prediction's result, the absurdity an absurdity that he at one time enjoyed recording, had gotten used to, but now possessed in his hand the ultimate alteration of two maniacs, Dr. Bessingham and himself. A quote by the undead Cervantes percolated through his paranoia: "we are the children of our own works."

Frank ran out into the street. There, lying dead in the gutter was Bessingham's crooked figure. He looked at his client's body, desperately needing the confirmation of his reflection. Coolly he lifted his face to see himself in the club's window. The lights were off. He could see only a dark absence. In horror, feeling an immense gravity, he crumbled to the ground. He had written off The Head of State for Human Affairs! What is the realization of absolute truth, he thought? Life? Death? Afterlife? He could not answer. Deep inside, in the presence of a hideous paradox, he found himself trembling in utter joy. And then Frank Spec cried out, "I am right!"

A short time after he would be taken to St. Mary's.

THE MUSEUMS

In earnest Edward began to look for harbors elsewhere. He turned his memory back. He could easily recall his childhood. He remembered the ancient museums specifically, the clarity of unadulterated art emotion born from the traditional paintings. He could recall vividly the change in medium that had given birth to an entire new age of expression. It had been as addictive as illicit drugs. Holograph, technotic overlay, interactive hallucinatory web pictures, download mediums where feeling was, like phrenology encouraged from interactive state cybernetics with the brain. And of course the "internal museum" idea by a prodigy of Albert Hofmann. Yet the old museums had survived the hyper advance of solace mechanics and pixilated relay montage that was the new rage. Edward climbed the stairs, passing his and Jack's stand against physical violation, and entered.

There was an almost holy silence, the amber light through the micro blinds filtering in refulgence with miniscule particles of what he assumed was a dust born from the earthen exhibits.

People floated in the hallways like the tranquility of a deactivated zone.

Museums had always been a part of Edward's family experience, the trip to the LA County, or MOMA a quasi-intellectual and cultural affair that would, his mother thought, bear the right kind of fruit in his sisters' and his life according to The Emotional Enhancement Policies that had begun with the dry up of relational feelings after the coup. Edward was not sure when they made their first journey. He knew that he must have been old enough to be on his own, and his sister, Ellie, old enough to begin the "appreciation". What Edward remembered was that he somehow got left at the door while his mother and Ellie were sucked into the swirl of paint, power, and particle that one might call aesthetic. Edward was given a time frame, some hour or so later when they would reconnoiter. He must have been five or six. Unlike his sister, he could not be with paintings for any emotional duration, probably because what was on the wall looked to Edward like nothing. He had no eye. He was, like the State Team Playing, a boy of action. Edward could only see the colors and lines and years of arduous tortured artistic labor as some kind of pointless emulsion that someone would die for. But Edward didn't register die for. Nor did he register that the gyration of color on the wall could have afforded him a million ice cream cones or a million Hershey's chocolate bars, or Jack and his patients a million hours of peace. No one broke it down for him, the brilliance of the piece of a shattered woman walking downstairs naked, backward, and holding a violin that looked like a gun with melted taffy on the bow. Neither could he equate it with the woman in Borders, the pistol of some strange apparition cocked like chance. No one said to Edward, "Son, this line here, the one that is jagged, was drawn by Picasso when he was insane in an air raid and after he slept with his sister and fucked his model he had an epiphany and the decapitated horse head symbolizes life during war." But the State wouldn't allow that. Radical explanation was considered a displacement. Natural emotion would not erupt from adulteration. No one told him that the painting with the light in it was once stolen and then recovered on a sunken ship and the giant squid that ate the diver who was a treasure hunter was later brought up and cut open and the painting in a waterproof scroll was pulled out of the Kraken, and the merchantmen who were actually pirates sold it to The Christies Brotherhood for one hundred million dollars which they used to fund the next war in South America. He had had to read about it on his own. How like the descriptions of other worlds in Edward's patients' illumined sessions! No one said, "Dude, check out that lopsided tit! Look at that piece of loin! That hairy arm in twilight was the arm of Byron after he had fenced and killed his lover's rival. No one connected it with a sublime harbor. Indeed, Edward was not let in to this "place", let in like the authorities to such interesting morsels of information, information that might have saved a psychotic episode with the float of art. But this did not trouble him. Edward waited at the front door of the museum and, with his London Transport hat in hand, persuaded every high-cultured, artistic idiot to give him their cash, as he had become doorman to the heaven they aspired to. But his sister disappeared within and would come out as intricate as the air conditioning in the building. She wouldn't speak, a sloppy, but beautiful smile on her freckled young artist face, and sort of waft with his mother as Edward skipped along behind with enough dough to go through at least ten candy bars. In this manner Edward was introduced to the museum, or what he now distinguished as a visual harbor dock, where the emulsion transcended through the optic lens and into an illegal elsewhere in his head, a place wherein your mind was encouraged through a static medium of enriched history that loosened time. That he couldn't understand the language of art was not a problem, the secret, highly coded harbor of language was decipherable by feeling, the paintings somehow broke open, as they were meant to, deep into your most unconscious emotions.

But what was most apparent was that Edward could not see. This ineptitude really squashed all hopes of understanding Monet, Picasso, Beckman, Warhol, Matisse, and the other Ancients. It was not that he could not actually see visually, his vision was 20/20 as far as he knew. But something strange happened when Edward entered museums, a particularly strange phenomenon of blindness that he could only call a horrendously short attention span, an affliction in the Post Vital culture which the Psychiatric Board had studied and then dismissed as a minor effect from computing systems. So where he had five minutes to look at a canvas, somehow the five minutes, like his patients' afflictions, had all these divisions, spaces in-between, and the canvas, although right in front of his face, would simply not exist. Was Edward mentally fractured, too? He looked at the goateed men and polka dot dressed, thick-rimmed-spectacled process women and tried to figure out how they looked at the stuff. For Edward could see the way they looked at the art, long beard-stroked moments with winced up, or silver-dollar-wide eyes, somehow ingesting the religious squiggles in front of them. After seeing the method, he too would lean back, angle his head, touch his chin, flutter his eyes and pretend to pulse in amazement. This, however, did not work. Edward was still occluded. The canvas of a naked ass with an exploded emulsion of shit called color was blank in front of him. As if a vacuum had sucked the entire thing into empty orbit he was left bereft of the more illegal experiences of art as he circled, the deeper experiences of ecstasies that were now under control. Too young and already programmed not to cuss, in despair, Edward began to flex his museum muscles another way, his way, a way in which he found he could break into the harbor.

Having grown up with jazz, the jazz that is magic and comes out of an antique vinyl record like a crackly analog heaven, Edward had obtained a beat by the age of his listening. Out of spite or depressed isolation he did not know, but he would, with all the rhythm in the world, begin to shuck-and-jive around the room like a rock star with an oil audience of life won and lost, paintings oozing with the emotions of mankind, and, like a rock star, Edward would gyrate to his tapping feet and hand slaps, and be-bop on his lips barely held back from discovery. Edward would do this, gyrate all over the room and slap himself and grunt and, like a pin ball machine, get so lit up internally that he felt he was Seurat's pointillist genius in brilliant form, the glitter of refulgence upon the harbor ripples or later, in retrospect, as one of his patients' important visions. And a sort of breathing occurred, like excited yoga, and he began to feel sexy and started focusing on the legs of middle aged women, and the flowered skirts on asses seemed to be not only alive but also incredible! Edward's beat would bop him around the museum and it was in this moment of discovery that he, the useless bellhop at the front door, became a participating member of snobbery, knowledge, lust, sex, power, death, corruption, love, and wisdom, all in front of him and clear as he jacked the entire scene with his newfound rhythm. This was actually the only way Edward could perceive the paintings and the harbors within. If he stood still it all disappeared and smeared and became horribly boring. But with his beat, he could see the scintillating colors of the artists who tried to capture this oddity of God, and later he could also see how God captured his patients, the awe of a breakdown coalescing into the foci of such artistic magnitude as they vibrated in their bodies to perceptions beyond his vision.

Edward's realization was to him profound, yet it became more profound as he discovered museums are amazing sonic boxes that may resonate intensely due to their special geometries and wood floors and drum-like ceilings. This anomalous acoustic quality made him be-bop extra well and he was not surprised when, at a Mona Lisa or a Campbell Soup copy, he was noticed by the cultured set as a standout, and that, after consideration, this example might be fairly dangerous. Edward became so good at this form of seeing he was able to make both first, second, and third floor sweeps of culture so quickly that his assertions buoyed him to heights of enthusiasm. After a run of percussion, Edward would stall at a painting and sort of breathe with it in yogic brilliance and let the lambent light filtering through the skylights elevate him and brush him with its refulgent honey. Indeed, when Edward paused after a run of paintings that were beaten to, pounded to, bopped to and pulsed with, he felt as if he had attained, no matter his flurry, a sense of something he can only call art vibe beyond The State. And in this art vibe was a place of profound, heart-beating resonance where Edward could now see moorings for emotional sensibility, no matter that his effusions were primitive. And maybe not even this. Maybe it was enhanced endorphins, or having shucked off some bad spell or a lack he possessed an abundance of, his nirvana commingling with vision and sound, like Prescription TV, only better. What was most incredible was that he could see, actually see the paintings, and whether he understood them or not, whether he grasped the deep philosophic present of the history and pain and love and lust—what Edward discerned was that the stuff he had up until now not known, was now capable of a brilliance he could only call real, heartfelt, sublime art, which has now induced him to play music in patient session, pursue his paper discretely, and get to the core he and his patients so longed for. Yet what was that core? Complete freedom of expression and health, absolute spirit, hyper-creation, and, of course, love, despite the times.

Edward's intensity and youthful amelioration grew from there. So when his sister and mother appeared and looked like Athena and Aphrodite floating down the escalator after their fix, he, at the door, would understand what they were so excited about. They would drive home in conversation about Renoir's sensibility, Monet's "Bridge", the pointillists, the war art, Picasso's cubism, Matisse's flowers, impasto paint and acrylic versus oil, and how Dali was into sex and if they got Whistler's light and if there was anything nice about the classicists, and ultimately, even though he didn't know all of the names, Edward, in the back seat, the younger brother who had previously only held open doors for the rich and undeniably aesthetic crowd, tapped his hand on the seat like Michaux after he had overdosed on mescaline, to balance the careening world, yet to his own beat which he listened to with appreciative reverence. Edward's understanding of toilet sublimity, outside of Jack's vicious art, outside of his naïve love, was now given another place, a place wherein life might unravel from the great machine, to breathe within the slow, indubitable peace of mind needed to live. Edward realized art, not a pill, could save his patients, and in this world he, too, wanted absolute right.

BOOST STATISTICS OF EDMOND LITTLE

E.L. folded into Magellan's to Cold Play and withdrew his shades. The light dimpling through the glass glanced off the canteen display. Not following the warm cascade he looked up and found himself on a Digital hung from the ceiling. The vibe was capital: browsy buyers, the expensive material of a specialty store, clerk's head bent in God knows what computation. Flow surged in his veins and he meandered like the bourgeois clickers looking for essentials. Passed the compasses. Passed sporting goods, backpacks, slick macks, and into the surround of articles aching for attention. His heart was pounding with the symbolic messages of the law...if you do this, one year....if you do that, two. Just managing the pound of this realization was hard enough. Then he turned off, went into intuition and let the vibe ride. Dark zone is what he termed it. The feel of the turn off of the whole program. What it required of him was a supreme trust that whatever he sensed was correct, whatever his fingers procured was right, whatever the other forty eyes in the store witnessed wasn't him. Upon reaching the fold-up umbrellas he paused, stroking the article with geometric care. Right size. Palmable. Thirty-seven dollars good for any rain. One glance up told him he had found the spot....not a single shopper or clerk face confronted his imagination. He slipped the umbrella up and then let it slide into his form. Looking around casually he did not pick up any vibe. He sauntered in a circle around a rack of jackets and let it fall into his right pocket. His heart beat faster. Hence "boost". The article, whether expensive or desirable, after the "idea" of stealing, became the term. Energy pumped through him like a freight train. A few more minutes to fit in and browse... nice water containers...nice bags...Then one last take of the floor and he found the door void of sensors. With one turn he walked out into the emphatic sunshine. His head played mock alarms that boosted him further. He turned and walked up the shops and around the corner, the event like a spirit jackhammer. In his mind he played all possible responses to be made in case of follow. "Oh, I completely forgot it was in my pocket!" "Just going to my car to get my wallet," "Oh, I am very sorry, I thought I had paid..." Around the corner he found his stride. He loped, feeling the prize in his pocket, his heart now settling into red-hot awe. One umbrella for travel. But where was he going? The question was rigged.... "what umbrella? I am sorry I do not know what you are talking about, as you can see I possess nothing..."

Boost. Steal. Hike. Take. Purloin. Rob. Filch. Pilfer. Lift. Prig. Bag. Nim. Crib. Palm. Pluck. The world for the crook was loaded, and like a gun often pointed in the most important direction. Any-thing that anybody in or out of his or her right mind wanted was here for the plunderer...even more so in State Stability. Some men wanted millions in return, others settled for a Slurpy. Pickpockets relieved millions of hapless finery while Corsairs actually took the whole boat. Thousands upon thousands of spoilers made away with goods so fine not even royalty could add up. The world was, in short, peppered with deception since the New Order and the hundred shops opening their doors to legitimate customers would find at least twenty percent of their stock had been lifted in one year. Nobody comprehends this unless you're a crossover...all the compliant, hard-working churchgoers, every one of them floating in the legal zone to be deprived of their material. Once over you get an edge that keeps bringing you back, mentally and physically. The edge, unknowable to a regular shopper, bubbles in the veins and mind of the thief until he appropriates the article and slakes his sensibility. Poacher. Rover. Harpy. Shark. Pirate. Racketeer. Thimble-Rigger. Greek. Blackleg. Welsher. Cacus. Artful Dodger... shoplifter.

It didn't matter to E.L. whether he had a diamond or a penny. What E.L. cared about was how he pulled his art. For that is how he saw it. All the things that added up from camera to clerk to manager to door guard—all of these in the "mix" made the balance sublime. Yet his favorite job was talking to the managers while he held an item, even in plain sight, and while chatting up the service person he would pocket the thing and continue on until he knew by the conversation that the idiot had no idea. Then he'd simply walk out, the trouble infused with extra vibe from the deceptive discussion. How many times had he done this? He had kept track, casually. Five years on the grab....about four hundred plus. How many managers did he freeboot in front of? Maybe three hundred. His work had perfected itself, had become particular like a polished diamond. But none of it was for cash. Cash always complicated the *brigandage*. If you went in for a money job then you were stuck with the effects. The object had to be sold. The piece had to be fenced. The job had to have multiple characters involved. So it was best, E.L. found, to lift only what you chanced, not needed. When you need you mess up. When it is pure the thing poached is made worthless until you get to its meaning, apply it to your life and feel. Imagination doesn't override the act with shivery nerves. Hence Dark Zone, or as E.L. liked to say to Wells, "intuition". This is how he operated. Know only as much as your desire to buy. Shop the store until you have your good. Then, flip things into the intuition and sack it or pocket it and pull the boost. From door to car you would be so lit up your legs wobbled. From car to road, granted no cops came with psycho work, you were on the edge. And until you got far enough away to know there was no law, you were high as a fucking kite. In this manner, E.L. had become a professional, and the smallest, most insignificant item often had the best value.

E.L considered his laws. A manager boost is no easy trick. What is obvious is that when you steal, whether or not you want one, you get a manager. There is very little explanation for this. One might think the chance of the stolen article at some weird intersection of space and time brings the manager into play. Perhaps more phenomenally the manager's entire job is to take care of the goods with extrasensory perception. Hence, when you procure the best good that is to be purloined, that good, somehow entering a new zone of retail, off the map so to speak, causes an anomaly that draws authority. In such regard, the lift is often fraught with varying nuances that make the take more charged. All one has to do is drop-pocket the goods and a manager will more than likely look, or appear. What they are looking at they cannot know. The law is a matter of possession. They are contagious with a puppeteer of sense, a behind-the-scenes entity that is Law. It sometimes comes through their eyes like small bowling balls of difference looking to knock out the pins. But the mere instance of boosting puts one somehow on their radar, since one may assume that any article "mishandled" in the store is in need of managerial attention. Straight up, a boost of an article in front of the manager is a very fine-tuned piece of work and when it goes well it makes the steal a flow of the most essential energy.

E.L. was in his intuition like a king. The parking lot was full. His ideas had settled into the Dark Zone. And the ever real and vital presence of his guts somehow pulled him out of his car and to Craft Essentials. Craft Essentials had everything including so many cameras one's profile was taken a hundred times upon entry. Nothing expensive. Lots of chachkas and material that was supposedly for artists. E.L. knew that the flow of this day was based upon speech. He opened the door and began the diligent search like all the people looking for their items. He headed down the aisle and browsed for what he played off as stuff, like anybody else, the clientele on the cruise for the best buy. When he came out of the aisle he ran into a rack of carpet material, linen, and a whole stack of assorted sewing thread on display. He didn't have to look up to know that there were five cameras checking him out. E.L. did the math. I am being observed on twenty different lenses. I am hot as a mother. They can see me sweat...but who are they?

What he had learned was cost. If it cost twenty thousand dollars to install a camera web, did the owner invest another ten thousand a year in observation fees? Probably not. Probably—and this is safe to say—the camera went nowhere...just like his supposed disease. No box with technicians panning in and out like in thrillers. No secret back room where they made you, like in spy movies. No super tech center where they possessed you, like in vampire flicks. The sole reason for this web-work was deterrent. If something happens, then the managers have it on film and can insure themselves over the grief of a customer. Rewind the shift and see what sucker tried to pull a heist. That and deterrent. So when the sweat beaded up on E.L.'s forehead it was for another reason. Already in his hand he had procured a sea blue spool. The thread felt like a small amusement park of joy in his palm. But the sweat was that while ruminating over the camera issue he had intuited the manager in the mix.

"May I help you sir." The man was dressed in polyester shirt and pants. Poor soul in a shitty job. Yet the poorer the soul the most likely to make you. Why? Because they had to hustle, too. They had to make bank to stay afloat. And, in a way they were on the fringe enough to be a looker, a maker, and probably also a taker.

"Just browsing," E.L. said with his hand folded over the item he had come upon.

"What are you looking for today, sir?" The question, like a pick, was trying to open him up. He had a sharp manager here. Had he come up just as E.L.'s fingers closed around the thread? E.L. decided to get into the thick of it.

"Yes, I am looking for some fabric." He lied... "I am trying to make camera cases for my line of Nikons."

The manager smiled. The words didn't exactly register. "Is it a small camera?"

"Actually," said E.L., poised in thief hyperspace, "I am starting a business...there are some," he looked up at the ceiling and added. "There are some forty cameras. I am looking at forty cases."

Hide in plain sight and do a PoPo. The rules were always shifty. E.L. had put all his cards on the table and the manager did not even register.

"Well we have some nice fabric. Over here we have the paisley red, and the silk although expensive is nice. What kind are you looking for?"

E.L. looked at the display with the thread in his hand. "I want steel blue." He smiled at the flirt.

"Well, we have a nice gun metal right over here."

"No. I want steel."

The pause was almost long enough to give E.L. away. He looked at the manager with a wry I've-got-your-goods-already smile.

"Well I don't think we have any steel here. We have Royal Blue, Teal, oh...here, this is steel blue."

E.L. was trying to hold back his joy. The manager had fallen hook line and sinker into the take, missing the semantics. His hand tightened around the thread.

"If you are looking to sew the fabric, we have lots of thread." The manager looked with excited I-will- sell-you eyes.

"Let me think about the fabric as I walk around. My Nikons are close to being up for sale. I would very much like to purchase now but I think I should...ask my wife." E.L. smiled.

"Oh, I quite understand," the manager said.

If you throw in the wife then everything goes legit. The trump card of love, innocence, and establishment. A wife remark was like saying you are a priest, there is no problem, she just wanted me to come shopping for her.

"Just let me know if I can help you in any way."

"Thank you very much," E.L. said

Then, precariously close to the conversation and meditating with the spool in his hand, he walked as naked as a newborn down the aisle he had meandered up, along to the door, and out into the parking lot. As he walked he felt shaky and happy and ready to lob the excuses... "Oh, I totally forgot that I had this in my hand."…. "Just going to get some cash out of the car..."… "I wanted to see what it looked like in the...sunlight." Then, upon reaching the door he used his keys, shaking with excitation, and hopped in. As everything came to a head, he shook and opened his palm...A blue spool of silk thread. Utterly meaningless thread unless you sew. It actually looked in color like his best steal he had ever made. That's it. He thought. I actually can sew it...there are other realities to seam together. The boost vibrated through his muscles and bones, like a positively charged ghost. He started the engine and rolled out of the lot, the images of his thoughts lifting.

As he drove he ruminated over the likeness of the thread and his latest steal, which lay wrapped in a cloth next to him on the seat. Purity, he thought. Incredible market for this. That he had pulled this heist was unusual. It was the most dangerous thing he had ever done. People would kill for purity, especially C grade vials. He thought of how it was made. They had done the synth-vials very easily. But then they got to poetry. Someone had come up with the great idea of a mixture that, like class 1 drugs of the past, became high value. What was it, he thought? He had stolen the thing from The Emotional Library Vats on a whim. He was curious what it might do to a person. E.L. could not imagine a person on purity. Would they become God? He tried to recall the mixture...condensed serotonin, poetical sensors, awe levels from the interface, and images of times in a memory transducer that fluxed into a foci of love, trust, happiness, and also, he thought strangely, hate. Then reduce them to a clear state and that was it. A liquid form of the very veins of angels.

He put the cloth with vial into the glove compartment and turned the corner. Better not to get caught with this.

THE VOICE ORCHESTRA

The bus had broken down on the way to Tower Records. The experimental group was to take a "vacation" from their illness, to experience a musical facility. None of the patients were advised that their medication had been supplanted with placebo. They had signed the appropriate papers releasing Edward for this surprise change. And in the time that they had been together they and Edward had become "psych-weathered". His patients trusted him. The fact that their normal meds were often debilitating was a common complaint all had expressed desire to change. So there had been no lack of interest in such experiment. It was seen by all as an improvised manner of reclamation of perspective.

Cherry, Mark, E.L., Frank, and Jack fidgeted in the back like popcorn in some theater pan, the oil of their perceptions hot in agitated realization. Jack had survived his coma. Edward had been quite nervous; the state would have come down on him hard. He observed his patients quietly. He hadn't planned for this event of misfortune with the bus. He had planned in the back of his mind for the dosages to fail while listening to the greatest hits in some studio in Tower, to record their meander as the body felt the med vacuum, and to artistically see the results. Now there was nothing to do but wait for the repair truck. That it might mean a possible crash in confines of their space was an issue. But Edward put all worries at ease and resigned himself to the mildness of the disaster.

With his eyes closing in his seat he suddenly picked up an unusual conversation in the back, which drew him instantly to notice. He pulled himself up and made his way down the aisle. There Edward found Frank, Cherry, Mark, E.L. and Jack huddled together in a concentrated group. The energy was quirky. They looked like satellite dishes picking up some weird frequency, twitching a little to something here and beyond. Their focus was intense. Their hands played on things as if on drums. All knew where they were supposed to be, up in the lofty kingdom of famous musicians. They were very excited. Edward joined in.

"The first first transmission wasn't quite quite recognizable. I didn't know if I was hearing things until I responded and it responded back."

"What did it say?" E.L. asked.

"My name name. It said, Mark."

"And nobody was there speaking with you?" Jack jumped in, excited.

"No no no."

"When did this happen?" E.L. retorted.

"Two to toto a.m. Western Standard Time, between 1901 and 1953."

"What the hell are you talking about," said Jack, "That puts you at roughly an ambiguous one-hundred plus!"

"I have have spent a lot of time time trying to figure it out, but I realized realwised, after study buddy, that these dates datas proved to be the most accurate. In 1901 Guglielmo Marcopoloconi sent the first wireless transmission from Paldu, Cornwall, to Newfoundland. He sent an 'S' over the Atlantic and it arrived safely at the receiver. But I could not understand why this was important at first until I lookedshooked at the physics that were enstabling the world to communicate at that time." Mark paused with his hands in the air. "Radio waves pass totoly through us." His face was in awe. "So...I figured that if they pass through then they are capable of affecting our communication, both literally in the world and within ourselves. Or or to put it another brother way: there is no difference between inside and out. Indeed of freed we, at that time time, I believe, became mediums, mediums for mass extrasensory transmissions." Edward observed the group. They were becoming very excited. Transmissions, after all, were common to all of them.

"Why 1953?" Edward asked.

"Crickly Dick and Watthefuckisgoinon had found the double Helix. The body alphabet, the code of our being, our genetic electric map to a future, our traits on a stir case that would give rise to om supreme knowledge of identity. In the span from 1901 to 1953 we see a tremendous mess advance in technologies that allowed the body to interact with various machines, to understandaband... possibly to fuse. So I figured that the invention tension of the crystal set along with a map of the body body transmogrifies us into other(s)." Mark made a shape with his body to elucidate "others". Essentially, extra-sensory perception as the voice fanspans out on wavelengths and the body load code is unlocked, the interaction of our retro fragment DNA with radio transmissions, these most most likely transmogrify the frequency scintillation of our hearing and supplants it with altered frequencies that are otherwise blocked by everyday dissonance and distraction."

The group were squinting, their brains wrapping around the physics.

"So why 2 a.m.?" Cherry asked.

"We are normally paranormally slipping into REM at that time time, a loosening up of the bright brain from the things of the day, synesthesia...synesthseesya takes over. We become the melting pot of dreams. We are susceptible to differeffervescence. But not only this. A code, I realized, embodied in a marking of time symbolically rollically linked: to "am" or to "is". More or less yes the verb disclosing existence. But what is existence? We are asleep weep without knowing what our full potential is. We are," Mark stopped to point and looked at Edward, "a 'regular', but cannot find the correct erecterset rhythm, the flow glow...the proper dissonance to lose it. Yet we want to express everything, as every body does! This is the actual course of liberty!" He halted abruptly.

"The real State," Edward said, "Communication...Language." Edward's look had twisted into intensity. Mark had picked up some cool information. The rest listened in earnest.

In concerted agreement his patients nodded their heads. Yes, they did want to express everything, everything that they were—faulty, potz, or not...what their constitution and adaptation demanded, the outflow of their souls the same as the natural desire to procreate. Yes, they did want to harbor their communication...in whatever way they could. To save. To record. To preserve and protect. In short, they all wanted to live, immediately, absolutely, now, at once. The chorus was more fine-tuned than the parts being fixed on the bus. Mark continued... "Put together ever the love articulations and one one gets expression and creation; existence becomes itself, we live live with complete health and we are awareness!"

How long had they all been locked up without voice enough to be in love, completely alive? How long had they only partially existed in mental illness or insanity? How long had Edward and they been subject to distraction after distraction for the sake of a prescribed life given to them by history's crude inventions, maze after med-maze that they barely navigated through as social beings? Indeed, how much did they not know and how much could they know after such mental transmogrification?

"Yes," Mark said. "Are you with me?"

They found nothing to object to. Moreover, Edward noticed that a moment of sublime peace had settled over as if the puzzling aspects of nature were no longer oblique shadows in mind. Clarity in words had occurred, a clarity that made them feel whole. He could hear the cranking of a tool in the engine.

Knowing that each patient's sensibility was, like a roulette wheel, going to slot into some number no matter the world chaos, Edward put all his money on their creativity. Then he returned to reasoning that perhaps they had hit a Doppler on the freeway, maybe his students slipping their intercourse a fey word, their perceptions unlocked in him, like the museums, elsewhere. E.L., and Frank looked up. "This is a very rare species of insight," they said in absolute tonal unison.

At this point Edward decided to call therapy in a public place, the only means of getting to a core he thought was opening. The bus was adjacent to a cheap Virtual with a sign that read Ginny's Restaurant. It was the only restaurant within ten miles that was a habitable spot to go deep. Yet, that it was a Virtual was a problem. People put in an order and went on mind vacations there, to live like in the old days the diner experience of Fifty's kitsch pancakes and cheap eggs. As with many Virtuals, it presented a retro-environment to relive the glory of days gone by. Edward had to consider how his patients would react to a hook up to yesterday, how would they feel with diners in a unified space of peaceful agreement.

Yet in complete disagreement with The State Psychiatric Codes he decided to put his patients into the best comfort zone, however public. That they had discovered this unique perception, which he thought might alter space, or change perception in a violent way, was his concern. He looked at the group cautiously.

"Lets go get a seat at that restaurant over there," Edward suggested, pointing to Ginny's. He could already see things starting to change. Jack had become more agitated. E.L. was twitching from subject to subject. Mark's eyes were wide and he noticed dilation. Cherry had begun to exhibit signs of auditory hallucination. And Frank, grooming his hair back, had a wild look in his eyes. Changing settings might placate their now fluxing actions. Food could very well calm them down.

Edward moved them with trepidation out the bus door. He

noticed his attention was breaking. His heart was beating fast. He didn't want to lose the core of this understanding. He didn't want for their ideas to float out beyond never to refocus. They crossed the street and he saw them slowly begin to, like some primitive tribe in a jungle of freeway and concrete, become startled in disbelief. They made the other side of the road and then Frank turned and to the straggling group and yelled.

"Come on let's take the place!"

As if some pack of animals, Edward realized, they had slipped into a completely different reality. Something wild and untamed had transpired. Even in himself a feeling of raw energy had swept over him, like he was part of their chaotic thoughts. Upon reaching the restaurant, Frank flung the door open in abandon. Edward realized he was no longer in control. They rolled in like a gigantic machine in the flow of the most vital electricity. Frank grabbed hold of Edward's arm just as they broke through the Virtual accommodation portal. The field of peaceful diners fluxed in front of them from vacation to normalcy. In the flux Edward could see faces of people who had been beaten down, long faces in sorrow and pain. Then, fluxing back again the Virtual reestablished and all was peaceful and calm and happy.

"What selection?" a computer voice said.

Edward watched Frank jam a chip into the slot and then another and another until the Virtual host balked.

"Please allow, please allow for…please allow for…"

A spark fizzled from the console and a man screamed at a table that had been deactivated. Then suddenly Edward realized, in the chaos of the moment, what might be considered a group hallucination that emitted around them. He looked to Frank who was smiling, "I put in the ego film western pulp relay mix," he said bluntly.

They enter the restaurant and unstick lipstick. A retro-crowd Fifties white trash eating pancakes and plastic eggs at the tables barely look up. The camera pans up the taut fishnet of history. She groans and gapes her mouth, a book up one leg and a pen strapped to the fissure between her thighs. The waitress offers menus. They toss their heads in slow motion, crap-dice-rolling smiles.

Mark, improvident, keeps his heart wheeling. Frank, with so much mascara, is a sobbing raccoon. E.L. the Kid gapped-toothed whistles Dixie. Frank, tanned as all women should be, looms, high-heels sharper than stilettos, skyscraping him. They head for a booth and remember Lincoln Logs.

"Wadda ya want," the waitress's bubble gum pops. The camera pans to her pink blow piercing her tongue. We see down her throat and then into her stomach, through the colon and out her ass, then slow down her legs and under the table and back up to the six. "Fucking fuzz is coming," Mark sighs. The bacon looks good in the picture perfectly pigged. "Four slabs, and the dregs of your best coffee, Bitch." "Attitude with that chick?"` "Yeah, it's how planes fly." Frank rubs his pen and pushes the head, clicking to elevator Muzac music. E.L. whips his pistols out and shoots the register. "Wadda you doin?" the waitress chafes. "Holy time, dar-ling." Observation's joke jokes into the room. The white trash keep eating, TV swallowed reactions. The food's American, besides.

Like a Turkish bulldog ground in a blender the coffee grains stick and blacken their teeth. The pep's in like a slut turning on frat boys. "We gonna do it by Jesus or not at all," says Frank. The ques-tion pointedly an exclamation and period has it that it's 2000 A.D. "Wait 'til the bacon," Mark says. "Wait 'til I've got the pig stuck in my gut like a rod up your rear end," says Cherry. "I've already burned in hell and there's time."

Ed grunts his snub nose to the plate. "Don't nobody care no more?" "That was last millennium, Ed." The camera melts to the coffee stirring in a Jack. "Wait, I'm uploading a vision." The cam-era blurs through the coffee to a double helix in the Fifties. "It's like poetry made by glowing computers; pixel clear and up dry on the cocksucker's spirals, says Cherry." Frank curls that down on his thigh. The camera licks slowly until Helix is blurred just like time's skin. "Fucking media," He chips like a golfer in the sand, "always erasing my body paint." "Give me syrup or give me death!" yells Mark. "Give him death," replies E.L., adjusting his rearview. "Either way," Frank rips, "you're a sap sweetly embalmed." He twizzles the words saintly, like a pacifier in the hands of reconciliation. "What a movie," says Frank looking at a toot who has just walked in to their fix. "She's got class and failed it for life." "We chicks must stick together, even in whoredom." "Lay it on Frank. Dike away." Frank gets up to smack and moves for the tooty. The others watch, chomping on bacon. "Let's lay bets they do it in the stall." "I bet you he rubs her right on the register." "Shit hot as newly weds." They watch as Frank whispers his magic. Greasier than train pistons at five hundred, they sleek into metaphysics and lay the busboy with a stare. "Quite good at propriety," says Mark. "My mother would be proud," says Jack." "Stop slopping you verb hound," says Frank, checking his book. "Almost time," says Mark, licking his barrels. This joint must be laissez-faire reverb from a mental. Classy as acts come they stewed that one.

"Almost time," says Mark again. The camera turns to slow copulating motion so the entire room shivers. E.L. is up on the table in a "crucifixion" draw, chandeliers and plates fly like Ultimate Frisbee. Frank begins to record in his book as Cherry accentuates the slop down his dregs, flips the tables on them and masturbates to the chaos. Frank and his toot head for the cook and one look levels him into a frying pan. Lots of gun-smoke. The eaters are nonplussed as flowers in a windless garden.

Outside the Virtual environment a siren blared. Two police figures entered and shut down the field. Glock out like a corral shooter, Officer Nesbit runs in with his partner in hyper-drive backup.

"DOWN DOWN DOWN!" yells officer Nesbit. He surveys the restaurant. With the field dropped every one is in complete despair. He looks around and finds amongst the startled guests nothing untoward. He speaks into his radio. "Back up."

Edward heaves out of the hallucination and an uncontrollable flash back invades his auditory..."Every shopper body falls down. The man with the purse runs upstairs. He discharges a weapon at me and I dive to the ground. I do not notice the victim woman running behind me. I sprint up the stairs without backup.

At the top of the stairs in the music section of Borders I see no one. I begin to comb the aisles. So intense is the feeling of pursuit I forget about Aremac. Then, at the end of the aisle as I turn the corner with my Glock in hand, the purse-snatcher disarms me and puts my identity in a vise-grip. He drags me to the stairwell and runs into the woman whose purse he stole. She is holding Sergeant Aremac's Thirty-Eight. The man looks at the woman with trapped eyes. I have become a human shield. The woman is pointing the gun directly at me. I look fiercely into her eyes in complete awe and disbelief. She closes her eyes tight. I do not know why she is closing her eyes. The gun wavers in her hand like a leaf in the wind..."

Edward regains composure and finds himself at a table. He looks to E.L., Cherry, Frank, Mark, and Jack. They are sitting casually in the booth. Edward is blinking his eyes, not knowing from the entry of Ginny's to the seat whether Frank dosed him or it's the broken Virtual, or whether it's his Empathy Test drug in echo, or heat.

"Where's the shooter! Where's the shooter!" The cop says to the waitress.

"There's no shooter here," says the waitress.

Officer Nesbit looks around. The customers look at him in shock.

"We got a call," he says, "shooter at Ginny's."

"There's no problem here," says the waitress. "Only nice customers. We thought you were doing a movie."

"Shit," he says, winded by his entry.

E.L. Cherry and the rest look at Edward. Edward is shaking. He sees a coffee in front of him. He sees that they have ordered pancakes.

Officer Nesbit turns toward Edward while putting his Glock in his holster. "Having a nice meal?" he says.

Edward looks at him. A flow of guilt is shaking in him.

"We did it," Edward said, shaking. "You see, I am a doctor of psychosis and my group here are out on a special trip and we were using placebo."

"What the hell is a placebo?"

Frank smiles at Edward.

"They're false medicine. We, ah, have hallucinations some-times...a State warranted psychological rehabilitation journey to Tower...we didn't mean to cause a..."

"Stir," says Frank. His spoon is gently rotating in his coffee.

Edward sees his mistake. Do not mention group hallucina-tion wherein they act out, violently act out their roles to jack the restaurant...do not mention subversive State mental cases from St. Mary's. Ah, do not mention they entered the restaurant, blew away the register, masturbated on the table, hooked the cook, booted the toot, and shifted reality in a pancake mix that suckered the cop into a fritz job of neural undulation at degrees of which...do not mention I am testing against the med standards to see if the potz orientation is of this world or another real..."

"I am sorry for the problem you didn't have," says Frank.

Officer Nesbit looked sharply at Dr. Wells. "Cause WHAT?"

Edward regained composure.

"We are on a tour. I am a doctor." His voice is moving rap-idly. "We are measuring the host adaptive against the metaphysi-cal layout of material of a vibe we are trying to get played out at Tower. Our bust...I mean bus broke down." Do not mention the possibility of given space-time relations... "ah, we measure our ac-tions in the mix of every day life as a tonal relation to reality." Do not mention we're insane...

"So you guys are a group? Of what?"

Mark piped up. "As you can see we don't have any guns. Just breakfast here, sir."

Edward's heart is pounding. Leave out the cerebral fracture born from years of seeing shit nobody really can understand...leave out illness...leave...

"Who reported," Officer Nesbit said, "this event?"

"I don't know," said Edward, regaining sensibility.

"Then nothing's going on?" He looked at the group skepti-cally.

"Just pancake excitement," said Frank. "But it does seem

that you are experiencing a fritz yourself, to which I would rec-ommend Gingko for amelioration. Look around you. There is no shooter here....perhaps I could give you my card, come in for therapy, loose transit verb play, and pulse essential cop make-up for longer duration." Frank motioned to Edward. Edward moved a shaking hand in his jacket and handed his card to the police officer in what he thought to be a surreal voice.

"I would be very happy to treat you if you are having hal-lucinations," said Edward.

"Must have been a faulty call. No problem here, then?" he said to the waitress.

"Everything is perfectly normal," she smiled.

Officer Nesbit and his partner walk out of the restaurant.

Cherry, Frank, E.L. Mark, and Jack watched Edward inhale.

"Now Now we know show that our hallucinations are real," said Mark.

"Yes," said Edward. "Now we know...somebody saw us."

TOWER

When they got to Tower things began to become expressive. The tour guide was startled when Edward, with his patients, asked for a private room.

"Why do you want a private room?"

Edward looked at him askance. "Ah, we are having a little bit of a projected tourism right now. My patients are excited by music. They have...ah...changed up," he left out transcended, "to a medium of expression which we must," he left out control "...facilitate."

"Shit," the tour guide said. "Just like a fucking famous musician. You're talking about cool vibe."

Edward paused. There was no better word for this experience. "Yes," he said.

"Shit we don't get any cool vibe around here very often unless the Swingers or the Jellybeans are in. Why didn't you say?"

"There was no other word in my head."

Then the tour guide leaned over. "You all dropped before

111

you came, right?"

Edward looked shocked. "Actually we did the opposite...we undropped."

"So you're trippin on free love?"

Frank intervened. "Costly love."

Costly love was another word for pure emotion in the street.

"If you got costly love then you are high as a fucking puritan!" the tour guide effused. "Costly mother fucking love! Jesus H. Pre Second Coming Christ. Let's get you to the recording studio and save this emoting. Just like a fucking revolution."

The bearded tour guide opened a side door and they entered into a padded studio.

"Now you just wait right here. Costly fucking love. I haven't seen such a thing since the goddamn B-News Group in the millennium switch bitch."

He turned away excited.

Edward considered the scene. His patients were on placebos and he was possibly connected to their, he didn't want to say, hallucination...experience. They had jacked into some Western Pulp Virtual by accident at the restaurant and the law appeared. Their actions were obviously not normal. Was it hallucination? And if it were, who would have called the cops? Someone must have seen their thoughts.

The tour guide returned.

"Let's hook you guys up! Nothing like a costly love session."

Frank, Cherry, Mark, E.L., Jack and Edward assumed seats in a circle. Edward folded his hands on his lap and looked up wondering how deep they would go. They were disheveled, the marks of their various problems setting impressions that came through their faces in both hard and soft animation, medically loose Edward thought, with the creases of hard mind labor.

"Ok," the tour guide said. "Now what I want you to do is to just say it how it is, don't hold back, open yourselves to the possibilities and flow." He looked to each of them. "Just say it how it is, there are no boundaries, no law, nothing." Then he opened it up to see where they were at. Frank offered the first take.

"There is a wince in the way life looks, a constant needing to turn away, an away that keeps wanting return. And we, Terra Incognita, say so many stupid things, as if tongue shook the Tower of Babel and an urn of words spilled its ash. Stuff that points to history and fills it up with mistakes like (I cannot repeat)—Someone is using my brain to cheat on an empathy exam!"

He stopped and bowed his head in his hands. A tremor shook his body, and wiping back his greasy black hair, he looked up and Edward saw that in his eyes was a gravity, a shiny gravity, whether due to medication reaction or some other spirit, he had unlocked. Force passed through Edward's mind like static in a dryer and he resettled his gaze on Frank.

"Hardly a fat chance in spell that this will beat your most regular sentences up." Frank laughed. "Just the other evening picking up supper for myself, someone asked what I was doing, and sticking in my trap no words arose, save, I am renting the food. How can you rent food? I asked, how fun are you? I mean fine, you know, did I just say 'rent'? I must...This is how things are living now..." Frank seemed to be chatting to himself or another in the room... "A virus from outer space? Sure, it could be that or just a ripple in the phase of what's pure, a language of block, a lingo tipple in the bar of many sayings. A shock in the shuck and jive of jazz. Words live such strange lives just as love, in abandon, sensibly, has no laws so it may sit and hike its skirt up all the way to phat city." He looked at them deeply. "But you want all, the away and the return and the pretty in-between that gives you center, and the last and the first saying, Fie that this worm would enter as gnome such a primitive brain!" A massive sigh heaved from his chest. "So it goes. You come out, cold-cocked, relay: If you don't know what it is, it's jazz...Baby, let this stand and maker her nonce in the lake of language that goes here like Kingdom Come. Let it ride and chance for itself. Let it, as they say, ride."

Frank settled back in his chair in some verbal electricity born from speech. The others looked on and no one said anything.

The tour guide was smiling like a Cheshire Cat.

"Shit, you're like that band made called the Tear Bottles. Jeesus!" He maneuvered around a data board and then pointed his hand at Jack.

Jack sat up and through his muscular form twitched out what appeared to be involuntary focus. He contributed.

"Out at the bars, fuzz mingled drunk mannequins. Cell phone rapture. Blinking light face lifts. Trying to hang on to a verb, a noun, sequins of thought tipping, an evening, a dress. Pits of pleasure and terror and soft madness and unknowing and desire's leverage in the eyes. Spin in the ken of foraging funk dealers, and rotting discourse, and pink bimbets. Out of your mind at sometime meantime. What year? You tell me. What now? Always. Grace stompers and mould munching the dish of raw in the room so loud plays with that delicate disaster in all hearts. Punching bag sound pound penthouse cream time and churn in the lost elegance. Steal a bench. Rest on the steel. Thinking without saying and want and not be bop pop be. Goddamn grace dealers and happy facers and fixed fops on the hunt for lust's bulb! Sticky glue language and lion pacers and pollination of the loins in a gesture, and lost love in the toilet and make-up solder all over her face and measure after measure of music mauling and crawling up the walls to the limit. Limit? Unimagined. A last ditch drink in your hands quaffed, shivering down your gullet to install your courage for one more go. Pinball machine madness. Eyes hung in air, here questions being dismantled. Pip and squeak spin of the vinyl pumping pairs of people together into trope machines bowed in the din and dump of sound and selections of yesterday suffusing the room, the relay reveling in their pawn shop merriment, the innocent children being hocked, yellers of today and fabric ripped raunch on the lips languishing out into the electric field like a fling with shock therapy. With crunch and coy faces and people pummeling together their last package of a day and hope and lust and the everlasting rip of play of American stuffed animals in a room blasting for the songs of trumped up pleasures."

Jack resettled into his chair as if he had delivered and now was rethinking an uppercut. Edward watched the ripples fan out into the rest. The group shifted in their chairs like unwinding ropes, untying in themselves places and pasts that were now present in the room. Edward wondered if he was going too far. After all, words, as much as they could make a person could unmake them. But he had wanted this...an opening on the radio. What would he do if they started to flash here? They were flashing! What would happen if...Yet, Edward thought that it was paramount to get it out now, after the genetic discovery of voice transmissions. Were they not a channel? Was this not what the voices they found needed?

"Ok. Anyone else?" the tour guide said. "Shit, this is beauty rockin lingo B plus makeover music babies."

"Is this going out over the air waves?" Edward asked

"Heck fucking yeah!" said the technician.

Voice risk shivered through Edward. They could say anything. They could cause him to lose his job. They could...

Mark raised his hand. Eyes looked to him and then, without a stammer he went deep.

"Down I this slink wrote me the car in at my fingertips flurry and prank so given, moments I was before too far of language in me swimming undone. But think this way. Or way but this think kissed to the future the steering wheel on lovely's elixir as I drove or drove madly my serum one word form. Or from might you hear the rope twisted to climb into unexactly clouds smooching horizon, like cotton puddles peddling their sunsets. Down I this wrote me. Simply so silence was lightning and you limpet in tidings of thought kept, moved to my purple swift miniatures simply violence so in tongue prattled this up and machine broke my beautiful true to be said not so lightly characters. Clearing lies so did not the traffic of mouth confuse us more into birdbaths and wires and that moonlight, where want we the North South, East and West rising tides on our shorelines. I here fasten. Fascinating, or whittle the bone long my fingers that writes this into a body I imagine elatingly is The Fourth of July, everyday crumpled like paper and trashed into air dunking the greater lives in a can pond. This slipper fits sky and Cinderella Stories winging angelic up as the ground is from mothers. Or mystery and mistake clasps onto addresses like fungus and children know feelings more than we do, stresses our accents. You see am I revelation in the hand swallowing my wings. See you am I tree in the bird steadfastly perched in the tomorrow mind swallowing past. Or lively ink scrawls in a classroom to the door saying watch me. But time. Time that in you my dear become gloriously fiddled to this safari and you are."

E.L. spoke up. "What is this supposed to do?" He was defensive; his hand was cocked in a fist, the other up over his head. He squirmed in his chair. "FUCK you guys. FUCK YOU FUCKING GUYS!" Then he pulled himself up and sat down, fidgeting with his nails. "Fuck." He repeated in disgust.

"We are expressing freely...anything that you want," Edward said. He felt a huge amount of space around his body. "To open. To open your voice to natural potential." Edward's eyes fluxed on the red light of the open-air data board. His vision relayed it to him as some great node of possible terror. Freedom of speech... Opening against State Policy might on a live radio not be the best thing. Edward thought of the worth of words going beyond the Uber Structure. The broadcast would reach the edge of the Milky Way in several years on the new wavelengths. This could cause a revolution, he thought. It could land them all in prison. Psychotic transmissions messing up the colony space channels.

"Feel feel feel it," said Mark.

E.L. closed his eyes, took a deep breath. "Do you know that meaning had dripped on to his chest, down to his fly, the smell of D Major, *Allegro Non Tropo*, furious and fast as his fingers un-battening the sweet spot in the wood. His tuxedo (the scent of 1850), the scent of Brahms's composition breath, the scent of opus 77 as he, the music, torqued from his body, the tuxedo with so many notes." E.L. looked sharply into a beyond. "Do you know that every string dramatically teases the play up the back of his black tailed fluke, so he floats in black shoes as if the sky is taking a sip of him gently, a quaff excite, and then, around 1851, he smells like coalesced love. No I bet you didn't know that. The smell of black! The smell of white! The scent of symphony stained like some million butterflies converging at the center of music and the scent of it, oozing into the tuxedo, oozing pleasurably, like a story, the front row weltering by the gush, the tricksy of the measure's mettle sliding into his shoes that were full of notes from last year." His eyes were wild with the words. Edward looked at him gesticulating in the air like a strange sea creature. "Stradivarius migrating from his hands, down his sleeves and to the groin, down the legs and into Wing Tips, mingling with the sweat of socks, Brahms in his grave rolling, 'more!' D major! melting to the suck, feeding him delicacies of sound, the tuxedo emitting every stink, of roses even, of the flowers given, of his girlfriend's perfumed hand, of his button plastic and of his wood, the violin weepening the score. He melts, he melts, he mels inno, a uddle of no am orry... I bet you didn't know that did you!" He almost shrieked.

"Fucking costly love session!" the tour guide said, "This is going out broad wave," his eyes were wide between his earphones.

Edward looked upon all of them. If this was therapy it was immaculate, clean disaster emptying from them like rivers. Their isolation room in their souls was being broken, their words were fanning out in the universe. Had they the normal oversight mechanisms this bit of creation would have been boxed away, lost, dissolved into nothing. Edward thought of his restroom study, the privacy of a place in a compromised society. This was the opposite of that. This was live radio with a bunch of mentally ill patients who were, it seemed, either poetical or hallucinating. He wondered if there would be a reprisal. He wondered how far they could go within this unusual Tower they had been cast into. Then Cherry spoke.

"Empty, the most important word, goes unnoticed by the throng. She fills the cracks in city walls and makes her body out of wind, collects the breath of ending life from so many mouths that have spoken. And, toying with the air like a god, she throws her body upon lonely men; shivers out each staple of loss and succumbs repeatedly to nothing. What strength in her absent limbs! What soul in her displaced time! Somewhere she grasps her maker's pen, writes how the world is a broken fable...Suddenly she loses her body and a baby sees her in her mother's eyes, the churches, married to god, feel the millions of moments where she ached. How may I end this poem I ask before I, too, marry her?" He paused and looked at the rest. "You must realize that I am in your love."

ASS

They kept returning from therapy—and return is what Edward was concerned about, for one space is different from another, even within one's head...and where you go isn't always here. Edward had to admit that perception depended upon the universe. What universe did they live in? How did this universe shape his patients and himself? Who decided what it was and how it would play out?

Simmering in the back burner of his consciousness Edward, like his patients, had begun to see things. Ever since the Tower tour he had felt hallucination tugging at his neural responses. As if the Virtual had not stopped, but kept playing over and over an environment of shifting chaos. That he had had surges of intense sexual feeling at the outset of his new test medicine did not appease a growing nervousness. It was called "synthesis adaptation" by The State, a cooperative effort by experimentals to push the envelopes of their minds. Where insanity they had wanted to put in a box forty years ago, now they wanted to let it loose, yet under guidelines. He agreed that no one could understand the mind unless they let it loose, let escape from the brain what otherwise was considered taboo. The State had opted for a test program. What it was specifically was difficult to say. Nevertheless you either were in or you were out, and Edward did not want to loose his liberal agreement. Edward's harbor of restroom, his harbor of museum, the Tower enlightenment—all vacillated in the trembling fabric of a new perception that pulsed here both on and off. And as he found one sanctuary another opened up only to reveal that it was not harbor at all.

Upon the change of Edward's self-prescribed test antipsychotic medication, the total of which amounted to two milligrams of Assperdal, six hundred milligrams of Fishium, four hundred milligrams of Queropel and an anti Tardive Dyskinesia medicine termed Bendopin, more commonly known as Amadine, his interest in the female proposition—the gate, the tush or rear, most commonly known as "ass"—increased. This focus Edward had heard was part of a new study of procreative measures seen as beneficial to the hegemony yet, with him, would prove almost devastatingly contrary to the design. Everywhere Edward looked, on pretty much every single, robust woman, he was given the lustful vision of this end, the very matter of fact and intense end that afforded him such focus that he could not without sincere help think of anything else. Edward's eyes, once innocent gazers of life, plummeted into every wiggling, every jiggling, every round mount of promise that came his way. As if Edward was struck with an invitation by God, his procreative sensibility screamed so loud that he could barely manage standing in line behind the firm bottom of a well-reared schizophrenic at the psych ward. His vision became acute and he could, like radar, detect the best ass in the room, anywhere, at any time, as if some fuck-magnet sucked into a valley of metal he so earnestly wanted to pack. The test meds were particular, emphasizing his id, unleashing him to write of this medium transcendence. And it didn't stop. And Edward thought it was—no matter the lascivious consideration, the natural inclination of any man—fairly sinful. Nevertheless, he took the medicine and his desire grew and pretty much all he could do was plunge deep into the abyss, his entire form shuddering like the convulse of a speeding med-engine destined to win a crack race so he could put his endowment over the trim finish line of fantasy and win the grand cup of nectar any spunk driver desires. That any tech-boy, for that matter, wants this is not unusual. But Edward was a man induced who had just found the button, or, as he thought, now game. So when he became fully conscious of his immediate need, his hormones pushed pictures so palpably lovely the horrible world couldn't shut them down and pleasure seeded its life in his pulsing loins in shivers of erratic electricity.

Ass. Ass with a shake. Ass with a sandwich. Ass with glass of more ass. Ass with a cocktail. Ass with a bowl of cereal. Ass with dimples. Ass with sass with another ass on top of that and more ass than a monkey's ass. Ass like divine ass that could make you spend yourself needlessly with the slightest tremor. He, Edward Wells, leading psychiatrist of the High Standing Award, psychosis expert, harbor searcher, could not help himself.

The more Edward thought of the bountiful assess out there the more he felt his nature in the grip of anima. Perhaps another harbor...one in which you get moored in a varietal rump dock, gluteus ripples with lambent light. There was so much ass out there that all you had to do was step out the door and it would rise into view like the surprise help balloon on the ancient Mac computers, that tells one the measure of the machine. And when one ass dissipated from view or over view, another ass would bounce into position and Edward would, however much he just wanted to get his food or take a nap, succumb to the curvature of the enhanced muffin bulging forth from blue jeans, the accent of the crack like some fissure one wants to dive into and swim through and flux in, like an animal crawling into a cave to keep warm...forever. So much was his attention on this glory, Edward soon forgot any iota of virtue that he once cherished, much undermining the regular sexual mandates. He knew that his patients, too, must have fallen, fallen into such crevices of lust. Edward looked at his dosage...four little pills rendered by a responsible chemist! Yet to be blunt, the more ass that he felt the more intensely he wanted to work his way in as if smut in the multiple museums behind old men's eyes!—living, palpable smut that makes one mature and enact the perverse of the raw... To be even more blunt, Edward wanted to stick everything in that dirty hole where from all the shit in the world excretes. He confessed...to dive into what graced his first Lorretos toilet perception of harbor privacy and glory. He soon became fitful and restless with his visions, visions that worked every angle of entry, every push and every pull, every tremor in the package he now considered to be the reason why men live. Yes...Edward thought: men are alive in our State Concept really to do one thing and one thing only, just as women are alive to give birth. Yes...men are alive to put their cocks into the inviting bush of a woman so that she may fulfill her one thing. Birth! And that is it. That is really the entire meaning of life. So, reasonably he thought...if he was feeling these feelings of immense attraction to ass he was pretty much feeling exactly the most appropriate primal pulse he may feel according to the new sex laws, and in this manner was not sinful but...virtuous, the same as the synthetic Aves species and butterflies are never thought of as corrupted, the same as our good priests in ecstasy. This, like a startling plunge of unearthly fact, drove him from the pit into the purity of it. Edward would allow himself the takeover of this virtuous sin and succumb to the multiple bouncing butts unbalancing the terrible world. He would make ass his mission, and he would do it with all the verve vim and mettle he could muster. For, he thought, life is horrible, wicked, and short (and so what if he was having a moral regression)...we must live no matter the apparent apparatus of law that keeps us blind, good, and locked up. Yes. Yes...we must, in all earnestness, fornicate as much as we possibly can—bury the organ, stash the cucumber, lay the point, even tuck the buck, not to mention hide the salami, bake the chicken, leaven the bread, pickle the planet, and pump some rump. The harbor potential, Edward thought...perhaps sex was it...moor your endowment in the best harbor for procreation...for life! After all, what was life made from? He convulsed. He could not help thinking of worms. And since, somehow, the Assperdal,

Fishium, Bendopine, and Queropel had an incredible side effect like this, Edward would continue taking it, to enhance his otherwise innocent consciousness...to live, he thought, like a man and to allow that man his power!

Yet for some reason Edward could not go from A to Z to complete the wicked alphabet of his medically induced addiction. He could not for some reason go from the gaze to the act to the success, and then to the next. Although capable, fairly good looking, and perhaps even a promise compared to other men, he could not even get to addressing the female species. Edward considered that he might be retarded or fairly inept in social ways. He even considered that he might have such strong visions that he could not get past the pith of the ass that was enhancing every hormone in his middle-aged, psychiatrist-balanced, male body because he was damaged. So, in a strange way Edward was an ass himself. He even could not stand to be around the female species lest she single out his filthy mind and he be dismissed as a naïve, imbecilic rake. So Edward began to stalk.

Yes. Edward began to be elusive and mysterious and he wore dark glasses like the police, and when out, with as much temerity as a spy trying to find God—to get his super secret of creation—he fished for as much ass as he could. In supermarket lines. At bus stops. In retail stores. Even in his harbors in memory, the latrine lust pumping every flush of the toilet of life. He became withdrawn and gaunt like some weird vampire whose bloodsucking addictions had transformed into butt and rump withdrawal, a withdrawal so tenacious whenever Edward witnessed a good ass he almost buckled in fanatic, even screaming lust and shakes. Yet he was not lost he thought. No, he was simply exercising the sanguine effect of an emerging, however lascivious, chemical State Value. His assspirations were simple: envision the gluteus maximus or minimus and plunge his thought of deviancy deep enough to cause him the gift of his attentions: harbor. Gift Edward thought. The gift of imagination that every human being possesses and which builds worlds! Yes...So he became suffused with his imagination's power to conjure ass at any time, anywhere, in any circumstance, doing anything, with any techno device, with super maniacal drive, and horrendous Pluribus Unum potential. In short, he had been absorbed by the press and the push into that rocking handful of future, imaginatively, metaphysically, and shockingly existentially.

Then something happened. Something Edward could not imagine. He could not stop thinking of his desire. The medicine had a one-way hetero mechanism. Even when at home or watching the news, or eating a dinner with friends. Everything, everything was assful! The news anchor's faces turned to hideous asses, faces of his friends at dinner looked like asses. When shopping for food, Edward would be rung up by an ass. While driving he would look at the people next to him and they would look like big asses. It became too much. Ass overload...he could not control his imagination! Edward felt that he had been made to hallucinate ass all the time in every place and every consideration he made. Did his patients do this, too? The medicine was stronger than he had anticipated, perhaps stronger than his psychiatrist's sense of prescription. What was he doing! Edward was sucked into an uninhabitable realm of ass he could not get out of. His thoughts of engaging sexually the multiple beautiful asses out there scared him now into the realization that he might not be able to not think about ass for the rest of his life! It was when he had seen every person as the gluteus maximus of the modern world when walking down the street that he knew his life had to change. Where Edward wanted to be cool and sexy and lascivious before, he now only wanted to get away and be rid of all ass, forever. He didn't attempt to think that he had fucked himself by his wicked desire, that he was, indeed, the ass that he so intensely wanted, neither that his test meds were a prescription that he had originally been writing against. Edward closed his eyes and tried to summon the opposite of an ass, not a vagina or a penis, but something that was contrary to ass, something like holiness...but he could not see his way through the invasion of ass that now plagued him. In a fit of despair he went to The State Church, a place that he knew would be so far away from his sinful visions that he might cure.

It was Sunday. Edward drove himself to the Good Brother

Church and sort of stumbled in and took a seat in the back, his dark glasses protecting him from optic confession. The priest entered and they all stood and said something he couldn't understand and then sat down again. To Edward's surprise the sermon was about the sin of the flesh and how we should refrain from sex. He felt like a demon. He burned with a massive repentance born from his symbolic engagement. People looked at him as if he was some vagrant, perhaps even seeing his visions of ass that had so suffused his being and which probably rendered him into that very cosmic cushion! Edward struggled to understand the sermon and to turn his thoughts to God, to Jesus Christ, or whoever, who was so seriously strung up on the cross at the altar that he thought he actually might be less an ass than the congregation who prayed to him each day. When the priest said, "cleave not with the flesh lest you spend yourself in the sinful act of lust," Edward took off his glasses and looked as deeply as he could into his pure eyes, into the headgear and the frock and the cross on his chest. Yet, as Edward looked, as he tried to shut out all vision of ass that had so gloriously driven him into this holy place, he could not see anything other than the very focus of his deep attentions. And then he looked around and the smiling people who nodded in agreement were all faces full of asses and the asses murmuring and smiling as they looked at the hanging Jesus and at the angels and the stained glass windows. All of them…a collective congregation of asses that were praying so that they would be saved and live eternally in the afterlife of heaven. In horror Edward flung himself into the aisle and stumbled toward the door. Something must be wrong with the medicine. Something was not at all right. The world he had known was no longer, he found, the pure unadulterated land of Edwardian Value. Rather, Edward found himself in a hell so profoundly ironic that all he could do was admit his mistake. Imagination is a beautiful power. He did not doubt his initial joy. Yet, how could he live with anything if all that was before him was his intense lust—born from anti-psychotics or not—but a vision of the most beautiful thing multiplying like the locust-smothered crops in the Salinas fields his students gazed into on the freeway; Amadine fields, Gyrexa fields, Bendopin fields... His joy and abandon was only as good as his ability to alter his view. This was not the harbor. For, Edward thought, we are all asses if we cannot see past the most natural desire. Who, after all, would be so struck by his or her desire that the entire world would assume its raw and even hideous mien, desire that is...without balance, the all-consuming bucking beast that fucks us and bucks us on the ride of life? Edward had over-harbored. He, it was he who had been reduced to the once attractive nexus of becoming! A joke? Yes that must be it. Medicine or not, psychotics or not, culture or not, his own crack of perception with its own shit, with its own abysmal sensitivity, had now assumed the toilet of the world to release himself in! Of course Edward struggled to escape. He thought of changing from the Assperdal, Amadine, Fishium, and Queropel, the medicine that was obviously a mistake. Would that do any good? Upon arriving at his home he stumbled to the mirror and turned on the light. There! There in the mirror his face was a giant ass, with an oblong scar going up and down like a fissure, all parts bulging in sensual form wanting him to admit himself so he could at least feel the wonderful, trembling delight of his initial attraction. He lifted up his hand, looking at it as if alien. Then, in some startlingly sick, disgusting manner, he let out a yell to the world from his enormous reflection. But all that sounded instead of his voice—his reasonable psychiatrist's voice—was a tremendous gas that blurted against the mirror, the steam of which smothered his face from the truth. Edward thought of the internal voices by radio transmission, cracking his genetic code. What would they say? Fool! Fool! You, Edward Wells, are having a nervous breakdown.

NIGHT SHIFT

You have to be insane to get into the PHF Unit. And you cannot leave until properly "groomed". The only other way to infiltrate is as an employee. No one had ever thought of breaking into this institution, a fairly phenomenal, and even insane entry into a place with enough potz-jobs inside to power a think tank. Hence Edward's desire, which slowly percolated in the vat of necessities one may be pummeled with in experimental settings. But it wasn't a score of the normal kind one may think of with boosting, bank jobs, or fine thievery. All Edward wanted was to get his eyes back. How does one get one's eyes back? After the detention some time ago of Edward's questionable self—his seven days of eternity—that the board had overlooked as purposeful trauma, and his initial motivation to be a psychiatrist, enough time to be sucked through the med pipes, to convene with the supreme elocution of the rhapsodic sick, to case the joint in cat-like detail, sniffing out the crackpots and crevice-crawlers that have play—one becomes, if not addled, supremely focused on facts that are completely in-explicable. And Edward had slipped professionally after the experi-mental pills. Hence his eyes after the ass episode, that which he thought had gone awry, and which now needed some sensitive redeeming.

What is sure is that you go in, but when you exit nothing is what it seems, as Edward's patients attested. Perhaps it was a touch of prescribed mixture, with some flux-ware, that made space change. He was "on" this prescription. He was also, as not-ed, on a number of other fine pharmies. And that a theft kick had gripped him rather deeply, after he had seen enough ass to plum-met into the abyss, Edward felt the necessary answer to his style zipping neurons into his want so that she lit with supreme con-sideration. To return...To return to the horror of his affliction. To return and take back his vision. All of this somehow jumpstarted him in a weird way. Had he lost it, really? The medicine. The State Mandates. His lascivious visions. The horror of the world. Patient contamination. Yet, Edward thought, if you don't go to the node you will never understand life's essential truths and his Harbor pa-per had moved him...back. That he might return his person to the scene of his affliction with enough courage to take him to the cen-ter of his curious illness did not strike him as strange. Edward was in search of harbor. And life had shifted enough that even the First Amendment of a butterfly on a flower cup could say something profound. And "place shift", as in so many of his patients, had un-settled him with its torturous bash of fritz realities. At this point, who really cared if his entry was a key, a saw, or a neural flash so prime the cerebral data board cracked the State? What Edward knew was that he was going in to realign his vision in the most re-splendent and artistic manner. Harbor, ass, medical reverb or not, Edward needed to understand his new fall.

Edward really didn't know what he would get or take. But this was not a problem. His patient, E.L., had him know that the over-planning of a job botches the flow, where the intuition, prop-erly felt, is the pick in the lock. So he didn't actually know how he would get in and neither did he really know what he would get once he got there. What Edward did know was that, if the whole fucking thing were a psycho-meta-morphical affair, he would un-psych the "meta" enough to re-morph the loop into a pool of good reflection. And why not pilfer from the clutches of the whole damn Doc team who had, so very generously in Edward's past, assisted his patients' and his health with balancing medicines? To be fair, why not relieve them of their most necessary tools, the chemical harbors that were now in question, had side effects, displaced him.

The visions heaped up in his now channeling eyes: Queropel, Bendopine, Gyrexa, Assperdal, Fishium—oozers, uppers, unders, overs, curlers, punkers, pushers, and "fuckers"—and in the heap of beauty that was probably controlling him, the doorways to the most ripe sex spots in the world pulsed chemical. But there was much much more inside than this...stuff you couldn't get on the market, stuff that was not yet tested. Edward quivered like the Dolby Surround sound of his soul, the woofer of life so horrendously loud one had to work a beat to properly bop back, or potz back, however you heard. Punching in digits. Measuring each day by the flux against the "real", his poor patients in the throws of lostness no beyond could answer, all a-float in a questionable way, a way that perhaps it was not at all what it seemed, neither true nor anchored. Inhaling "drug air"... the pink cotton candy slurp marsh of the beyond. Industry morphers. Indeed, having to "secure" (a most common term) life to live life—all was simply atrocious. But why not just perk out and end up in the turquoise water of some beach spot in Bimbamboo? This was perhaps one of the great secrets: the tech medicalities followed you. Indeed, one could be getting hallucinatory service from a coral reef and would not know if it was real or fake even though it was "real". One could, in a batting eye, get a trashcan made of flesh, birds that were children's blocks, cars with ghosts in them, and a plethora of other changing mesh from the phase of the meds. In short, turquoise water in Hawaii was fairly much like saying you are watching the sweat of a unique creature, meant, of course, to Cook you. Hence Edward's empathy for Mark, Jack, E.L., Cherry, and Frank, the deep empathy uncommon in his world. And so returning all this shit was like asking on

Neo Jeopardy if the history question was actually correct...or was it perhaps a life question that time, in this hilarity of med game show, was, like the audience assumption, "off". However this is only the skinny. The real thing Edward wanted to say was that he was going to break into the PHF Unit (Psychiatric Health Facility), and return his eyes to their proper place upon his face, and breaking in was the way to do it.

But how, after all these years, would Edward get his eyes back? In a way, if he let things go the way they were going—the recent mania, the delusions, the divorce from reality—he would, to be honest, not be breaking into the PHF, but would be breaking into himself...to steal himself, to return. No doubt the eyes would follow. He had never thought of stealing himself before, yet, given the current load of information that is in the flux bank for one to think of, stealing himself seemed to be the best thing...to get himself in enough to get out of his mind without being apprehended. Or, to take from his person the download and empty into divine vacuum. Yes, you have to be insane to get in to the PHF, as Edward knew, and so very trickily, in his master plan, his search, his assness—that was now manifesting like a freaked-out circuit board on juice—Edward realized some things.

Upon the back patio, wherefrom the local nut case can take a good gander at the life they are missing, is a very ornate collection of iron eyes laid up in grating, all of course something to see through and to be informed that you are looking out of a building that is, like yourself, just checking you out. Edward had procured much irony from this layout and he now was receiving much irony about what he could do with it. Indeed, he had a saw with ample edge to go through this hideous message. And as he sawed he could make passage enough for the entire sublime cadre of lost souls to pour out of. Once done, he wouldn't even need to go in for the pharmaceuticals...Edward realized a brain frisson intensely...ALL of the pharmaceuticals would be within the patients. And since these eyes, his eyes and theirs, had seen the infrastructure of God, whatever poured out must be beautiful. These patients and his self, maybe even in his self, his early patient friends! These drug powered livers a cache of ultimate med perception enough to trip him, re-loop him, and pull him out and back into his now missing vision. The necessary soul that you get only if you are, like an industrial plunger, to plunge all the fucked-up cosmic shit out of the "problem" to clear the pipes, or, he thought, "brain cells".

The saw was cold in Edward's hand. He could perceive the shivering apparatus of the ward from his car. The ladder in the back was ample enough to pitch against the side and pull from it the iron girding. Edward put out his cigarette with a flick, and then sleuthed to the object of his purpose. That his eyes were not iron did not really phase him. Edward had already imagined himself sawing the eyes to see in, to literally see into his own brain, left there some ten years ago with the detritus of healing it was so famous for. In his work he moved and when he got up to the bars he set the teeth into the very eyes that had once kept him and sawed away. Edward could not help thinking of privacy. The privacy of blindness in a security state, like the privacy of a toilet. The symbolic draw of vision from the Uber cameras that kept one guessing.

Edward removed one eye, and then another, and then another, until four eyes had been removed and left to gravity. As he looked in, the place reverbed with memories so insane he could barely reflect. But it was these eyes that Edward wanted out, the eyes that had kept him so solemnly conscious that he would be trapped forever in a hell made by synthesis drugs so sublime you could not not want them under warden guidance. He didn't want them. Probably nobody really wanted them. You became quiescence. A float of fog in the fields of questions: is this I? Is this what I normally would see? Is this life or...death? Is this my making or another's? All of these ludicrous philosophical questions like jellybeans from China that have lead in them on Halloween and you are a ghoul in the off-season of lostness, yet cannot help but maw. Not even this. This was only the small part. For, once you had popped a pill you did not know, ever ever ever again, who you really were...

Edward's hands sawed the eyes open and he looked in and it was sterile and dead. He could not help imagining his own brain. He could not imagine the loss of time and places, the ghost-shift that he had been on for the past ten years now somehow before him that he was seeing/sawing in. After Edward had removed four eyes, he yelled like a maniac into the darkness. IS ANY ONE THERE! Nothing came out of his "head". Nothing but a great echo that spilled down the hallways to the beds the patients were knocked in. IS ANYBODY IN THERE! Edward called again. Still nothing. The eyes lay before the ladder in their black iron, dead on the ground. He could not help imagining that they were his own oracles of vision. Removed from his head, the PHF Unit now without sight, he looking in like a starved creature. Then there was a flutter in the back darkness of the hall, and then another flutter. Then, from his carved out eyes came one patient after another, robed like Buddhists, wild in their faces and sorrow and tiredness. They came shuffling out of the building, patients in all manners of dismay, patients with the most lost looks on their faces. One after another! Mark. Frank. Cherry. Jack. E.L. They came up to his eyes and Edward stepped aside and they paused and then jumped through, one after the other, their robes pulsing with pink medicine and, Edward imagined, the chemical love of a pharmaceutically manufactured America. As they spilled forth he hung back on the ladder and withdrew a Nikon camera and began to take pictures of them, to freeze them in space and time, each one hurtling into the garden and landing upon the ground. To freeze the moment of seeing. To preserve. To Save Them. To take back each patient from the cog-work pixel template of modernity so that they might live forever at this moment. Free great flying angles of insanity! What ever the hell Edward was going to do with the pics was beside him, but he fired anyway, until all had popped from his head like a gigantic living play of Zeus giving birth to a totally insane, yet beautiful Aphrodite. From the forehead of one machine they flew out into another machine and then off and free. They began to run in every direction on the hospital grounds, yelling like maniacs, his brethren in the Potz Trade.

Then the fucking doctors and wardens. One after the other, flying like great herons out of the eyes that they prized...Edward's eyes that had torturously stored them for so long. One after the other they splattered into the black canopy of the night and from his tortured body. ALL of them yelling like maniacs! But he didn't take pictures of them. No. He kept them in reality, stuck as they were in their administrations.

At this moment Edward jumped from his perch and landed on the ground. The wardens ran like madmen after the escapees. Edward was grappled and thrown to the earth. He wriggled for his life and pulled his hair and screamed like a lunatic. "I am Edward Wells, psychiatrist! It's an art project! IT's a modern medical art project!" He could hear yelling everywhere. The premises percolated in the most beautiful and surreal way. MY art project, he thought! MY fucking modern art project! The warden bound his hands in plastic and lifted him from the ground as the words and spittle oozed from his mouth. Edward looked at the warden as if he was a blurry friend and the man hauled him up to the lock-down doors. Upon entry Edward felt terror and doom. Then, he broke free. He broke free and ran like a lunatic, extracting from his jacket two small spray paint cans. Edward then proceeded to gingerly spray "love" and "Fuck Authority" all over the wall, the word LOVE as strong as the other word...to keep the message going. From behind him the warden yelled and with his cans he painted him blind. After spraying the entire hallway with expletives and love Edward was very happy and ran for the porch with the eyes that had once kept him, his eyes he thought, his ten-year struggle to see what the fuck was actually going on. As two big wardens bore down upon him he leapt through these eyes and into the pitch of his brain. The way he felt! The way he felt! He fell down and into the garden and gasped the fresh night air. He had, he realized, dived out of his own eyes and into real life! Lights shone down to his now absent body. Edward ran for his car and made for the road. He was trembling. He was trembling like his paper delivery, much better than the High Standing Award; he was trembling like the gun in the hand of the woman in the Empathy Test. He had paint all over him. He had one loose manacle on his wrist. But, Edward thought, his smile hyperbolically curved in a superior depth of animal, he had dived out of his own head and back into the real world...the real living, legitimate, Goddamn World. This, strangely, had taken 5,110 days.

Edward's story faded out. In reality or the surreal he had been caught after the ass breakdown. They found him in the Lorettos latrine licking the walls, arms wrapped around the Toto sink yelling "OZ IS NOW". They pried him loose and dumped him in a strait jacket, then drove him back to the ward. Edward lapsed into the PHF Unit, through his aforementioned projections and into a deep psychosis. In this state he shrank away in some cerebral cocoon zone of trauma. The doctors put him in a special room. He was labeled "non-responsive", put in a chair looking out of the grating. He did not know what was in his mind, for Edward was blind to everything around him. This horrible experience, so quick to manifest and overload him, in which he no longer knew reality, how time functioned, and who he, Edward M. Wells, was. The orderlies in Edward's brain kept looking him over. Who was Edward M. Wells? What did life mean to a schizoaffective PhD in psychiatry in the grip of psychosis? How could he save himself? Edward would be convinced of one thing: beyond all chaos, beyond all the reason is a place where there cannot be any sickness for the mere fact that love exists. This was the harbor in the very core of his breakdown. He held onto this love with his synapses, a curl of some sea creature tucked into another world. She felt through him and assuaged his tremendous loss. Edward's memory flickered in some cave of half-conscious feeling.

When she looked out the window of his eyes Edward imagined what she was seeing, he imagined where she was going in her seeing that he could never get to, he imagined what she felt like. He had sat next to her in innocence, delivered his heart to consideration in ways in his memory that were pure, he had seen her disappear and reappear in his life like clarity. And then Cleo was gone.

Everything had gone dark in the trauma. Edward had broken in and broken down the world he hated, broke down, and his confidence, shattered like glass that is supposed to tell you the truth, put him back into this horrible place. Post Tower tour, perhaps the relations to the students had crashed him, the contagion of relation to another mind. Edward could not tell whether The Harbor Paper was real or fake. It floated in some syrup he could only call reflection. Yet he gripped on to his love like a limpet. His dream of being a teacher, a cop, and a student, the shooter of Sergeant Aremac, played through his brain in popping frames. What does one live for? For an ultimate reason no less, the love of a woman that his consciousness had told him was real. All of this crunched down in Edward's bones and he, in the stricken state of psychosis, took his bearings like a sailor set afloat in ancient seas.

Edward was unconscious when the nurse came in. The psychotic trauma had left him in a mentally paralyzed state where no external limb worked. Limp like a piece of seaweed he lay. The inside seemed as sick as the outside. Yet, inside him, when the nurse came to change the sheets, he found his harbor in the beat of his heart, and with every beat Edward knew he was knocking on the door of a heaven he could not describe. Why? Something deep in his inner self sensed life, a familiarity of a personal nature.

A nurse, in his blackness, shivered through like a mirage. Edward was aware, vaguely, of his familiar feeling. He felt it in his room in the changing of the sheets, talking to him as if he were conscious. Edward's heart began to beat differently. Indeed, with each beat of his heart, with each beat of her visitation, he felt, through the darkness of his vision, a light born from this woman. Every day in the usual care of a nurse Edward was turned over and talked to, by the touch of her soft hands he was made to rethink his loss, and with these touches, as if some Braille illuminate in the fortitude of spiritual words, summon himself to return.

Then one day when Edward was in the contorted reality of his breakdown, he sensed something different. The hands touched him from his face, and slowly down to his stomach, and then to his loins beneath the sheet. A gasp came from him. Something in the trembling beauty of this touch he rose to and he kept rising like drilled well water and Edward gushed forth back into the world.

It was sudden, deep, and vital. The next day, Edward opened his eyes for the first time and winced through the light. He was conscious that something had occurred which was so magnificent that he was returned to life. He looked around. The nurse who changed him each day was gone. It would be some few days before they released him. Status: healthy, mentally stabilized, cogent with sense of surroundings, speech, people, and State purpose. Edward left the hospital and returned to his work as a psychiatrist. He would not know until some years later what the nurse had done and then by the sheer act of love Edward would realize the gravitas of human nature, the actual ultimate necessity: We must live no matter what.

STATE PSYCHIATRIC BOARD

Mrs. Falk, along with two other male board members, with cold, officiating stares, watched Edward enter the office. Edward seated himself in a swivel chair in front of Mrs. Falk's desk. The desk displayed a neat mind. A dated fountain inkwell, one magma rock paperweight, and one dossier, which Edward imagined was his file, graced the top. One of the men was smoking and the smoke drifted upward and dissipated in an overhead fan. Mrs. Falk's gaze, with serious confidence, caught Edward.

"Dr. Edward M. Wells."

Edward watched as Mrs. Falk's black nail polish handled papers in front of her. He imagined a black widow spider rolling in its legs web for a victim.

"Yes," Edward responded.

Mrs. Falk leaned to the man at her right, "Case number 4472, Experimental." She then looked directly at Edward.

"You had a nervous breakdown. Are you better now?"

The question held no emotional concern.

"Yes," said Edward.

Mrs. Falk smiled a prim smile and then tapped her black polished index nail upon the dossier. "Better," Mrs. Falk, said, "is a joke, Dr. Wells. I am referring you to your gambling with patients' lives."

Edward acknowledged the abject pun in his mind. Mrs. Falk did not joke, normally. He had heard some very disturbing things about her.

"We have heard some very disturbing things about you, Dr. Wells." Her eyes sifted over him in a concentrated look. Edward wondered if she had read his mind. "You see, Dr. Wells, the disturbance seems to be multifold." Mrs. Falk dropped her Mont Blanc upon the folder. It landed crisply, accenting her insinuations. "Do you know to what we are referring, Dr. Wells?"

Edward held back a response. The man next to Mrs. Falk took a deep hit off of what Edward could see now were imported Spanish Ducados. Mrs. Falk leveled her gaze upon Edward.

"You are responsible for ten patients of whom several are standing out. I have a list here, Dr. Wells, of incongruities that are beyond the normal experimental values we want to see in psychotic patients. You are licensed C3 psychiatry, yet you seem not to understand the proper procedures to oversee Frank Spec, Jack Spillain, Edmond Little, Mark Nichols, and Norbert Cherry." Mrs. Falk paused, and lifted herself off the chair to smooth out her gray skirt. "We are very disturbed at your flagrant abuse of your status, Dr. Wells."

Edward bowed his head and then lifted it up. "I have been having difficulty," he said, "understanding the limits..."

Both men on either side of Mrs. Falk's desk swiveled in their chairs as if to regain balance. Mrs. Falk coughed.

"You don't seem to understand, Dr. Wells, nor do the patients mentioned, what experiment means." She turned a page on her desk and read. "We have reason to believe that Edward M. Wells is supplanting medicine in his patients. We have reports that there was, at LAX Airport, with one Mark Nichols, an incident wherein he hallucinated through customs." Mrs. Falk glanced up.

Edward remained silent.

"Hallucinated violently in front of security wherein one Sergeant Satano was imagined to have his head blown off by a nine-millimeter Browning with dum dum bullets. It is said that the tracers found his conscience to be clean, his actions to be abnormal, but the viewfinders at the airport disclosed pictorial interview between his neural template and it came up abstractly disturbing. In black and white," Mrs. Falk paused, "In black and white...we see the face of Sergeant Satano and one other officer blown apart in slow motion resolution for about one second wherein they reconstituted." Mrs. Falk looked at Edward. "Mark Nichols was allowed on the plane as we did not trace the mental aberration until after the fact."

Edward could not believe they had seen it? He blinked his eyes closed and figured that they must have a new neural scan now in the security, able to see, but not able to define in time. It must have been quite disturbing for them, he thought.

"I gave him a placebo, Mrs. Falk."

Edward watched her face flinch. The two men shifted again in their chairs. One man adjusted his black-rimmed glasses.

"A placebo?" Mrs. Falk said in astonishment.

"Yes," Edward replied. "He is a very sensitive man. I did not inform him. To help with the passage through customs."

Mrs. Falk frowned into her papers and then looked up. "Impossible she said. The only way the neural scans at airports can view the internal images of a brain is with chemical agitation." She stopped. "Placebo you say."

"Yes," to help with the passage.

"Are you implying that we did not see this act of violence?"

"I am aware," Edward said, "that it is possible that you either picked up his other medicine or that your security had a glitch."

Mrs. Falk looked directly at him. "Glitch?"

"It is not impossible for a machine to have a nervous breakdown as in the Relay Studies of Jeremy Smith."

Mrs. Falk looked flustered. She continued her report.

"It has been discovered that all of the aforesaid patients under your guidance participated in a mass hallucination with Amodine wherein they entered a restaurant and opened fire in a retrospective setting, a setting that came through our observations as a diner in mid-space format where virtual holidays are taken, where all aforesaid patients in an act so incredibly lawless, mounted tables and fired at random through the medicine and into the virtual café. Although nobody was hurt, our sub-sensor absorption modules recorded about ten minutes of outright mayhem on a med level incongruous with their normal meds and dosages." Mrs. Falk stopped and looked at Edward.

Edward returned her stare. He couldn't really believe that they had seen all that.

"Ah, that was also placebo, Mrs. Falk."

Mrs. Falk gazed somewhere deep inside of him.

"Impossible. The sensors found an infraction in the retrovacation, a hole in which there was this aforesaid occurrence."

"Yes," replied Edward. "I am not sure how your sensors can pick up such a thing when all my patients on that day..."

Mrs. Falk tapped the dossier agitated.

"There is more! You are said to have taken an experimental dosage of Assperdal, Fishium, Queropel, and Bendopine which incited in you a massively grotesque reaction where you hallucinated the obscene throughout town, with friends, in public places, and not least of all one of the State Churches after which you invaded neurologically St. Mary's Mental Health Facility, freed up your patients by cutting out the iron eye grid symbolically and then were bold enough to act out graffiti contrary to The State before your drug trance crashed and you were physically apprehended and restrained, brought back to the aforesaid Mental Health Facility where you spent one month recovering."

Edward listened to the damaging reports. He could not fathom how they had all this information. How had they seen Mark's hallucination? How had they seen the restaurant? Detecting an aberration when none existed? They could, he thought, be hallucinating themselves. They could be witnessing a desired thing, yet not actual. He looked back into Mrs. Falk's piercing eyes.

"I admit," Edward said, "to having taken these medicines myself. I was experimenting with the erogenous factors. I had quite an unpleasant experience."

Mrs. Falk gazed at him silently. Her face was stiff with chilly authorial concern. "But we are, Dr. Wells, worried mostly by your patient Frank Spec." She smiled a terse smile. "It is reported that Frank Spec was the pre-mortem obituary scribe for one Dr. Bessingham, a State Official for Human Relations." Mrs. Falk's eyes twitched. "The report states that Frank Spec persuaded Dr. Bessingham of his fad obituary work and after reading through Bessingham's personal diary's it is reported that he predicted Dr. Bessingham's death at the Z Club in LA where they met. Dr. Bessingham, The State Official of Human Relations, it is reported, after their meeting, exited the building and collapsed and died in the gutter. More startling," Mrs. Falk shuffled her papers, "the document found with his body the pre-mortem obituary written by your patient, Mr. Spec, for Dr. Bessingham." Mrs. Falk stopped cold… "The obituary is presciently correct."

Edward was frozen. He didn't know about this. Frank was good, he knew, real good with words, but he had not quite believed the obit ideas Frank had told him.

"It is not a threat against The State to conceive of outlandish things, Dr. Wells. We all learn from the fringes of the mind. Your experimental status is licensed as you well know to go beyond…" Mrs. Falk coughed. "But to predict an official's death…I do not think we are ready for this. Hallucinations…yes, we all need a good trip now and then…but a prophet of our doom…." She paused and her eyes furrowed… "A prophet of The State's doom…I just don't think that we can allow that sort of…ah…formidable prescience." She paused again. "You see, Dr. Wells, if we know when we are going to die at such a level, we might decide to control…what we cannot know…an impossibility with the status quo…you see."

Edward looked at her and recalled Frank as a student in the Empathy Test, how he had gone to Borders and how he had pulled the trigger on Officer Aremac. Frank Spec who had mesmerized him during a session so that he might open up about his love for Cleo. Frank who was big, and awkward and full of hidden love, if you knew how to address him.

"So what do you have to say for yourself, Dr. Wells."?

Edward took a deep breath. "I am aware that my patients have abilities, Mrs. Falk, that are unusual to standard conduct..." Edward paused... "I am also aware that the experimental group is sanctioned to develop a state wherein the patients have enough mental room to grow. My patients, Mrs. Falk, feel trapped by not only their illnesses but the current State settings." Edward closed his eyes searching for the right words. "They are simply trying to express themselves...beyond the limits put forth, they...want to live greater lives than their illness allows."

"And what greater life do you want to live, Dr. Wells?"

He had fallen into a trap. What life could be greater than the State's? His mind swam with inaccurate answers until one slipped into place.

"I want to live for love," Wells said.

Mrs. Falk burned a whole through his head. "Love, Dr. Wells?"

"Yes, I want to live for something beyond living...I want to live for life's highest..." He paused... "triumph. To love."

"Let us remember your Empathy Levels, Dr. Wells. Under Operation A Gel Tab for the cop program empathy levels you declare to the Board that you shot and killed, in both partner and student form, the synth-officer Aremac. You perform these outrageous acts in order that you might save a woman. You say that you found empathy enough for the woman to feel...love?"

"Yes," replied Edward.

"Do you overthrow the State for love?" Mrs. Faulk said coldly.

Edward felt himself falling into a deep deep pit. They were slowly reeling him in, nice and slow, like expert fishermen on some expedition. Nice and slow and easy, he thought, tension on the line, the line being jigged here and there, slowly but surely. Had he been given C3 status, let alone C1 status, as a test himself? Was this some grand experiment of emotion that the state was fishing for because it was empty of that very necessity? He rocked forward in his chair.

"You overthrow yourself for love," Edward said. "You do everything you can to subvert the ego, bring down the Id, and supplant the superego, or God for that matter to become in love." He thought to himself and then continued... "if God were to dictate a life without love and the only way in which one could achieve love was to overthrow God..." The room was deadly still... "I would overthrow God."

Both men rocked back in their chairs. One blew a plume of smoke into the air. Mrs. Falk brushed her hand through her black bob.

"Is The State then supposed to overthrow God to...love?" She said.

A fish on a line fighting in the sea currents flashed through Edward's head, a fish on a line and at the end of the line death.

"Yes," Edward said.

Mrs. Falk picked up her Mont Blanc and began to twizzle it in her hand.

"So you are then telling me that I must over throw God to love?"

Edward set his eyes upon her pen and then refocused on her lips. They were painted in bright cadmium red. Her lips were pressed together expecting a retort.

"You must overthrow yourself in some way, understand your most base self and then rise to the highest feeling of sensitivity of spirit and try and feel love."

"So you are saying that after killing the virtual synth-officer, providing a fake half dosage of Operation A to Mr. Nichols so he hallucinates a border assault, encouraging Mr. Spillain to express pugilism of the most raw nature, giving fake Amadine capsules to your patients to submit a virtual restaurant to violence, and not stopping Mr. Spec from prophesying and maybe even conspiring to overthrow State officials, that you are attempting to overthrow God in your patients so that they may, after absolute mental dissonance, break into love in themselves…is that what you mean to do?"

Edward felt the line tightening. The hook was somewhere mixed up between him, his patients, his values, God, The State, and love, and he didn't know which value it was in. He passed a stare over the three. Formula State inquisition, he thought. Did they have one ounce of creative fire in them? Did they not see what he was trying to do, to help encourage his innocent patients to defy the very things that were supposed to be their jails? He focused back on Mrs. Falk.

"God, it seems, to you, Mrs. Falk is not in love with much other than regulation of every part of this forsaken society. Should one, if they are being prevented from their love, not do exactly what I did in my Empathy Exams?"

"You mean kill for love!" She slammed her pen down.

"If my love was going to be killed, yes, I will kill to save love."

"Is that what you are preparing your patients to do!" Her eyes were fiercely sharp. He imagined her own relationship with her husband. It must be over. It must be dead, on the rocks over. And now she is acting out of terror of the truth…that she has dried up into a prune and no longer possesses a drop of love in her vapid spider body.

He felt the line zip from his mouth to hers. She was on the hook now.

"I am preparing my patients to express every thought they have, on medicine or not, in order that they live. If something should, in that process, harm their relation with themselves and their own love, I would do everything in my power to abort it."

"Yes, Dr. Well's. Abort seems to be the very word I am looking for. You see you are this close to being aborted for your idea of love…this close. Your patients are under your care. They are, at this stage, verging on illegal, and with your encouragement I do not see

144

them achieving love, I see them achieving insidious acts of creative destruction. How deep do you want to go, Dr. Wells? Do you want to go so deep that one of them dies? Is that a way to love? Do you want to go deep enough that they are brought up on charges of..." She paused...

Edward could hear the word in her head. "Virtual assault?" He said.

She glared at him. "Charges of assault...do you wish them to be tried for..."

Edward interjected, "Creativity?"

She glared at him again, "Murder? Do you wish for them to be put in jail for..."

Edward quickly injected, "Expression?"

Mrs. Falk held up her hand. "Ok, Ok...you've made your point. But I warn you you are on thin ice here. If we catch you instigating one more random attack upon the infrastructure you will be brought up on charges of...treason." She looked up.

Edward relaxed back into his chair. Treason he thought, treason for thinking, for expression, for medical experimentation... treason.

"That is God, Dr. Wells."

THE FRANK SPEC FILE

Frank came to Edward after his recovery. He was nervous. He seemed to shake involuntarily. Frank who had evolved in their time together into a fine case of paranoid schizophrenia. The same Frank who had tried to erase himself in a doctoral thesis on "The Limitations of Ego" in front of an audience of one hundred State literary scholars. And even though they had been together, translating their mutual illnesses at a Virtual, in therapy, and in other private circumstances, he had returned to Edward after his fall. His dramatic, yet sensitive self all came out at once in an emergency late night session. He sat with his legs crossed in a Zen position in front of Edward and then, with all the grace of a careening psychotic experience, proceeded to reveal himself in his own way.

"My name is Frank Spec and I am a self-made man, for the record. In November of this year of grace I wrote an obituary for the still living Dr. Bessingham. He came to me for my profession. I was able to procure his diaries and began the computation to write a pre-mortem. He seemed very pleased, as if he wanted to die. Over the next few months I was, in private consultation, able to discover facts of a disturbing nature. That his life was sordid, maligned with problems, and failing didn't stop him from divulgence, Dr. Wells. I am innocent of his death. I didn't mean to do a job for the Head of State for Human Affairs. I didn't know. I was the heartbeat of a boy and somehow I got out. I was the curvature of waves on the hull of my beauty. I was in the stitching of live circuitry and his hand flipped me into his history. I was thus working in this pitch, and I want to tell you exactly how, Dr. Wells, I predicted his death.

Like any life, mine exists in love. Not love that I imagine, but love that you imagine. It would be impossible for me to assume such a position alone. I am only so creative. Yet as a creative body in the download from the brilliant light of my previous consciousness to this body of black story, I am the maker and the line. This is my profession. I write, Dr. Wells, to know the truth. I write because if I do not know the truth then all love fails, everything fails. And there is no difference between inside and out. I am made a line, and my line makes me. In this state of fluid script I am born, and, as I am born, I, the maker of these lines, the very body of your conception, as now we hear each other, see, and feel, live. I understand this of any human.

Dr. Bessingham was no different. He heard me, I heard him. He saw me, I saw him. And he felt me, I think, and I felt him. As now, where you look I spread. Where you rest I ruminate. Where you pierce I slip. Where you lull I float. Symmetry is the first glorious notice in correspondence. Please do not misunderstand me, Dr. Wells. I cannot admit that I don't exist. Neither can I quite comprehend how every particle of my being is being relayed in your soul. To be frank, from my study of Dr. Bessingham, I was aware of this symmetry. I also became aware that I, Frank Spec, like him, shared a symbiotic relation. I had to be empathic to understand. So there, as things popped into consciousness, we were everywhere and nowhere, all at the same time, but together. An almost synchronic harmony of place, time, thought, and feeling began to occur. I see no difference between this awareness and the night I speak in either, to you, in this office. Hence, like Dr. Bessingham, like his slow departure into death, I was on a shift that was, in the curvature of our very souls, a shared relation. I, Dr. Wells, began to see ahead."

Edward crossed his legs. See ahead to where, he thought?

"In such a state I was very much aware that our meeting was un-complex. We were loosening up, loosening out, loosening everything. I had his diaries, papers, certificates, pictures...his history spread out before me like a great puzzle. But I had to get close. I had to work my way into him like a tick to draw the proper perception. So in this manner, if you look outside of yourself you will see me, Frank, sitting here as the glowing exclamation of moonlight balances its sheen upon the window. You look out. You find me. I am complete. You see the blessed idea from my pool of story. You see well. I am the curvature of your desire in the sleek refulgence of my desire to know. Yet your eye rides on doubt. I am punctuated by your hesitancy. You flow in the river of my promise. I feel your reluctance to see more. WE, I, FRANK SPEC, I realized shared with Dr. Bessingham the mutual understanding of effects of reflection. And here! Here! You pause. For, it is in this sacred pool that he was made! I was getting close to his creation. The closer to creation, the closer to what un-creates. I could feel the papers becoming flesh. I could sense the details slowly congealing into an emulsion of understanding. I could feel his shuddering soul in my very hands and say...death, Dr. Bessingham, is a rude truth. But I didn't and he didn't get there without empathy for a beyond. This is it. This is all you have to do. It doesn't matter where you are, what you are, who you are, or even really how you are. What matters was that I was getting close. Pictures, diary, scribbles, notes, recordings, Bessingham's entire life lay before me and I could feel his pulse fading every word. That he died was not my intension. Yet that he would perish...I wanted him to become the best death because I wanted him to achieve his highest moment of..." Frank paused with his hand up against his head… "State Craft."

"Free…what is free now is the real question. Free for me is being the pitch truth we are in. Free to know in the utter river of doubt that overwhelms our lives that we are not absent, that we are presence. Here. What is a gift about conscious life? Did I ever have body, they ask? The workers, the State functionaries, the techno wizards, the umbilically wrapped up circuitry and wire strung officials who guide us? All of us, slotted into the grid like termites in some big silicon hill of disaster, loneliness, horror… Dr. Bessingham asked me, 'How will my body look to The State when you are done?' But that's not the question, I said to him. The astonishing question is…will you have body without Frank? Will you have, in all your official powers, body without the people, the ants that work for your machine, the multitudes who are loosing daily due to the regulatory laws, the insidious controls. That's what I asked him, privately. And then I began to write. I began to write it out, how I might disappear him completely from his horrible position of State of Human Affairs. I am on this most mysterious nightshift explaining this to you, Dr. Wells, because you must know. I am innocent. I did not ask for him to come to me. I did not ask because if I realized that he was actually material, if I realized that of all the State Officials then I was afraid I, too, would cease to exist! This is, I think, the cardinal horror of a pre-mortem…to realize that, in the blackness of the night of the soul, in the pitch dark of the spirit, the nocturnal dregs of our being, the abyss of our loss, the sunless terror of our visions, the negative of day that destroys us, the unseen force of our broken relations, the hidden lies, the realm of ghost and shade that pass through, the absolute horrific occlusion of "purity" and light of being…we are already dead." Frank looked up at the overhead light. "Absence is a great solace to those who live miserable lives. But, it was this answer that I was looking for in Bessingham, in his pathetic, Parkinson riddled body, and now with you, you who are plying the waves of my consciousness in this reflective sea of truth at this ungodly hour, Dr. Wells."

Edward could feel Frank beginning to trance, the pulsing electricity of his determination, the sadness, the reality folding.

"I am talking like a maniac, Dr. Wells, to figure out this absolute consideration! This consideration that would be the casket for Dr. Bessingham. In a way, I really should only write stories that help people possess their "material". So, in essence, knowing that our relation was linked, Dr. Bessingham and my own, I began the logic."

Frank looked at Edward with deeply troubled eyes. He could see him writing to get out of a trap, his desperate eyes shining in earnest balance with himself and something beyond. Edward nodded his head for him to continue.

"I saw only one way of answering this most important question of death and existence. Knowing that Bessingham was seeing me now, Dr. Wells, seeing my sensitivity to the line, to his life, to the symmetrical circumstances at hand, I told him that there would be a simple method to write him off.

He had come over for a drink before I was to meet him downtown at a club. When he arrived he sat down at the table and we just stared at each other. He was quivering from Parkinson's. His cane fell on the floor. Then I proceeded. Most sincerely I asked him to ask himself if he possess, in his eyes, my form. He nodded solemnly. Now that we know you possess in your eyes my form, I said, I want you to ask yourself if you will continue to read my form even though it may show you that you actually don't exist. He nodded again. OK, I said. Now that I know that you have answered in the affirmative because I am continuing, now you must realize that if I am continuing then you should suppose that in all reality we either have a shared character or in some manner are reflective, since my continuance is also your own. OK. One may invariably argue that, although I, Frank Spec, am continuing, that doesn't mean that you, Dr. Bessingham, actually are. It may be that despite our mutual relation that you are not reading me and your existence is separate, and that you may be able to see without actually being here. If indeed this is the case, then one might also assume that if you are actually seeing me but are not here, then I, Frank Spec, might not be here as well! If I am actually not here, like yourself, then it would be safe to assume that if we are not actually present and we are elsewhere, then my body is being seen by another body, which means I do exist, but just in a different way. If you are still seeing me you may safely say that although not present you are aware that I am, in whatever reality, being seen, and if I am being seen then I am being read, and if both of us are absent, then somehow, in our absence, we are aware of our forms, however separate." He smiled at Edward. "OK. So, now that we know we are aware of our presence, although absent, I may assume that I am not required to be present to be seen or read, and you are also not required to be present when you see me. IF then we are absent together but present elsewhere one can conclude that, as I said before, my existence is ubiquitous, as much as yours, and being everywhere we are then able to be absent because even in absentia we would be there...which means that although we are everywhere, in order to actually be everywhere, we would have to be absent from some place. If this is so, one may safely say that even though you are reading me now and we are together we must also admit that it is impossible to be ubiquitous yet absent from one place. IF this is correct then your earlier lack of continuation, your physical trauma, means that you are in that one place wherein no ubiquitous relation may exist...which means that either both of us are in that place or you, and I, are completely separate. In short, Dr. Bessingham, in my body, that you have read, in complete understanding that your reading of my person, and my seeing of your person, is without connection...One may safely say then that if you are seeing me now then I am wrong, that we both exist as much as we are not together, which means that I am not you, I the maker of lines and the lines that make me, and in such regard am...false. Which means that in *my* contrivance you have been *made*—if all actions make a person—and if that ultimately is so...your existence is fake also! AND this, Dr. Bessingham, means that although you exist, you do not exist in truth! And if you don't exist in truth...then you must not exist at all!

My dear Dr. Bessingham, I said, you have been seeing without body. Yet our intercourse has been real. How is it that I am, in your reflection, also absent when so definitely you have been possessed by me? How is it that you are without form, existence, even love, yet both of us, dependent upon each other, exist, Dr. Bessingham?"

Frank stopped. He took a deep breath, "that is when I knew I had the obituary. The logic was secured. But what it meant to me was that if Dr. Bessingham didn't exist in truth then it was possible the entire infrastructure that he was responsible for was also fake," Frank's eyes were wide, "the rest of it had to be intuited, piece by piece until in the most profound relay of sensory perceptions everything coalesced into the foci of my empathy for the supreme moment of his last breath. Bessingham left and then I wrote, 'Dr. M. Bessingham died at 12:00 am upon leaving a club downtown…'"

THE PSYCHOTIC CONCEPTION

Cleo sat in the women's bathroom at the psychiatric hospital looking in disbelief at the pregnancy test bar that she had just peed on. The steam from her urine sifted off the tab. Her hands shook in complete awe and terror and all the other emotion that comes when such discovery is found. But this was different. She had become pregnant from a psychotic patient, a man who was "not here" but "there". The patient on death's doorstep. The reality out like a light. The non-body of Ed. The man who had some other working concept? Cleo tried to take a deep breath as the ramifications spun her in and out of the irony of the situation: the psychotropic conception mistake of love.

She, Cleo Smith, had been fertilized by a man who was 'absent', a person who could not 'conceive' but who had, literally conceived 'with' her. Moreover, in his non-responsive state he had delivered life, a life he did not seem to possess, which now grew in her womb. SHE, Cleo Smith, was in possession of a coupling of his erupted body delivered by his disrupted mind in a corrupted act! The microscope in her nurse brain began to focus: he not moving, sperm moving, he not life, her another life, he out, she and he in, he incapable of gesture, now inside her one of the greatest gestures, he mute, she now rife with words (FUCK FUCK FUCK!). She looked out through the lace curtains after she mounted him at the PHF. The wind rocked the lace and with determination she put all of Edward inside her. And what were the reverberations? She saw the news broadcast—a typical virus that inflicts all hopelessly narcissistic Americans—the film about her, the reports, and the camera following her in "real life", the spread of media. There she was on Zopra. There she was on Fairly Bling Live. There she was on MZB. There she was on paparazzi film exposures born out in digital body in seedy rooms in trashy apartments in Hollywood. And there Cleo told of her impossible story.

"So you're pregnant with a psychotic patient's baby. How do you feel? Will you consult with Edward Wells about the term, about your future? Was it an ethical lay, did you consider the moral implications? So you're the reverse situation of what we normally think about life. A compromised man made a baby with you. Isn't that like an oxymoron or a paradox or something? So you're going to have it, of course? So you will be on the news, in the papers, in books, virtually everywhere for the rest of your life. So how does your significant other feel? How do you feel about him?"

The propagation of rumor made her shiver into LAMAS LAMAS LAMAS...she sucked in breath after breath, the LAMAS a somewhat cryptic conflation of Spanish, telling who she would soon become: LA MADRE, LA MA, to bear el bambino incredible. LAMAS!

The panorama of the future beckoning her was too much. Yet she had taken Edward into her own hands at the hospital, realizing that without him she would never love. A child, she knew, would seal them...forever. However Cleo realized that she was screwed in more ways than one. On the one hand, if she spilled, which eventually she must, literally, she would have to answer some very hard questions: whose baby is it? On the other hand, if she aborted, it would be like killing some exotic plant that could cure cancer. Only one woman had, before this, become pregnant by a psychotic trauma, a woman in England, a woman who was orthodox Neo Catholic. And then the future historians and estheticians had the worst question possible: to have or to have not, the latter of which would bear severe abortion consequences, given her belief in God. And however different this was, however reverse, perverse, trippy, abnormal she too, was on a tightrope of emerging value. In short, the normal nurse Cleo, who did not have a life before, could now have one of the greatest lives ever: she carried the phenomenal question of another world creating life! Indeed, she carried the impossible articulation of a man she loved who was kaput.

With her new load of information, with the bun beginning to rise, with shock and delight and love and the secret... shit, the secret! She would have to tell Ed eventually, for the baby's sake. What a sacrifice! With these striking thoughts, Cleo changed with one urination in the toilet into a sacred woman who had been chosen royally by curiosity.

Cleo left the hospital the next day and did not return. When Edward awoke, his memory could only recall an immense feeling of love he had felt in his darkest moment. Where did that love come from? Who had touched him? How had he reanimated from terror?

NORBERT CHERRY

Norbert Cherry was Edward's sixth patient. He glimpsed things that were not there or maybe were. Before breakdown, Cherry had been a law student of high mark. He had broken down during the Bar when answering a question about criminal insanity and reason. When he held forth he was professional and direct...as he told Edward... "My name is Norbert Cherry and I am a recovering observer. I don't have many friends since my decline. I am without proper relation, both physically and fantastically. I like to discover and learn. I have a mouse named Little Cherry whom I love. And I am, I have found, utterly alone in the world.

I know exactly when I first found that I was somehow elsewhere. I was ensconced on a bus stop bench and the bus rolled up. I stood and distinguished the doors opening. A very nice driver smiled at me and said, 'alright mate'. I traversed the steps, took my change out of my pocket, deposited the change into the slot, and when I looked again the driver was a mass of paper with a cover, with two pen arms holding the wheel. I recalculated in astonishment. That I determined the driver to be a book in the place of the driver, a book that was smiling, with a hat on, was both hilarious and scary to me. And somehow, without being able to turn around or exclaim in shock that the driver was a book, I shuffled down the aisle and found a seat. I recognized it was the stupidest thing in the world to do. I fathomed that I should have questioned the book driver. I even understood that I should probably have exited immediately. But for some reason unknown to me I let the fantastic hallucination go, either out of shock, State embarrassment or ignorance, and the book driver closed the door and we lurched forward into the blackness. This was my first detection that the world as I once knew it was other. Not only was it other, the world was completely inverse to what I had once observed. In this way, after the bus driver, I became aware of many things that are pretty much impossible to understand, yet I must inform you, Dr. Wells.

I am not sure really if I got off the bus or not. What I remember is that I found myself in a department store downtown and, needing shoes, found the appropriate vendor and spoke to him.

"What are you looking for?" he asked politely.

"A good walking shoe."

He motioned to an array of shoes on the wall. "You may notice," he said, "that the majority of our shoes are style shoes."

"What does that mean?" I asked.

"They are not meant for walking."

"So you sell style shoes mostly?"

"Yes. Most shoes that are worn in the world today are not walking shoes. The majority of shoes people wear are style shoes... not meant for walking."

I considered this bit of information. I already knew something was going to be incongruous here as well as on the bus. "How do people get around?" I said nonchalantly, taking in the boyish figure of the shoe vendor.

"They don't."

"What do you mean they don't. There are millions of people out there walking in shoes as we speak."

"No," said the shoe vendor. "Most people who wear style shoes don't walk."

"How do they get around!"

"Everybody who wears style shoes, which is pretty much everybody, don't walk."

"What do they do?" I asked severely.

"Um," the vendor paused, as if confused by the information he was giving me, "I guess if they don't walk then they are stopped."

That things had been in this relative decline into absurdity since the bus, scared me and I got up quickly and dismissed the stupid vendor. Then, turning toward the door, I stepped briskly away and exited the department store building. As I gained the outside I looked up and as my eyes rose I found my attention fixated upon the shoes on people's feet. It was in that instant that the next contradistinction occurred, and which began my slow divorce from reality. There were, as the vendor said, style shoes upon pretty much everybody's feet. Contrary to the vendor's percipience, the people with style shoes were moving as usual around the mall. Laughing to myself a nervous laugh, I felt the confidence of my rationality and made my way toward the street where, still focused upon the style shoes around me, I suddenly realized something very strange. Although the people appeared to be moving, when I looked at them I saw that it was a veneer of movement. Indeed, every apparently moving shoe was as static as the vendor had said, yet static behind the actual body. So, when I looked, what I saw was that the seemingly moving shoes and legs, and bodies only moved on the surface. Underneath, or rather, behind, the fake movement was complete stasis. I gazed on in utter shock. All these people ambling to all these different places were actually fixed exactly where they were, in their style shoes. The resulting observation moved me quickly through the mall. And it was the same with every person—all unmoving, all without motion, all seemingly active, but actually without one iota of motion. I stepped with my walking shoes through the deception, and when I got to the street, looking about frantically, I observed that it was the same on the street: every single person was adorned in style shoes and were inert underneath! Wanting to perceive really what was going on, whether it might very well be myself who had cracked, I paused on the sidewalk and simply gazed. Everybody in their style shoes was walking, skipping, even jumping. All style shoe people, as far as I could tell, were in observable action. People passed me, brushed by me, walked down the street as happy as any shopper. Then, when I turned my head to double-check this normalcy, there it was, plain as day! Every single person walking by me had not moved an inch, Dr. Wells. As if stuck in some cosmic glue, the entire crowd was unchanging. Not only this, the veneer of them moving, happy with their shopping, skipping with their children, chatting as they strolled, was real! All of them, as if paused upon a TV screen, were stuck still as flamingos. In this minute I realized the world that I had known was not only insane, but also changed completely. Not only that, but the people who lived with me on this part of the planet were unaware that they were not going anywhere. This abstract idea quickly moved me away from the crowd, and I ran for my life, in my walking shoes, as fast as I could, away.

I didn't want to admit that I had lost it. Neither did I want to admit that the world was deranged, Dr. Wells. Yet, wisely, I realized that I must either define my reality or else I would be without any balance with which to live. Thinking about where I might best rediscover reason, I walked to the Courthouse where, etched into the stone arches leading into the chambers, were the words, "Reason is the lifeblood of the law." When I read this epigram I was supremely relieved. Surely, if the stonemasons who had been instructed by the court to write this wisdom had put chisel to stone in accordance with the highest law, and the law made reason "lifeblood", certainly this should be the place where I could right this strange delusion.

Upon reaching the steps, I climbed up and walked to the Superior Court where a trial was being conducted. Walking into the courtroom I quietly found a seat in the back. When I looked up I beheld a Judge in Judge's robes, a lawyer standing and questioning a man, a Jury of some twelve people, and what appeared to be the Defense in chairs. I quickly tuned in, and, to my surprise, the argument was over how to get the style shoes off the street.

"Nobody is going anywhere!" The Prosecution screamed at the Jury. "Behold the guilty party in his chair. He is wearing style shoes, has been asked to quit the stand, and has not moved once since he was brought up for questioning!"

I shrank down in the back of the room like a pressed accordion. How could this be! They were talking about my hallucination! The Prosecution is addressing my very hallucination, Dr. Wells! I looked up to see what was happening.

"Goddamn it!" The Judge yelled. "Will you quit your line of address! Of course he's not going to go anywhere, he's guilty! The Jury has spoken! The defendant is guilty as charged!"

"But he's not moving!" yelled the Prosecution. "He won't quit the stand!"

"You did," the Judge looked fiercely at the Jury, "you did all, in consent and proper deliberation regarding the law, find this man guilty!"

I saw all of the Jury nod their heads in agreement. "He's guilty of the crime of stealing a pair of shoes, style shoes, from the aforesaid mall shop. Guilty."

"There!" the Judge yelled, motioning to the Prosecution, "They did find him guilty."

"But he won't quit the stand!" screamed the Prosecution. "Someone get him to quit the Goddamn stand!"

I looked on, incredulous. The poor man who was in the stand was not moving. The Judge's hands were flailing around in the air.

"He's your fucking client!" the Prosecution yelled at the Defense, "You get him down!"

The Defense looked up from their papers. "Well, you know, the defense rests."

"SO! Tell him to get down!"

"Can't," said the Defense.

"Why not?" replied the Prosecution.

The Defense team lifted their feet up onto the table. Every

single foot was encased in a style shoe.

The Prosecution seemed baffled. "He's been convicted! Someone put him in jail!" The Prosecution looked at the Judge who motioned for the courtroom Security. The Security guard, sitting in the back of the courtroom, looked innocently at the Judge. "Ah, sir," the guard said, "ah, we are also wearing style shoes."

"You what!"

"Style shoes. We are wearing style shoes...ah, so we can't move."

The Judge, in astonishment, stopped. "Ok, you get him off the stand!" he said to the Prosecution. The Prosecution made to move and nothing happened. They looked down to their feet and found themselves fixing their gaze on the style shoes they had worn for this proceeding.

"We got style shoes, too," said the Prosecution in embarrassment.

The Judge stood up. I watched his puffy cheeks turn red. Just as he was about to step down, he stopped, looked down and lifted up his robes. I watched him ascertain something about his feet. Then, looking up again, the Judge screamed. "I've got Goddamn style shoes on, too!"

"What do you want to do?" said the Prosecution. "The Defense has style shoes, the Security has style shoes, we have style shoes, the guilty party has style shoes...does the Jury have style shoes?" Everybody turned to the Jury. They all looked down where they were sitting.

"Yup, we all got style shoes on," said the lead juror.

"Who in this courtroom doesn't have style shoes!" yelled the Judge.

Nobody in the audience moved. I looked down at my walking shoes, but didn't say anything.

"Can anybody move to get this guilty man, guilty for stealing style shoes, off the stand so that his sentence may be served?"

The entire court was dead silent.

"Everybody here has style shoes?" the Judge asked in disbelief.

"Looks that way," said the Defense.

"So that means, " said the Prosecution, "That we haven't moved this entire time?"

"I guess if we all have style shoes then we haven't moved for more than the entire time," said the Defense.

"So," said the Judge, "if none of us have moved the entire time, how did we get here?"

The Defense looked at the Prosecution, and then to the Jury, and back to the Judge. There was silence.

"So," said, the Judge, "if we have never moved, how long have we been here?"

The lawyers all looked at each other with confused faces.

"I move to reconsider the argument at another time..." said the Defense.

I watched them look at each other with severe, trapped-animal stares. Nobody moved.

So that the Court would not be alarmed, I left quietly, out the back door, my walking shoes squeaking loudly on the time-worn wood floors. As I left I felt like some kind of liberated monkey. Upon reaching the street I turned and looked up at the etching on the arch to the Courthouse. There it was, as plain as day, 'Reason is the lifeblood of the law.' What reason was there for all of this? I could not, at that point, possibly imagine, Dr. Wells."

EMOTIONAL
LIBRARY GARDENS

It was past twelve midnight when Edward arrived at the Psychiatric Test Center Facility for State Research. All experimental status was allowed access during the day, for all manner of purposes dealing with psychiatric exams. But Edward did not want to be seen.

He pulled up into a doctor's slot and opened the door to his car. The external lab lights flickered in the cold night air. Looking around carefully he spotted no other person. He walked to the lab door and inserted his flex pass. The door acknowledged him and slid open to reveal a chaotic environment of appliances, gadgets of various kinds, and the synth-beds for full submersion.

He had cast his thoughts back as far as he could go to try and reconcile his feelings of love, past his several girl friends, past Cleo, and to the Empathy Exam he had taken to pass C1 certification for psychiatry. There he stopped and tried to play back the effects of the Operation A Gel Tab. He still could not understand why he had tried to save the woman in the test, at the cost of Officer Aremac. Edward fumbled with a medicine cabinet and flung it open. All sorts of vials and chips and capsule bottles of various sort pronounced a fine investment for the Core. His hand trembled and he extracted a Memorine B tab. They were said to offer the best definition along with the most up to date tracking of empathy sensory. In the back of his mind he knew the reason for this selection; he wanted to go to the foci of the very troubling thoughts he had been having. Love. How could he have advanced from the last test, some ten years ago, after killing the test monitor? He had given the Board its reason, irrational as it was. Love. For love he had pulled the trigger. To save an innocent woman's life…a virtual woman. Why had they passed him? Who was the woman? Why had he pulled the trigger to save her all the while eliminating the responsibility driver? He fumbled with the top and emptied an Operation Memorine B Tab. Looking around for a clear bed he lay down and attached the sensory patches to his head and chest. He took a deep breath. He had never taken another test. He had never taken one alone. As he swallowed the tab and reclined his head into the supports he thought of reality. What reality could be judged on medication? What reality could be lived on medication? Putting this aside, he relaxed into the recline. In one minute he would enter the program. He knew the program would provide him with another slant, perhaps another view into the drug empathy and his own. Yet what he was looking for was the decision. Why had he chosen love over life?

Edward counted down the seconds. You will activate a voice said, in ten, nine, eight, seven…Edward closed his eyes.

Officer Aremac gets into the L.A.P.D. vehicle. Edward feels the gravity of the law in the weight of his utility belt. The sense of the light density of Kevlar is heroically feeling-full on his chest. Edward looks at Aremac and smiles. They pull out of the lot on a Stat call to The Emotional Library Gardens. The car is revving high flow of a visceral 8 engine. When they turn the corner they see the door to the Gardens has been left open. They pull into the parking slot at a slant and exit the car. Aremac reaches down for his Thirty-Eight. Seeing this, Edward also draws his Glock. They walk to the door and nudge it open. There is a dim light inside. Techno music is playing out of the pixilated advertisement on the door and wall. Officer Aremac enters first. Edward follows cautiously. Upon entry they see a man at the counter with a gun to the head of a woman. They assume the woman is the librarian. Officer Aremac levels his gun and takes aim at the man. Suddenly the man pushes the woman aside and starts firing. Both Officer Aremac and Edward fall to the ground. Chips of love and hate fly in the air off the shelves. The officers return fire. A vat of sadness explodes on the counter and the man screams. The intensity of the shootout increases. A vial of tears falls to the ground and breaks apart viscerally in a huge gasp. The man dives over the counter and opens up on them from the other side. Bullets crack vials of hate and anger, disgust blows off the shelf, and glass anticipation splits into the air in a slow crystal motion and cracks open in steam on the tiles. Edward returns fire and kindness breaks in a bottle behind the man. He keeps firing. A pity chip explodes, and an envy module is blasted apart in fractured light. Officer Aremac runs to the other side of the room and dives into the Tear Market Section. Edward covers him and fear dinks off the counter and shatters to the ground. The man behind the counter continues to fire. Bullets blitz every which way around the room. Then suddenly there's silence. Glass on the floor clinks under a foot. The room is rocking like a pendulum. Edward looks in the direction of the counter. A man is standing there with a gun to his head. Edward can see the woman is holding his gun. She is shaking emotionally. She has disarmed him. Officer Aremac arises and shakes emotional residue off. The man held by the woman suddenly yells. "I'm a State Official of the Emotional Core." Aremac stops in an undecided freeze. Edward looks to Aremac. Aremac levels his gun at the woman. His hand seems to be in slow motion. A wind blows through the door from outside. The advertisements broadcast "best hate to go down with," "Kick it with happiness for any level," "Emphatic loss in the moment of a realization." The light flickers in the room from broken phosphorescence. I am watching the woman with the gun to the head of the criminal. She is shaking. Officer Aremac levels upon the woman. I am watching him take slow aim. I do not know if he is aiming at the man or the woman. I find my gun rising slowly in the direction of Aremac. The criminal states again, "I am a State Official of the Emotional Core!" A shot fires. I look at the man being held by the woman. He is quivering in the broken light. I turn back to see Officer Aremac crumpled on the ground. I look at my hand. In my hand is my Glock. When I look back to the woman I see she is pointing her gun in the direction of myself. I look at her with terrified eyes. A shot fires. I grab my chest in reactive shock. When I feel no bullet I turn around. Behind me another officer is laying on the floor. When I turn around again the woman is gone.

Edward's eyes wince into recognition. The next phase of the test he feels in his pulse. The Memorine B Tab he can feel numbing his hands. Then a light flash and he falls into quick REM.

I am a psychiatrist with a patient going to get an emotion. The emotion we are looking for is to instill in us the best feeling of responsibility. We know that this emotion is trust. We also know that trust, fortified by truth, is a concoction known to be dangerous to The State. Nevertheless we must find trust in ourselves to find the truth. We are going to The Emotional Library Gardens to acquire this feeling.

Upon opening the door there is the sound of Kick advertisements. Jake music plays out through the pixilated templates. Slow circuitry of solace fluxes through white sleep offerings. Truth is advertised at a high price. We enter and walk up to the librarian. My patient, whose name is Frank, asks for high-grade truth. As we are asking for this I browse the chip shelves. The door opens. A man walks in with a gun. He walks up to the woman and pushes Frank on the floor. Holding the woman hostage he begins to rob emotions. He does not see me. The door opens suddenly and two policemen enter. Their guns are drawn. In the following seconds a firefight ensues. I am aware that the woman is in danger. I see fear vials explode in the air. Pity shatters off the desktop. Light love fluxes from love signs to disintegration a vat of tears. The air is cracking. Anger chips blast off a shelf in front of my face. I make my way around behind the criminal holding the woman. I see Frank by the counter holding the criminal's gun. Officer Aremac and his partner are reloading their weapons. Frank holds his hands up and says he is looking for truth. The officers aim at me thinking I'm the criminal. Suddenly it is quiet. I look up. The officers are pointing their guns at me. I think they are going to fire. I am not armed. Suddenly there are three shots. I look down at my body. When I look up Frank is falling to the ground. When I look up both officers are dead before him. I look to my hands. I am not holding a weapon. I look on the floor and see Frank lying motionless. In his hand is the criminal's gun. I look at the criminal and he runs out the door. When I turn around the woman is not there.

Edward heaved up with a gasp from the sentient patches. He pulled them off his body. He was shaking. He felt paranoid as if someone was watching. Yet of course the chit in the computer term was the only witness. What was the reason for being here, he thought. He could not recall. In slow motion his mind swam out of The Emotion Library. Bits of imagery zipped in his head. He reached for the rail and pushed himself up.

He had had a double scenario, like the last time. He tried to remember the reason of his test. Had he wanted to know the truth? Yes. But it had to do with love. Why would he kill someone for love to save a life? The question was the typical irrational split of the exam system. His heart was still beating fast. Empathy was the key word. The irony of empathy in an Emotional Library where all emotion is being shot. The confusion of a space where all feeling in chip form is under attack. Whoever thought up these tests was insane, maybe a poet; some radical that had gotten through and wanted to get the psych board back for fucking up his emotional existence. The flow in him began to ebb and then evened out into a flux state of accessible thought.

Officer Aremac had been the test driver. They responded to a call at the Emotional Library Gardens. What call that was they did not know. Upon entering they found a woman who was being held hostage by a man. They both raised their guns. There was a gunfight. He could recall the sizzling phyzz of bullets going through vials of high grade. Hate, love, fear, anger, sadness, joy, surprise, disgust, trust, anticipation, kindness, pity, shame. The emotions had popped off the shelves like explosive desires. Then the woman had disarmed the hijacker. Aremac aimed at her. He should not have aimed at her. I did not speak. I was stunned by the fight. I looked at the woman. The man yelled something about being a State Official. Aremac I felt changed in that moment. He aimed at the woman. A shot fired. I wanted to stop him. I wanted to...I could not say kill. Edward's feelings balked. I had shot Aremac again. I had shot him to save the woman. Edward raced in his head to see the image. But it blanked out. A feeling in his guts. He had felt... what was it? Joy? No. Responsibility? No. Then a feeling erupted in him...pleasure at knowing that the authority of Aremac was wrong. He had felt the pleasure of his righteousness.

Edward rose from the table and looked around. The lab was lit by night lamps and had a cold sterile feeling of work that was without human touch. He turned to the computer term and saw no picture. There had been one more test.

Frank and he had been looking for truth. Trust and truth at the Emotional Library. Upon entering they passed the pixilated ads. There was a feeling of rightness there about getting truth. Frank approached a woman librarian. He asked for the truth. A man entered and pushed Frank down. Edward had been browsing in the hate archives. The man took the woman hostage. Two officers entered. A firefight ensued. Emotion scattered from the shelves. Edward had looked at the hate chips and imagined what he hated most. In the back of his mind his mind froze. The question was not love. The question he was looking for was the truth. He paused in his brain and winced in clarity. Love wasn't the answer of this test. The real question was how much did he hate the system. How much and how deep did he hate the entire thing. Bullets were flying. A bunch of vials of sadness splattered in his face. He made his way to the woman. He wanted to say he loved her. The feeling however was contrary. He didn't love her. He dove behind the counter and Frank picked up the criminal's gun. The two officers reloaded and took aim. Frank had said innocently...we are looking for truth. It wasn't a question. It was a statement. Three shots fired. The two officers slumped to the ground. I looked in my hands. I held no gun. Frank in front of me had blocked the shot. He fell to the ground as innocent as his illness. He was my patient. He was my friend. I looked at the woman and she was not there. I looked in my hand and there was a vial. The vial I clutched in my hand was a vial of hate, high grade. And that was the truth. I hated the whole thing. The entire fabric of this bullshit reality that was happening I hated. I looked at my friend, my patient on the floor. Frank lay motionless without hate.

Edward sucked in the synthetic air of the test room. He looked at the synth-screen above him that showed his thoughts. The Board could not see this fundamental kernel of truth or he would be dead, he thought. It was not love he had saved the woman for. That ideal emotion sounded very nice. But it wasn't that. He felt shock. The shock of reality. He was after the truth. And the truth was...his hand shook like after his delivery of his paper. The truth was he hated it all, and in his hate he had shot the authority. All authority. Joy. That sanguine feeling of pleasure they had questioned. It was the love of the joy and the love of the hate that was being balanced. But, he could not now fail the strongest emotion in him. Like the purity vials that everyone wanted...he, Edward M. Wells was full of hate.

He turned and pulled out the gig chip from the terminal. Nobody could see this. Upon turning toward the door he stopped dead cold. A form stood before him. He could make out the visage of a middle-aged man. The face was void of emotion. The man was in a jacket and somewhat slumped at the shoulders, like he was scared.

"You are trying to understand your love," the man said.

Edward, frozen in his place, could not speak. They stood facing each other without a word for several seconds.

"Yes," Edward said. He looked deeply into the man in front of him. Who would be at the facility at this hour?

"I make the experimental exam medicine," the man said.

Edward eyed him from his shoes up. He wore sneakers, jeans,

and a jacket. His countenance took on the look of a young man.

"Who are you," Edward said.

"Jeremy Smith."

Then it came rushing back to Edward. Jeremy smith. The study who did not pass. The study that had in his Empathy Exam disappeared through a hole in his head. Rejected.

"I know what you are looking for," Jeremy said.

Edward could not stop his hand from shaking.

Jeremy moved to the table separating them. He put his hands on the table and then looked up. "You are looking for the ability to feel all your emotions without the system formats, tests, authority, programs."

Edward nodded his head and shivered.

"You are looking for justice mostly. Love is your lie. Hope is a fallacy. Fear is your motivation. Happiness is just a vacation." He smiled a sad smile.

Edward watched him straighten up.

"You are looking for the very visceral center of your being in a society that oppresses this center. You say you are looking for love but this is just a blanket covering your desire for truth and trust. You want to know the deepest feeling yet you come to take a test, a test that is controlled by Memorine B. You want to say and see that in this test you are noble upstanding and good. You save a woman against all odds. You go against The State, your empathy fluxes from heroism to disaster. Your values are medicated into action. Your actions are void of the deep feeling of being in the world. You try and see through your patient's lives. You try and understand love in a program. But it is not real love. As part of a great machine you are prodded into being an experimental genius who wins awards…yet you don't love, you don't trust, you don't know the truth, and you have no justice."

The room was silent. Edward looked at the mem-chip in his hand.

"I bet that recording holds enough hate to burn right through the eyes of the system holding you. You are trying to hide your worst emotions by supplanting the noble feeling of love while joy shows you actually liked killing the synth-officer."

"How do you know this?" Edward said.

"I went through the system test. I went, as Officer Aremac aimed at my head for trying to save my own love, right through the bullet hole, right through my death."

"How did you do it?"

Jeremy looked far off in his eyes. His face twitched and then he spoke.

"I made up the entire thing. I took a placebo. I had the story, the exam notes, what was going to happen, at what time, in what intervals, and then I made it up."

"You mean you were not on medicine?" Edward said, incredulous.

"Not one chemical pixilated bit of it. It was my will against the machine."

"So you supplanted the medicine with a placebo and they bought it?"

Jeremy continued... "I knew they'd get the imagery. I knew they'd array correctly through the digital chalk. I knew that all I had to do was tell their story and then, right at the most fracturing act of terror I simply changed my mind..." he paused. "I simply fell through a hole that I invented and let them see. My free will against theirs."

Edward looked cautiously at Jeremy. "What are you doing here?" He asked.

"I was following your exam. After I fell through the hole of my own death they had become rather impressed. They gave me a job at the low-level exam experiments, and I rose like the technocrat they wanted me to be. Now I make the exams. I do the chemical blueprints." He motioned to Edward's hand that held the chip. "That is original brain time, you've got."

Edward looked at the chip. "What do you mean?"

"I made Memorine B. Another guy and I. A synth-placebo. Fakes the medicinal array of chemical nuance, but is essentially an empty medicine. It can go through the machine without detection, perfectly."

"I took a placebo?"

"Yes. But ask yourself what your creative imagination has done while on placebo. The entire digital pick-up that recorded you was pure. Indeed, you came to the truth of the matter on your own. You, Edward Wells, invented the correct response to the entire system in a most emotionally amazing way. Do you know what this means?" He paused and shook his hand in the air. "It means that you, off medicine, have deduced the most beautiful reality of imagistic violence and truth in response to pressures weighing upon you to know. But what you now know is that your emotional responses simply want the best, may I say, the most ecstatic answer. Just like anybody. Just like a child."

Edward was silent. The room was dim and empty save for them. He had just hallucinated, according to Jeremy, without medicine...purely. And he had gotten to the core of his problem. He simply hated the entire system. Jeremy looked at him and then spoke.

"I wanted to prove that people are more capable than what the system is trying to create. Nobody knows the meds are false... not yet. But someday I'll let it out and the whole system will crash. That people are more capable than a crutch, then a prompt, then a fabricated support, then a lead to the vapid future where no one is original...will awake them. I wanted to slip originality into the machine and let the machine sort it out. And look at you. You have your own vitally aware imagination that is capable of such independent visions."

"So the synth-hookups still pick up a radiation of memory pics, even off substance?"

"Yes, still the same. But just think of the fracture in the entire hierarchy when they find that they are seeing real images, untainted by the medicine. Just think what will happen if we are all liberated from the pill." Jeremy turned away. "Back to work as they say, back to work." He stopped at the door and turned back to Edward. "One more thing...The Psychiatric State Board are mostly emotion substance abusers. They are all addicted to the libraries, if you don't know. Truth, Love, Trust...they take it to make decisions about the field. They base their decisions upon other people's emotions. They were probably on it when you passed. Someone's innocent coalesce of purity and truth decided for them your success, success in killing Officer Aremac...for love. Does that makes sense to you?" Jeremy smiled a sad smile. "The world feels exactly the same as you. They say hallucination as if illness...but it is just agitated creativity, suppressed for hundreds of years." He walked out the door.

BETWEEN ANGER MANAGEMENT AND REALITY

After Jack recovered he had gone many ways. But it was in Anger Management that he focused his chaotic energy into the one meaning in his life that had helped him: Edward Wells, the psych who shared the fight as much as Jack had fought it, like a laissez-faire witness who understood that if you stop something that is natural, even if it is illegal or bad, you might be snuffing out the Amazon flower that would save humanity. Why stop anything that is natural? Is nature innately evil? It would have died off long ago. He had ruminated over this in his class while the other members looked on. Cherry, Frank, E.L., Mark and he with all the anger in their heads curing. No, nature was not innately evil. It would be the same as saying that a sprig of grass is evil, a dog is evil, even a thought is evil. Mankind had made this world with a moral though, and probably if anything was evil it was that the moral was to teach that evil existed in man only if man was, under some great social alteration, made to be what he was not originally. And if this was unconscious, as most who were beset by this fault were, then even then they were innocent of evil. That nature must be changed, like in his class, he now considered to be contrary to him, was only the ironic realigning that most social law required.

Edward had been ordered to put all of his patients through the class. They sat in a circle looking at each other in quizzical, somewhat guilty looks, in a silence that spoke of the curiosity of this amelioration. How deep could a person speak about anger after the invasion of a mind? How would they be repaired?

A woman entered and sat down in a chair. She had blonde hair, shoulder length, and was dressed in fairly formal attire. Her name was Cindy. They observed calmness in her, an almost cheery demeanor that was nice to look at.

"Alright. What I want to get out of this class today is some difficult answers." She paused and turned her head to face all presiding. "Answers that will not always be easy, but answers that reach into the core of your being, the feelings we all have that will—although maybe socially awkward—open us to understand our deepest angst." Cindy swept her hands around. "Although it might be scary for some of you, you will find that expression of your own truth will cure. Where for some of you this will be difficult, please know that you don't have to speak, but speaking about your issues will help to air your troubles and perhaps we may respond better afterward."

Cherry was breathing deeply in his chair. Empathy was his demon. He felt everything. And what he felt now was the future bearing down on him. Almost crushing. He looked to the others whom he had spent experimental time with.

Frank was slumped back in his chair, seemingly in another state, his eyes holding the class in a distance that told of medfatigue. Next to him Mark was playing thumb games and pipping every once in a while words of a new language. Adjacent from him sat E.L. His eyes were focused in almost shock on the director. Jack shifted in his seat in agitation, the most outstanding of all of them when it came to violence.

"Now, we'll just go around and I want you to say your name and then something about your feelings, in whatever manifestation you are comfortable with." She cocked her head to the right and all eyes fell upon Jack. He looked up startled and somewhat scared. He wasn't used to speaking in public least of all with a cleft palate. There was a disruptive silence and then he spoke.

"Jack Spillain."

The pause in the room was awkward. He shifted in his seat.

"What are we supposed to say?"

Cindy popped up in her chair. "Just say anything you want. Talk."

He sat up slowly, shifted in his seat and his muscles flexed down his arm.

"When we have nothing we either fuck or we fight." He looked at Cindy. She nodded to him to continue. "When we go out we either fuck or we fight. If when we fuck we fight, our women get laid. If when we fight we fuck, their women get laid. If we do nothing then everybody is fucked. Hence we are fucking fighters and fighting fuckers and nothing, the universal reference, is perfectly poised to be fucked for fighting for us." Jack looked up for reassurance. The others looked on with encouraging eyes.

"Just say it," said Cindy.

Jack looked at her hard.

"Why, you ask? Because it is the best ref. Should we fuck fighters or fight fuckers or simply fuck the ref? If the ref is a fucker then we'll have him fight for us. If the ref is a fighter then we'll have him fucked seven times a day seven days a week until he sees God. If the ref is God and he fucks us then we'll fuck him back. If God is a fighter then we'll fight him back. And, if the world doesn't yet know how to fuck and fight then we'll teach them that there is no God."

"Ok." Cindy said. "Did everybody pick up the anger in that? That's real anger." Cindy combed her hand through her blonde hair. "Does anybody have a comment?"

Cherry popped up in his seat. "Good," he said.

Frank, recovering from his dose, clapped his hands hard.

"Right on brother," said E.L.

Mark looked at Cindy. His face was tense.

"Good," Cindy said. Now anger is a base emotion. Anger comes from all kinds of places. Anger informs us of feelings that are latent and reactive. Anger is a response to differences that are unfair." She looked at the group. "Does anybody want to go?"

Mark somehow gained the attention of the room. He stammered a little and then settled. "I want to block anger."

Cindy held out her hand. "How do you block anger," she said.

"This is a ward poem." Mark unfurled. "I pull it to the root to back see the slime. Phlegm means fire. I sickness in the light reflect. Reflect light in the sickness of I. Word. Turn slowly all around the root. You see nothing in conception. Conception sees nothing in you. This, interwoven with the poison of a stare. Eat me. Ecila. How I ask you will. Turn the 1851 sentience around like a word. Eighteen Fifty-One. One fifty aid in..." Marks hands created a symbol in the air... "Now over into your wetware eat ware no here love. Evolve flow in the reflect of Alice. Again, die your own soul black with my words reverse and clean as the apple in your throat, like Old English devolving in your pate. Blind open and clear as this line. Annihilate yourself in your knowledge of myself."

"What makes you angry?" Cindy said, focusing on Mark.

"When the world like mixes up and you can't figure it out."

"Does the world mix up for anyone else here?" She looked out at them and found Frank's eyes wide with horror.

"For you?" she said to Frank.

"Jesus Christ," Frank said.

"You're exacerbated at something?" Cindy said.

"Before the Nazis come, give me a kiss." Frank said to her. "There, they are at our door. They love to burn children and adults, disabled people, and dogs that inform. Invite them in. Please, have a seat. Look at all of our art. I think we know you from WWII, WWI, and the Romans. Please, sit next to the fire and get warm. We will tell you secrets. Look, do you see this pot; it was fired at 1000 degrees and then spun on a wheel where my mother glazed the skin. Much like your work! How joyful it is to have you here! Please, have a drink! It is Absinthe 1939! After the Putsch! We wanted it to be of a better gravity so we put it in a tumbler and spun it at 1000 MHz and it came out as bitter as my family line. Pour yourself reality. I will pour it for you. What is the best thing? All of us are in a circle. We are at the center. You are around us. You and I can see my tattoos. They are "Freedom", "War", and "Truth"." Frank held up his inked arms. They flexed in front of the group. "I toast all of you. My dear friends. Please, let me take a picture, I will light a fire. There, all together in front of the fire! Click!"

"Ok," Cindy said. "Let's acknowledge this." She encouraged the others in the circle to clap. Each clapped awkwardly.

"That's right," Mark said. "Don't forget the cardinal rule."

"What's the cardinal rule?" Cindy asked.

Each of the patients looked to Frank. "Live," he said, "before the Nazis get you."

"Yes," Cindy said. "We must all live, in whatever way we can. Although we are all different we share similar feelings. Who here is really angry?"

Everyone raised their hands slowly.

"But angry in an original way," said Mark.

"Like how?" said Cindy.

"Because I'm original."

"Does that make you angry?" She looked at Mark in fake concern.

"What make's me angry is that no one gives a shit."

They all nodded. Cherry looked directly at her. "We are sort of stuck with this illness and it forces upon us alienation, loneliness, and fractures that are difficult to live with."

"That's truth," said Frank.

Everyone looked at Cherry.

"But what I have found are unabsolute truths," said Cherry. "What is absolute is the "un". I "un" then everything. I am not

178

ashamed to not be. The beauty of nature is not abashed to be without. The church is not guilty to lack. Even God has his faults. Ungodly acts are more defined than Godly ones. Be good, my son, for the truth is that if God exists he is disabled. I pray to people in wheelchairs, lunatics, lepers, sick children, and my own schizoaffective attribute. Please tell the mistaken universe that God is moored in the harbor behind the eyes of the plague victims of 1666. Please tell the church that behind the tongues of invalids is the word. Please tell the destitute that they only need graffiti their neighborhood with this truth. We will see each other in jail and the priest will come to anoint us. Yet, when the door closes he will have to ask himself how he, too, is disabled, to distinguish between the multiple criminal lost priests who now begin to prey on him. And one Parkinson patient who shakes uncontrollably will respond to his prayer: Yes Father, you may now illuminate me about Africa, The Middle East, Spain, South America, Germany, the Native Americans...and tell me your dream of conversion of pain into gold, and your disease into capital, make me still."

Cherry shook involuntarily. The others fidgeted in their seats.

"Now we're getting off the track. We are here to discusses anger."

"That was anger," said Frank. "Pure, unadulterated truth anger."

"Yes," said Cindy, "but what about your feelings?"

"I thought those were feelings," Jack said.

They looked at Cindy. How many times a day she did this they did not know.

"Our feelings have been crushed," said Mark

Cindy looked at Mark furtively.

E.L. said, "fuck it," out loud. Everyone looked at him. "Fuck the whole thing. If we can't speak then we get fucking angry."

"You go," said Cindy. "Get the anger out of you. Uncrush."

He looked at her coolly.

"This is a love song," he said. The room was silent. "They write like lepers of geometry, The State. Graph your own body like the Man. Us peasants have been etched by the sun. I read their eyes and see the kings. My friend, write like the plague their beautiful marks to take you to the kingdom. I hate them with my peasant soul, etched by the dust, my hands dripping with future, my soul as poor as the crown jewels. But they do not know what a king means, the lepers, dead morsels of code, fucked by their cash, stuffed like the olive eyes of their treachery. I can see, when I look in their eyes, tables full of other promises: death, punctual as the genetic code they cannot touch. Hence my knife, my knife, from the table of their making, stolen at the last instant when Jesus is supposed to be over. Peasant that I am, I could use it to make one point: look into the North Star and see how my fake direction is absolute. I have closed my peasant eyes and I am king and the knife is at the throat of God."

E.L.'s eyes were closed.

"Alright," Cindy said. "That's not what I want. I want you to get to the core."

"That wasn't to the core?" said Frank.

"Well it was to the core in some ways, but what about the law?"

The room was silent.

Frank held up his hand. He slowly stood up, and brushed off his clothes. You could see muscles lining his arms, and his shoulders were considerably endowed. He looked directly at Cindy and put his fist up to his head.

"This inverse reality knows one thing, Cindy, if you point the dream gun at the real it is real; if you point the real gun at the dream it is not. Hence, I am a dream." He held up his hands to show the group. "The mechanisms in my hand are confusing. At one moment birds, at another moment a cross, at another a nine-millimeter Browning. The children come and take in their hands the birds. The church comes and takes the cross. My muse keeps writing for the gun. When the children take the bird it is a sign of innocence. When the church takes the cross it is a sign of terror. When my muse takes the gun it is a sign of poetry. My hand never wanted any of this. I look across at my gifts. The church is very happy to have a cross. The children are very curious about the birds. My muse can only aim for the cross because the cross is a focus. I ask them to haul it up and give me a target. Two nuns and two priests arrange the wood up on the altar. Accidentally, the birds of the children explode in the air. My muse, never one to hold a gun, pulls the trigger, startled by the present. Bang! Bang! Bang! Bang!" Frank holds up his hands like guns. "When the birds clear, two nuns and two priests lie dead at the altar. Never accept a gift that you cannot live up to."

"What does that have to do with the law?" said Cindy.

There was a shaky pause and then Mark pitched in his chair and almost fell over. He started muttering. "I am looking every which way. Multitudinal and absolute. I am looking every which way because I am a trigger to reality. People think I am a dream. I am also a real dream." He stopped. All eyes focused on him. "Frank is a dream, E.L. is a dream, Cherry is a dream, and Jack is a dream."

Frank spoke up. "We are all stuck in dreams we cannot get out of. But when the shit goes down my focus is every which way… my poem, the trigger, my soul is perfect." Frank knocked down his chair. "My eye, a finger of perfection, is waiting. Sure as my doubt and pure as my reflection I, with myself on the poem, wait." The room fell silent. "My poems are slow," he said. "My eye is fast. My soul is pure. What I know is that the devil exists, angels are real, the church is bad, love is purer as hatred, and my poem is the answer to all of this. When the priest in the guise of a devil enters, my hand, my eye, and my pen are sure. When the devil in the guise of a priest enters I am even surer. At this moment every direction converges on the crosshairs of my conscience. Pure as my muse, my muse the bullet in the gun, the words in my poem the bullets of my promise, I pull the circle around me, make a cross, and the chamber empties." Frank dropped on to his knee and made the sign of the cross. "When I say, you are a poet you know the absolute you live. I blow smoke from the barrel and the question: Who could convene in such hideous forms!" He gestured to the circle. "Intuitively, the asking fluxes and the multitude of words silver as truth turns cylindrical in the ears of my guilt. You see meaning open up and salt the story in a blanket of ocean."

Cindy stood up. "Alright," she said. "Now ask yourselves what is really going on with you inside. What is really going on in your emotions. What do you really think of anger? When you get to a good answer then tell me."

"Nothing is secret," Mark said. "Shouldn't that piss you off?"

"I had the knowledge to give everything away," said Cherry. "I was attacked. The psychical force was against my way."

"Say more about privacy, Mark."

"Everything is foreknown."

Cindy did not respond. Then she said, "Ok, just imagine a world that is…"

"I used every word to counter the sickness," Jack interrupted. "It was the hardest thing I ever did. Every word like a rainstorm. They went dark and leveled me."

"E.L. how can we be private if all the voices coming in like a blitzkrieg all the time do not shut up?" said Cherry.

"When you reach the center everything stills," said Frank. "The light became nice. I felt warmth and relief and purpose. Yet up until this I fought with all my might against a demon horde of words that made me steel down to my quick. I didn't want to do this. I wanted my innocence. I wanted my love." An involuntary shudder shook Frank.

Jack cut in, "knowing that I had to fight, I burned my soul in my fist. Then, finally, when I had acted with every means I possessed, my anger rested. I could do no more. The feeling was very tiring, very bitter, and even deadly. I did not want to stop."

The phosphorescent lights in the room glitched off and then on. The circle appeared like ghosts. The feeling of anger turned in the air in the room with the overhead fan. Each one of the patients looked at each other in a feeling of despair. What was anger like really? What would motivate a person to violence? How far had they come to speak these feelings, openly, without prompt? Was this even what they were supposed to do?

Edward entered.

They focused on Edward the same way that Edward had focused on them, in their individual fights to live with mental illness. Jack at the museum. Frank at a late night session. Cherry lost in empathy. Mark stuck in the airport with chaos of the beyond. E.L. off of parole and shaking. They knew Edward understood the expression of truth from a group who could not communicate or interact normally in society. He had been there at the recovery of Jack from his coma. He had been there with Frank at St. Mary's. He had been with Mark as he fell into oblivion. And now when he entered Jack recalled when Edward had placed the coin in his hand, when he had received the coin; in that moment he knew what Ed knew: a deep love was on the other side of this mentally ill rage. That moment of connection to another, no matter machine or currency, was the necessary answer. The Anger Management had become an experience of learning, which told them that the world was on fire with the most unnatural emotions, but was it still a world to live in? The room was silent. The lights flickered.

PRIVACY & MEDICINE CONTINUED

The following tests were conclusive. Knowing that he needed a scientific difference to prove *The Harbor* findings, Edward made his way across town to Jake's Café. Entering the café, he casually unhooked the spoon key and wobbled into the restroom, and, closing the door, he again sensed the sublime click in the lock, which, though closing, freed one into privacy. For it was here, as in the Lorretos lavatory, that his divorce from the outside world afforded him a bewildering feeling of untrammeled intimacy. Not intimacy as one would think of it, but intimacy with a self beaten silly by the new world freak show that he had been thrown into ever since his psychosis. Communication of the third kind. Blip culture members being pushed alive as they pushed the buttons to the next "screen". Empathy tests in which he killed in hate for love. And here the reclusion was, although walled in, a freeing into "place" that was neither out or totally in but afloat in simple brick form in an establishment. And it was hardly observed, hardly spoken of, hardly "passed through". That is how private it was; no one spoke of his or her personal deliveries to the pipes.

An American Standard toilet graced the corner. Another Georgia Pacific towel dispenser was slotted on the wall. And the Toto sink jutted whitely from the wall like a firm ceramic jaw. What was startling was that Edward felt truly free. Free for the first time from the din. Free from the awkward rattle of machine. Free from the consideration of the law. Even free from himself. It was like a precipice, which, once reached, allowed you to jump into a wholly new anti-gravity that made thought all float. Upon turning on the faucet he was reminded by the miniscule wine from the water and the pipes of his early childhood when he could hear the comforting flow in the lines at night in his parents' home. This distinct, coupled with the floral soap smell and the mirror where, when he looked, he was actually not "there" but here, he found completely purifying. Purifying like the Emotional Libraries were purifying. And glancing back into the mirror he noticed that he was disencumbered even from the problem of his identity. Who really cares in the Head? He meditated. Was there anyone who really cared? No. Here he was himself...alone, but himself. The white tile made him feel surrounded yet not trapped, the factual I-am-here feeling of white. And that he was in a cubicle of some five by seven feet did not make him feel that he was without means of escape, for the escape seemed to happen in the mere thought that no one else in the entire world knew that he was there, what he might be doing, how he was "looking", where he might be lounging, what his ideas were, and ultimately where he was in the totality of space and time. Nobody. Not a damn soul. This consideration was deeply moving, and Edward slumped on the wall in utter relief. Here he was "locked in" yet totally free! The irony in itself was like the medicine of which he had written in the harbor paper: "the placebo medicine dislocates reality and gives you your health elsewhere." He looked at his watch...did it even matter? No, for in this space of sublime relaxation there was no time, he found, save now. If he had had another clock he could have taken a bearing, but here there was none. What did two mean in the toilet? Nothing. Edward's cheek on the tile felt the coolness of the ceramics. His tongue slipped out of his mouth and he tasted the wall. How utterly hilarious that he would taste a wall! Then he jigged over to the toilet and looked in. Water that carried away our horrific digestive residues. Who knew where it went, really. So much distance from these pipes to the plant, so much possibility... He flushed the mechanism and watched the water swirl away. Then, upon reaching a climax in the realization of the Toto functions, Edward opened the door and slipped out, his privacy unregistered by any electronic device or human eye.

Upon reaching the conclusion that his first early toilet observations afforded a sensibility similar to that of the second, though each possessed some very different effects, Edward decided to scribe his new secret's attributes, the history, and the philosophical sense afforded him in comparison to Post Vital medication.

If pills containing ameliorative spatial differences such as Gyrexa, Queropel, Amadine, Fishium, and Assperdal are surrounded by the negative space of a toilet, wherein the sanguine reverb in the "rest" room, from toilet flush to washing of hands, but most directly the privacy afforded by the "compound" free zone of this room, it could be assumed the medicine and the person taking the medicine would be made better. More simply, the irony of a privacy that is actually "free", contrary to property law possession, if surrounding the spatial differences of the aforesaid medication in "harbor", suggests a possible inversion of "a rest" room, and could symbolically detox the pill in the space used for human relief. In short, he thought, this would overlay the medicine with a substantial environmental health, like placebo, and if the environment were healthy the toilet would be effectively clearer, even made super healthy for the patient, while on meds.

He could understand that where *Toilette* is originally a French word meaning "cloth put over the shoulders while dressing the hair or shaving," the Latin root of toilette, *tela*, meaning "web" could make the issue more definite. For if indeed he had been experiencing the salubrious feeling of a "web", he was being "covered". That the irony of the bathroom "web" was actually off the "world web" yet in the world, the ameliorative feeling of "privacy" compounded. Simply, he fathomed that tela was a covering over the covering...or overlay, which copied the world differently! Indeed, "tela" either reflected the web and therefore was "free", or it "covered" the web and therefore the web was "here" but "gone". Whatever the case, Edward now realized the beauty of this simple room: in privacy it was free, as much as in its web was the liberty of verbal relief from the greater web, by reflective nuance, used, he thought, largely for connection or catching.

Edward continued with assiduous focus. Today we have many names for this indispensable and quite evolved room: 'john', 'lavatory', 'bathroom', 'latrine', 'loo', 'W.C.', and, 'head'—all depending upon where you are. The list could go on ad finitum if one were to enumerate the multitude of labels for our civilized world's 'inner sanctum' of the home. But, who really broods about it when they go to 'do their business' there; the business that would—if we were to count all of the minutes culture relieves within—amount to millions of hours of freedom. It is so regarded that even the cell phone craze, which holds Star Trek curiosity, does not penetrate this zone of cleansing, shivering relief, sublime relaxation. Where the early Walter Mosely noted that "punning is language on vacation," one could very well say that 'toilet relief' or 'web' relief is soul on vacation; primping in the mirror is aesthetics on vacation and showering is body on vacation...

Edward settled and returned to the medicine problem. The fact remained that if symptoms of psychosis and mania were mitigated as with his first toilet experience, then perhaps they might be healed or sated by such continual reflection that his paper might embody. Here in the harbor of words he was seeing through to answer historical plumbing's ability to be sanus.

The first semi-functional toilets were natural: bushes, holes in the ground and rivers, which could only temporarily conceal the putrid character of the material all must release after digestion.

Even today these junctures are still used, both in civilized countries during emergencies and in uncivilized countries. Where the Nile in Egypt presents a bathing spot along with many rivers in other parts of the world, an outbacker in the US will use a bush, a hole, whatever can be found during the moment of truth. Hence, although we are all privy to the most 'advanced' toilet system in the world just as we are privy to State TV or the computer, the pressing nature of the body will tyrannically demand we utilize any means available.

And that was it: in order to abide mental illness life mandated that one use any means available...even the most absurd. That we are dependent on the toilet three times a day would only boost the failing senses. It would be a supportive Tela-free "Head" therapy wherein we plumbed not only the problem but the need for free private space, which could transfer to the psychiatric trauma study, by reflective pipes, the space so often compromised for a schizophrenic person. So why could it not be that the toilet was the next best place to unhook from the percept chemicals of medicine and fuse to the possibility that a Toto sink or a Kohler toilet, not to mention a Georgia Pacific dispenser, along with the white tiles and the smell of the soap, might be alternative medicine? This, all to say, that really the combination of the toiletries and the irony of privacy being free and being free in privacy while still in the "web" or head, is one answer in a million, yet possible. If space shapes who we are as much as we shape space...could it not be that receiving toilet treatment instead of medicinal treatment might ameliorate the ragged human need, might allow us our shit?

Then, in a small advancement, the bucket arose as the receptacle in which humans emptied themselves. The contents of the bucket, of course, were disposed of, either out the window, into the river, or whatever place the carrier deemed far enough away not to cause a stink. What if we had to use this method and tote the bucket to the appropriate place? We would live in hell.

But the fact was, Edward had to admit, that many patients on meds did live in hell despite the supposed effects of the chemicals reorienting them to life. If the toilet was hell then could it be a better hell than the radical reactions to the medicine? Edward stopped. He had found the difference: the perception of shit was different for different people. Some shit was psychological and shiny cerebral and some shit was colloquial and slangy, and literal shit was the most abominable though much more of a relief, because you knew exactly what it was. Whereas on a med you did not know what the shit was, in the toilet you knew exactly what the shit was. What would be better? Real shit that you could flush away or mental aberrant shit that you couldn't ever flush away? He looked again at the history and began flow.

After the bucket, the Western World moved into the plumbing age. The Romans, according to The Encyclopedia Britannica, "... had a considerably developed plumbing system, advanced disposal with water that was brought to Rome by aqueducts and distributed to homes in lead pipes—hence the name plumbing from the Latin word plumbum for lead." " 'During the Middle Ages plumbing became almost nonexistent. In fact, London's first water system after the Middle Ages (c. 1515) consisted partly of the rehabilitated Roman system. What we know as modern plumbing began in the early 1800's when the new steam engine was used to supply water under pressure and cheap cast iron pipes were employed to carry it." All of these inventions and adaptations helped the world to sparkle, Edward thought, unlike the actual problem with the pills for mania, depression and psychosis. Why not, when down, just go to the Head and let it out, as a member of a primitive tribe who is "losing it" is sent out into the bush...?

Edward's focus, he realized, was literally absurd, but the physics of the restroom provided the solid solution: once in the Head you knew what you were getting no matter the putrid truth at hand. It was really a matter of the solid material versus the psychological guesswork. If it came down to simple chemistry, the human body was born to excrete its waste product, but the chemical concoction of a pharmaceutical had no physical basis...it was without proper understanding, even by doctors. He continued with the history, trying to get to the essential argument.

The Net stated "...in the late 1800's we meet the infamous Thomas Crapper, who all agree had a successful career in the plumbing industry from 1861 to 1904, but many are skeptical about whether he actually invented the flush toilet, the hybrid device that has made it into our homes today. The most famous product attributed to Thomas Crapper wasn't invented by him at all. The 'Silent Valveless Water Waste Preventer' (No. 814) was a symphonic discharge system that allowed a toilet to flush effectively when the cistern was only half full. British Patent 4990 for 1898 was issued to a Mr. Albert Giblin for this product. Nevertheless, Crapper's name is engraved on the thrones during that time and the "origin of 'crap' is still being debated," "Possible sources include the Dutch Krappe; Low German krape meaning a vile and inedible fish; Middle English crappy, and Thomas Crapper." We may suppose, however, that "The World War One doughboys passing through England brought together Crapper's name and the toilet. They saw the words T. Crapper-Chelsea printed on the tanks and coined the slang. . ."

If there was one difference between the medicine and the toilet it was that medicine is not private and the toilet is. After one pops a pill the space may flux any which way and there is infiltration in the patient; no longer is there the sensible understanding that one is not actually "somewhere or someone else", but the somewhere and someone else is in the patient. Whereas in a toilet you know exactly where you are, exactly what to do, the exact result, and how to take care of the problem with one simple lever. And it is the "lever" that is the exact knowledge one gets from a toilet, a physical lever that takes the shit away, not a psychological one that keeps it returning. With medicine...Edgar pulled his papers together and thought about the problem...with medicine the "lever" turned a multitude of things on and off: light, reality, language, depression, hope, joy, and even healthy wisdom. Who wanted their chemical mix to pull so many levers that one couldn't properly reason what even life was about? At least with a toilet you had the straight answer: the throne you sat on would take all the shit you could give it and then you'd be clean. Yet there was more.

To be blinded by 'inventor-centrism' tells a tale: that the West does not want to relinquish its hold on a product that is revolutionary, just as the pharmaceutical companies do not want to relinquish their hold on a product that is "transitional". No, as much as the chemical has been invested in "grooming" the depressive individual, and the nation for that matter, the fact remains that a digestible pill that will "balance" a person may be psychologically helpful, but the toilet remains the ultimate answer to the physiological and psychological "release". It has morphed very little. It provides a way to relieve the body of solid mass. It cures one for a good time afterward. And, there is no flux to the privacy gained from the interlude of profound moment. History shows that archeologists found an antique latrine in the tomb of a king of the Western Han Dynasty (206 BC to 24 AD) that is not much different from the ones we sit on today. This throne's consistency with physiological evolution suggests that historical stability may very well be more efficacious to the well-being of the mind, contrary to the flux mechanisms in pharmaceutical compounds. And the diary recounting the joy of this device informs that even historically toilets were healthy in essence, enough to not only move the bowels but the psycho-chemical neural relations in the head. That there be proof of lack of flux is no small matter, for it is the issue of flux that is the direct problem with the modern chemical. Indeed flux makes medicine contrary to a balanced stability, where the toilet is consistent. Hence, China "flushed Britain's claims to have invented the 'water closet' down the pan," just as much as Fezer Jelly, Quark, and Mizer drug companies could not flush the irony that the common denominator in the rendering of all of their drugs was that while making the pill, chemists and architects relieved themselves regularly throughout the project, ignorant of the power in their latrines that would certainly mend these problems.

Yet, why is it that our appreciation for the toilet is so low? Most houses today, especially in America, are equipped with a toilet boasting the name 'American Upright'. This does smack one with a sense of pride in the business of naming, like a flag flying high on top of the hill, waving accomplishment. However, is our standard of appreciation so low that we have emptied ourselves to the point where nobody truly recognizes anymore that lifestyle is ultimately made by and ameliorated by the toilet, more than by drugs, and that we are living highly evolved lives and have as a result the gifts of cleanliness, even sanity? Where we have secured an incredibly practical invention, which has numerous benefits for our health, have we forgotten that a benefit is only beneficial when it is recognized? And then what this really comes down to is that most people do have an incredible appreciation but simply keep it to themselves; for the toilet is our own private chance to, as they say, let it flow, to be in a private place, with ourselves yet liberated from the invasion of noxious technology in the real overly-governmental world.

THE WISH FOUNDATION

Cleo was dying. The diagnosis was last stage brain cancer and her doctor had given her one month to live. They had noticed after she had found enough courage to address her fainting spells. It had settled in like an unwanted guest without her knowing. She returned home that day, after the diagnosis, and crumpled into her daughter's bed. How could she tell her? And she wasn't now just a single mother. She had a baby in the womb, a baby who had been conceived in action of almost spontaneous emotional uncontrol in the psych ward. That she had brought her first child into the world with grace and quiet satisfaction helped to ease her immediate horror. Their apartment, a small side-street synthetic low-income residence, barely fit both of them. Her calling had always been her daughter's welfare. The doll in her hand crushed against her determination.

Tell her? Could she explain to a five-year-old what this disease was? She had done everything in her power to put food on the table, pay the rent, dress her, and with all the care and tenderness necessary to get her the best education. Her face in the pillow sucked the air she needed and at the same time deliberately, even irresponsibly, wanted to shut off. Nothing had been easy in her life she'd had to fight for. A stream of very strong words pelted the pillow, spittle highlighting the cover. This. She breathed. This Goddamn life is not going to take me down!

Rising from her daughter's bed, Cleo punched the computer until it lit up with a start. She then pushed the keys to spell Wish Foundation and uploaded that company of final generosity, the gracious allowance for the terminally ill which places a person in a pre-death nirvana so that they might enjoy the final days. The application was meaningless to her. Paper had suddenly become nothing, a block in the confusion of this busy, techno-jacked existence. Seeing a number she lifted the phone and dialed. A warm and even saccharine voice answered.

"Yes," her voice shook, "is this The Wish Foundation?"

"Yes," the woman responded.

Cleo did not know how to proceed. Am I dying, really? Is this actually happening? Do I admit my diagnosis to a stranger? She gathered herself and said flatly, "My name is Cleo Smith and I have one month to live."

The silence was long. After all, how many calls like this does the receptionist get in a day? The confessions must be horrible.

"I see," the voice said. "You may arrange with me to see someone who will help you process your desire."

The formal, somewhat distant speech, was not what Cleo had imagined. How can one process desire? Shouldn't she have said we can help you die gracefully? Wish?

"When can I see a representative?" Cleo asked with agitation.

"We can arrange a meeting tomorrow, if you like."

"Yes," she said, almost strong enough to crack glass. Cleo was between realities, part alive and part already gone, the words of the doctor an unwanted violation of her consciousness. "Yes, I would like to see someone immediately."

The arrangement was made; the date for the next day at their offices in downtown Los Angeles however did not make Cleo lighter. She turned from the phone and looked out through the refracting light shifting the LA skyline into hazy honey.

Though she didn't know how to tell her daughter, or even if she should say anything, Cleo made soup for them that evening and over the meal she fluxed from her daughter's innocence to her own very focused need. She had a life inside of her that had to live. It was too early for a premature birth. The spoons tinked on the rims of their bowls. The silence was felt as some suppression of a mystery Cleo could not yet entertain. In her mother's shadow the daughter slurped the soup pensively. Then, finding no words to disclose her situation, Cleo read to her daughter the Wizard of Oz until she fell asleep. The walls were too close. The apartment box they existed in was suddenly completely suffocating. The windows only opened into the LA smog. She recognized the need to sleep yet she could not fade out. The knowledge that her eyes might not ever ever open again stopped her from letting them close. Close. That's what the disease was. Close and critical like a knife blade. A cold, empty, horrible law of the most inane sort. Death, Cleo realized, was uncompassionate. It did not have the same force as life. Indeed, the contrary absolute of death was fairly much impossible to accept. Shut out completely from life! Allowed no feeling! Put out like some stupid birthday candle in the wince of a wish? Her thoughts roared and fidgeted and stumbled until something she could only name angelic let her close her eyes and she slept.

Snapped awake by a siren, Cleo found her daughter already dressed and ready for school. Sensing the worry of the night she had risen on her own. Cleo kissed her and they hopped into the VW bug and zipped into the LA traffic. She dropped her daughter off and then, catching her breath, looked on the map to find where the Wish Foundation building was located. Looser now that she was alone, with the rest of the world just inches away, going places that would allow them to live, they motored to the ton of the incomprehensible problems of the world. When Cleo arrived at the Wish Foundation Building she felt the deep loss of her mission already pressing down on her. She found her way into the offices and was told to wait in the lobby, where she looked in complete disbelief at People Magazine and the plethora of other lifestyle media that was available. As her eye blurred into a star a man entered and asked if she was Cleo. She rose and respectfully walked with him into an open office. He introduced himself as Jake and then introduced two other people, a young woman named Lucy and a middle-aged man with a beard called Mark. It was Mark who matter-of-factly asked in a strange stammer what her illness was. She looked at him like a gun.

"Last stage brain cancer, they say."

Jake, accommodating and friendly, said, "Please understand we must know these things so we can make a proper consultation. How long do you have?"

Cleo smiled for the first time, somehow feeling the absurdity of her position...of theirs. "The doctor says one month."

"We can put you on the immediate Wish list. If you don't mind reading and signing these papers and then we can talk. Just releases, you know. Regular."

Cleo looked into the bureaucracy in immediate recognition of the forms; time seemed to matter more than legalese. She jotted her name down.

"Good," Jake said. Now there are many fantasies people have: Crack a Nut Game Show, swimming with dolphins, going to the Alps, skiing naked, meeting the president..." his voice trailed off and then he looked up bright-eyed. "What do you want to do?"

Cleo's eyes had become very clear. She looked at all of them as if they were some sort of Willy Wonka first aid team. Then, shaking off the vision, she said point blank, "I want to rob a bank."

Mark looked over at Lucy and then to Jake and said, "No."

Jake coughed and then said, "you see we are restricted by law from breaking the law...as a wish."

"It it is nat natural to feel feel angry at socfuckingciety," said Mark.

Lucy nodded her head in agreement.

"How about riding elephants or going on The Jingo Society,

or you could even try and see the Pope in a Virtual."

"Forget the Pope," Cleo said, "I want money and I want it from a bank and I want to jack a fucking bank."

"Well," Jake said, "ah...you...ah we understand how you might be angry and we understand how you might want to...ah... take it out on society...but we can't rob a bank."

"You don't seem to understand. I am terminally ill. I have one daughter who will be alone when I die. I want her to live a good life," she paused in mid space... "I am also pregnant."

They looked at her with searching eyes.

"Preg an aunt?" asked Mark.

She looked over the man who seemed to be in a skipping alphabet of problematic speech.

"Yes."

"You you could get donut nations. There are lots of pe peo-ple and organizawfulations out there that want to kelp, Dicrosoft, Soneyspell, Bewlett Asspackward, heck there is an umpire list of donkeys that will give you some cash. They like to help. We could could get Sean Zen to talk to his his friends. We could even have a callathong."

Cleo looked at Mark, taking his quirk in with the care of an almost dead woman. "Mark, what do you think. Should I have Ma-dame Shore give me money? Should I try and win at Jingo and save my daughter with that...that goddamn show? Should I sell my body for a month and put a few men out of their liquid cash to se-cure for my daughter and unborn their future? Is that appropriate for a dying woman? Or, Mark, Jake, and Lucy...should I go get a gun and do it myself?"

The three Wish Foundation employees looked confusedly and carefully at the woman they were trying to console.

"Jack a bank. I mean do you think that you would get away with that with the State Watch? Do you think that you can pull something like that off? You'd spend the last two weeks of your life hooked up to a peace look system behind bars. Do you even have the equipment?" Jake looked earnestly at Cleo.

"Listen. You're not going to die. You're not going to get my daughter a million so she can go to a good school. Do you think I want to swim with dolphins or save my daughter and possibly not upcoming baby?" Her eyes fell on the now shaking gaze of Jake, flung Mark a cold stare, and burned a hole in the head of Lucy with considerable optic force.

"Ok," Jake said. As much as we want to help you in your time of crisis, we are not able to rob banks."

Mark shook his head, "No toto banks. We could could get you a sleepover in a nice nice safe though."

"I don't want to slumber party in a safe, Mark, I want to jack a bank, save my daughter and die with a reasonable story."

Mark, stone-faced, suddenly said, "it's it's been done be-fuckingfore."

Jake spun around, "What!" he yelled. "Before. It hasn't been done before. Not by this agency!"

Mark looked at Jake. "The Charity Case for William Stunning."

Jake's eyes went wide. "That was a give away. William just wanted to get a bed of cash to sleep on."

"Yeah but he took the bed home."

"So, he gave it back to the museum."

"It was an art show," said Lucy.

Jake looked wide-eyed at his cohorts. "William lost the money."

"It was a donutnation besides," said Mark.

"Not a heist. Not a heist, Mark."

Mark looked with a smirk at Cleo.

"So there was a bank job."

"No, No, No," Jake said. "It was a museum mistake. They lost the Dada money bed and he died."

"I just want to boost some loot," said Cleo.

"Well, this is certainly not an organization that authorizes grand larceny. We are a law abiding Wish Foundation according to The Death Manuel of Recovery. We..." Jake paused. "We only repair the end of life."

Cleo was standing. "I see," she said. "I know that death is abnormal. It's just a wish that's all. I'll make my way. I don't need this law-this and law-that...I am going to leave now." She got up walked to the door. Mark rose and held the door open for her.

"Sorry we cannot pelt you with your wish he said. Please call back if you get bet any other ideas."

Cleo looked into the street in front of her, the force of the world somehow pathetically withered, the skyline and buildings like putty that some idiot had put into place to make fun of God. She stepped with determination into this, turned and thanked him and then left.

That evening, Cleo told her daughter. She couldn't tell it like a story, nor could she tell it like a lesson, and neither could she tell it as straight as the deafening truth that crept into her space and flattened all that was real. So she told it like it was, that she was sick and that cancer was a disease and that if she were lucky she would get better. Her daughter asked her if she felt bad and she said she did. She did not tell her how impossible the answer of life had been for her over the past five days. What she said was to soothe, to be clear, and to be real. Her daughter looked at her as she looked at her daughter, serious and deep and mysterious as the disease and possible death described. Something transferred, something like a spirit, and they cried together. When the phone rang, Cleo, out of habit, reached for the device.

"Uh hi...is this Mrs. Dish."

"Smith, who is this?"

"Ah, yes, Mrs. Smith, this is is Mark." There was a long pause after his announcement.

"Yes, Mark, I thought we concluded our meeting earlier today."

"Ah, yes." The pause was unnatural. "Well, Mrs. Smith, my friend Frank and I, we got to talking and we don't donut think anybody should be die without getting their their wish. We got to talking and we both agreed like china that your idea is crazy, and completely against against company policy...but, you see see, I just happen to know, ah, somebody, some people."

"So you know somebody. I am not going to shilly-shally with imbeciles."

"No, No, Mrs. Smith, the person I know can...ah...rob banks."

Cleo listened into the phone like a grand canyon with wind in it from a long time ago. "So. I don't have time for..."

"Mrs. Smith. We talked it over. Frank, myself and my acquaintance E.L. William Stunning Jr....we all all think it's a good Zippo. I mean idea, after all, what is a wish if it doesn't come true?"

Cleo was silent. An unearthly smile spread to her ears. "When can we get together?"

They met on the Venice pier. Cleo watched an old Lincoln Mercury pull up with several passengers. Mark stepped out of the car with dark glasses on. The other doors swung open to reveal what Cleo thought of as a strange, slow moving group. She recognized instantly one of the men. Frank Spec looked at her from suspended animation. Shit, she thought, a mental ward. But in her head he was still holding her in his arms and his shaking was going into her. He didn't take off his glasses. She brushed her hair back. Frank Spec, word master. Let off on a clemency charge by the State Psych Board. How utterly strange. Behind him she could see two other people she recognized vaguely from the psych circuit. But when the passenger door opened she almost fainted. Edward Wells stood up and smiled into the sun. After all these years she thought, just as I am about to die, just as I am about to commit a crime to live, just as I am about to have his baby, how utterly ironic. The universe, she thought, is so incredibly strange. They approached her.

"You you seem seem to know know these people," said Mark.

Edward stopped in front of Cleo. In his mind he was falling back into his memories like off of a great cliff. "Cleo," he said.

She reached forward and hugged him. The hug went through him and deep into his earliest feelings of her. He stepped back and noticed her bulging belly. "You're pregnant?"

She smiled at him an irrepressible smile. "Ah, yes, Edward. I am pregnant."

"How beautiful. Whose is it?" His voice seemed sadly distant.

Mark had a shocked look on his face. He and the others had picked up a secret feeling.

Edward looked at his patients. His eyes squinted into her.

"It's yours," said Cleo.

"What?"

"Shit," said Frank.

Edward felt a feeling of terror pass through him. "Mine? How could it be mine?"

Cleo smiled. "Please understand," she said. "You were almost dead. Your trauma in St. Mary's. I was there. I ah...was acting nightshift nurse." she paused and then began to laugh. "You just got excited when I was changing your sheets, Edward, and I, ah, I took advantage of you."

Mark began to laugh.

"You mean you slept with me while I was psychotic?"

"Yep."

"And now you are pregnant with...my baby?" Edward's face was frozen.

"Yep. I thought you were going to die. You sort of began to get excited and then I just, you know, just put you were I wanted."

"Jesus Christ," said Frank.

"Wow," said Jack. "Woman power."

Edward suddenly found a ton of gravity raining down on him. "So you are telling me that when I was out you and I copulated and now you and your baby...our baby...are going to die if you don't get money for your operation and we just happened to get together through the most miniscule ounce of chance by Mark working for The Wish Foundation?"

"Life is strange," said Cleo.

"I'll say," said Frank.

"Oh yeah life is really really strange," said Cherry.

"Incredibodily," said Mark.

"Well," said Edward, feeling happily nervous. The new gravity of responsibility passed through like…he could not explain. He straightened up. "I see no better thing to do now then…" he trailed off…

"Rob a bank," said Cleo.

"Yes," Edward said, "Yes, of course…we will need money, we must save ourselves." His voice had a resonance in it that echoed from his early childhood. Innocence comprehending truth and necessity.

Mark stepped back. "This is E.L. William Stunning Jr. Otherwise known as Edmond Little." Edmond smiled a mischievous smile. "He knows about safes," said Mark. "It was his father's wish to sleep in a bed made of money that somehow got lost in the museum shuffle…transferred to Edmond. Grew in him to a very good relation with safes, among other things."

The wind whipped off the Pacific and they leaned into the bluster while they talked.

"This is Frank," Mark said to Cleo.

Cleo looked at the man in front of her with skepticism. He was still wolf like, yet a bit more portly, had a stain on his pseudo Chinese silk shirt, and was as unkempt as the wood they stood on. Mark was smiling. "Frank, is is a pro."

"I know Frank," Cleo said warmly.

"This is Cherry," Mark said. "Cherry can feel anything…anywhere, in any dimension."

Cherry smiled.

"Edward is the boss," said Mark.

"What's your idea" E.L. asked Cleo.

"I don't have an idea, I just want to jack a bank."

"Robbing and jacking are not too cool. If you want to boost something you can't in a bank, and arms cause problems. But…I can crack a safe. But cracking a safe is not easy. And there are a lot of banks…" E.L. trailed off and toed his Eccos on the planks. A psychotic tremor passed through him. "But I know a place that's itching to be cracked."

"Where's that," Cleo asked curiously. The others leaned in

to hear what E.L. had to say.

"Bank of America doesn't just keep cash in their holdings. My friend, who does the carpets after hours, told me that there is a safe auxiliary to the big safe, separate from the safety deposit and particular to the State Board of Trustees who are affiliates of AIG and who, when they come to LA, like to keep their jewelry cozy in-between parties. My friend says it's a modified Sentry Safe G-D model 1800781 that they use. They come in on the weekends, wives, kids, and wouldn't you know it the famous Blue Tavernier Diamond...loaned to impress. My friend says that they come in on Fridays, drop it off at the bank, and pick it up for their Saturday dinners at the Design Center on Melrose. One night. Go in to clean the carpets, sack my friend, crack the bling, leave them tied up and we're sailing."

"We'll be maids," said Mark.

"We'll be congressmen," said E.L.

"What do you mean," said Cleo.

"We'll dress up nice. You can be Hamilton. You can be Burr. Lucy can drive. And I'll be Truman."

"Your friends will be hung."

"No, they'll be...at worst, relieved."

"What do you think, Ed?" Cleo looked up at him.

The wind in her face was beautiful to him. An invigorating shiver passed through his body.

"We gotta live," said Edward. "E.L. is a pro. Frank is a pro. Cherry can feel the inside of any security system. Mark can conduct...pretty much anything."

A black Ford drove up. They looked skeptically at the vehicle. Jack stepped out into the wind. He looked fit and had slicked his hair back. Mark motioned him over.   "Jack." Mark said. "We're going to jack a bank."

Jack smiled. He was missing his front tooth. "Just a minor offence," he said. "I can whistle better."

Cleo felt a surge in her. Deep down inside she felt hope for her children. The plan smacked of all the things she had imagined about death: danger, riches, artfulness, and criminal beauty. That she would jack this bank while pregnant made her smile even greater; her unborn child would be criminal. They would all add their two cents.

"We settle on next week. I already have the buyer. You'll have three weeks to live...with about three million dollars." E.L. smiled off into a cryptic distance where he had plummeted into post parole. Professional schizophrenia was occurring. In his mind he could see his father giving him his last words in the million-dollar bed... "Take the whole fucking lot," he had said, "and don't hold back."

Cleo felt butterflies in her yet to be sick stomach. Robbing from the richest people to make the terminally ill live. She looked at Edward, Frank, Jack, Mark, Cherry, and E.L. and smiled.

HEIST

It was an LA evening, the circuit board of lights spread in the basin like some electrical Medusa head, data one could read and turn to stone to. Illumination to understand, in the reading, the beauty of city chaos, and what the friction of future involves. Unfortunately for the heist, E.L.'s insiders had vanished off the face of the map, leaving their plan without an entry to Bank of America. Frank had become their only other option. But Frank had a plan.

Frank could feel the flow in his veins like when he wrote off a person's life, the synergy splashing through and up the cliffs of impossibility. In place of practicality Frank had formulated a most imperfect alternative plan for the robbery of the Tavernier Diamond from Bank of America. It had soaked in his brain until it seeped through like the matrix of a synth-machine for massaging the neural landscapes until the ride fluxed magically in the body to the desire of the download. His smile creased through his face as he looked at the team.

"I'm going to do a pre-mortem for the security," he said.

E.L., Cleo, Jack, Edward, Cherry and Mark looked at him with quizzical looks.

"You mean you're going to write the security off," said Mark.

"Exactly. All I need," said Frank, "is for Cherry and Mark to go in on a placebo and get scanned. The drug monitors will register a hole. Just bring back the feeling of the hole and the empathic element to me and I'll translate it. Once I've figured the semantic of the absence in the system and a way to crash or go through the Net, E.L., Edward, and Cleo break in with hardware and go through the outage, whatever that may be, and crack the safe." He paused and looked at Cherry and Mark in bewildering confidence. "You both know how sensitive the system is and how sensitive you are. What I want you to do is go in past the security. Now the security normally reads the cerebral effusion of every person on a med. Like an array, it picks up the identity, the emotion, and the agitations of the neural undulation of each brain. Yet, on a placebo you will register a difference. I am thinking of a sort of blackout of the sensory system, like a cloud over the sun. The sensors will read the negative of the chalk array. But you," he pointed at Cherry and Mark with long fingers, "will feel it. You will feel it and what you do is return to me and give me your reading. I'll extract the difference off of that. And if you hallucinate all the better. What is important is that you get the machine security to react to you. Use everything you have, hallucination, psychotic breaks, complete neurosis, dementia, everything. But not on purpose." He paused... "ah, it has to be natural. The machine's anomaly should show, just the same as we, as anomaly, show in the system. If I can figure out the glitch..." He put his fist up against his head... "ah...its place, time, dislocation, reaction, and even essence, if it has that, I can figure its death..."

They group observed Frank moving his fingers elaborately in the air.

"Jack, will run the car outside the bank," Frank said. "What I need is for you Cherry and you Mark to go into the bank tomorrow on..."

"Memorine B," said Edward.

Each looked at him. He had been silent for some time.

"What's Memorine B?" said Cleo.

"It's a pseudo placebo. Has all the effects of a regular placebo yet it fakes the medicine out, fakes the machine out."

"It's not real?"

"It's a chimera medicine," Edward said. "It mocks the medicine but has not effect, like placebo. I, ah, had the privilege of taking some the other night on an Empathy Exam. It worked for me nicely."

"Ok," said Frank, "Just as long as it's a placebo. What I need is for the machine system to react. I want it to react like at Ginny's. I want someone to report the hallucination. Then they'll go try and fix it. Which means the system will have a gap, despite the report. So as they see our hallucination I'll be able to see through Mark and Cherry, like in an Empathy Exam, what the gap is. We'll do this tomorrow."

Cherry and Mark looked excitedly at each other. Free reign to hallucinate and crack security. Smiles illuminated the sanguine joy of the proposed mission.

At twelve o'clock the next day Mark and Cherry were given Memorine B with sense patches under hats. There bodies had become used to taking pills for regulation so the reaction should, as Dr. Wells, said, cause a contrary response in their bodies. It should, he said, make you think you are on the pill, while feeling the deficit, a sort of tug-of-war with the mind, until it either balanced or crashed. What he thought it would do was cause an excitation of dopamine that would not plane out, but rather fall off and cause their neural messages to crash into a zone of different perception all together, increasing their empathy levels by significant amounts, blanking the normal security. But he didn't tell them everything. The less they knew the less they would be expecting a reaction...the more the symbolic sensors would react to the absence.

Jack drove them to the Bank of America. It was a hot LA day. Arriving without incident Cherry and Mark both exited the car and walked toward the bank front doors. A voice in Mark's head said, you will be entering in ten, nine, eight...In Cherry's head he had already reached one.

You enter the bank. The air conditioner is on. It is cool and crisp like an arctic den. A woman looks to you in slow motion and smiles. There are many people behind desks and some four tellers working behind counters. Seven cameras film you from seven different positions. A guard stands in the corner of the room. Mark turns and feels the terror of authority. The guard has his hand on his gunstock. Other people stand in line. Cherry turns in a three sixty to see. As he turns the cameras turn with him. His vision becomes blurry. He tries to pick up the room like a satellite. A woman asks him if he may be helped. The voice sounds very far away, like in a canyon. Mark walks toward a camera. He imagines his brain being seen by light. He sees the agitation of his brain through the lens. Cherry has picked up the safe in the back. When Mark turns the guard is at his elbow. They brush each other and Mark feels the visceral power of the law. Cherry has walked over to the line. He is to get money out so everything is normal. Cherry is standing with a camera pointed at his head. It feels like the barrel of a gun. He looks at it and imagines his thoughts in the camera. The camera explodes into a million pieces. He turns and wants to run. The guard has drawn his gun and everybody is scattering. Mark observes this and looks at the other cameras. They begin to explode like fireworks. The guard is nervously trying to find cover. Cherry dives over the teller. Mark sees the entire security apparatus explode. Sparks fly in the air. Cherry runs to Mark. When they get in touching distance the entire room implodes back to normalcy. Cherry looks into Mark's eyes. He is smiling. Cherry can see a camera in his head. The camera films the filaments of his soul. Light pours through his eyes like the sun. Cherry realizes that he too has a camera in his head. Mark looks at Cherry and they both film each other. The lenses begin to suck each of them into their heads. As they pour into each other they realize their emotion is fear. Then at the very last they are sucked into each other and disappear.

Cherry and Mark find themselves outside walking to the

car. They do not know how they got outside. They are both shaking as if they've broken the law. They get into the car and Jack drives them away. They are speechless. In ten minutes they reach Edward's office.

"Ok," Frank is saying. "Tell me the score." Cleo, Edward, E.L., and Jack look earnestly at Mark and Cherry.

"All the cameras exploded," Mark says.

"All of them," repeats Cherry.

"So you both saw the same thing?"

"Yes."

"This is a good indicator of virtual congruence," says Edward.

"What was the feel?" says Cleo.

They looked at each other.

"There was a massive vortex," says Mark. "All the cameras got sucked into an implosion of ourselves."

"Good," says Frank. "What else."

"I was scared of being noticed," Cherry said. "I could feel the entire bank dissolving. Every camera looked at us."

"All of them?" said Frank

"Yes," all of them," said Cherry.

"Ok, so all of the cameras imploded when you looked at them. You were on Memorine B placebo, which means if you were in there for ten minutes then wherever you walked in the bank there are neural gaps, gap lines like in a drawing. What shape did you walk in, Mark?"

"A musical treble clef."

"And what shape did you walk in, Cherry?"

"Ah, a circuit."

"Ok, so when you opened the door was that where the circuit and treble clef began?"

"Yes," they both said.

"So what we have," Frank smiled, "Is a neural gap line of open security from door to teller from twelve noon to twelve ten or so, in the form of a musical clef and a circuit...and the cameras exploded?" He stopped to check his notes. "And then imploded, which means there is a cut off of power in the drug sensory system from door to teller for about ten minutes." Frank smiled, "according to your prescient similarity."

"I think you both sensed future," Frank said. "I think that the circuitry went down sound wise for ten minutes, all the while the cameras filmed a blank in your heads for the same time, which sounds to me like we've got about a ten minute hole without security." He got up.

"How will you know?" asked Cleo.

"They'll send a technician to solve the blackout. All I have to do is contact the security dept." He picked up the phone and dialed a number.

"Hi, is this Security Enterprises?"

The voice was reserved. "Yes," a woman responded with static.

"Did you send out a repair man to downtown B of A this afternoon?"

"Is this B of A?"

"Yes, just following up."

"Ah, yes, the repair was sent out about ten minutes ago."

"Thank you very much." Frank put down the receiver and smiled.

"Now how did you feel," Frank looked excitedly to Mark and Cherry.

"I felt the electrical guilt modules in my guts, sort of buzzing there in agitation," said Mark.

"Yeah, like the system was pressing into figurations and the data met up with a friction in us or something," said Cherry

"Good," said Frank. "Now what I think is this," he paused in mid brilliance. "I think that...and this is the obit...I think that the system relay for drug sensory of customers at Bank of America flubbed. I think that this is a gap due to the lack of chemical play out in both of your heads, which was exacerbated by the placebo so that you picked up the desire of the machine to film, which you saw in violent exertions of camera implosion. I think that from those two facts we can guess that the sensory security exerted its feed and blew itself essentially into oblivion for about ten minutes, tested by the security tech. And I think that if we ourselves take placebo going in this evening then the same thing will happen. In which case, I think that all we need to do is jimmy the locks and we're as erased as laundering. This, and all we have to do is play back the tape from that point in the day when you walked in while we are breaking in and we shut circuitry. That will cut the electrical sensors." Frank smiled a large wolf smile.

"Then it's up to us," E.L. said.

"Yeah, you just do your magic, E.L., and crack that safe and Jack will get us out of there in pugilistic time."

The Tavernier went in at five. The bank closed at 6pm. E.L. had said that he could manage the Sentry Safe G-D model in ten minutes. He seemed to be particularly happy with his forte, some kind of Houdini boojum surrounding his wares: scope, drill, and wire in a wrap of terry cloth.

They made the parking lot at exactly 2 am. The bank lights shone down on the parking lot in the fog. Jack pulled over to an unlit area and turned off the ignition.

"OK." said Frank, Memorine B hitting his bloodstream. He reached in his pocket of his coat jacket and held up a chip. "The ten minutes of cover is going to go into the front entry circuit. After that, Jack, you come and do the locks. Then you, E.L., Cleo, and Edward are in. You'll have ten minutes on their data bank, and an extra drug loss security on our placebos. You work the safe and then we're out of here. Pull down your masks."

The night air outside was shifting like a pixilated mist you could get from a synth-fogger. They rolled out of the car and Frank inserted the chip, which told the machine its pre-mortem and then mortem status. The machine blipped on and then off. E.L. ran up and jimmied the locks, a proud line of smithing in his family history. The door cracked open and E.L. Cleo, and Edward passed in.

Upon finding the outstanding safe where the Tavernier was to be stored E.L. yelled.

"Son of a bitch!"

"What," said Cleo, worried.

"It's a Brinks D-49 Special."

"What does that mean?"

"What it means is that it has a botch switch just in case anybody drills it."

"A botch switch""

E.L. almost tore off his mask. "A botch switch means I drill, it botches."

"Botches what?"

"Alarm. Internal alarm and the entire mechanism fucking fritzes."

"Can't you go around it?"

E.L. looked at Cleo through his mask. "The only thing that is going to work is if I finesse it. But finessing it takes...could take an hour. You think the other side of those cameras are going to wait an hour?"

"Jesus Christ, E.L., aren't you supposed to be a crack thief?"

"Yeah, well the buck just might stop here."

E.L. turned and walked away. He then turned back and in his hand he held a large round piece of Symtex plastic explosive that looked to Cleo like Play-Dough. "The only thing with a Brinks is to botch the botch. Stand back. I am going to blow the pot."

E.L. crouched down while Cleo watched with interest. "Step back behind the teller," he said dynamically.

Cleo did as he said. The safe popped and the surroundings were clouded with smoke. Cleo's ears were ringing. E.L.'s hand reached inside. He groped around and withdrew a black velvet case. Carefully he ripped open the casing. There, inside, set against the black glittery felt background, was the Blue Tavernier Diamond on a thin necklace. E.L. clutched the necklace and turned feverishly to Cleo. "Go!" He yelled. They both fled to the waiting car. Cleo was beside herself. "You didn't say explosives!"

E.L. leveled a stare at her, "but we did say this!" He held the jewel up in front of her Wish Foundation face.

"May we be delivered," Frank said.

Jack floored the vehicle to a din of distant sirens.

TRIAL

E.L.'s buyer was cool, efficient and corrupt enough to respect the business. The money felt appropriately heavy in his hand, the case full with the agreed-upon sum. When he met with Cleo the following afternoon at a parking lot in the Beverly Center, he smiled. For some reason the job, if it may be called so, seemed very far away. He put a shopping bag in her passenger seat and said he had to disappear. Cleo thanked him, her smile unforced, her gratitude genuine. Then, as abruptly as they had met, Cleo found herself alone. She looked in the Banana Republic Bag he had handed off. Stacks of crisp green one hundred dollar notes bulged from its depths. In the back of her mind she could not get rid of the doctor's words... one month, one month maybe two if you're lucky. The reality of her wish was not strong enough to keep these words back. Like inky impressions they bled into her day.

The robbery had been flawless. The one-month to live, maybe less, precariously rocked between the thrill of the event and the actuality of her illness. Edward had said he would accompany her up north. She had declined at first, then allowed him to commit to this final attempt at life. She put her foot down on the pedal. The Stanford Stem Cell Research Lab was five hundred miles away.

She made the drive with Edward in a state of repetition, the explosion popping over and over again, the absurdity of the act, the even more absurd meeting of her and her initial love. The help of the Wish Foundation staff, Edward's patients, and her now focused designs crackled like the hallucinations her patients told her about at St. Mary's. Across the windscreen the landscape swam: Malibu mansions, empty military bases, California Oaks, Salinas Valley fields and the freedom of the drive. She had contacted one Doctor Spencer, a specialist in Stem Cell research and cancer rehabilitation. When she said she would like to make a donation to the special test group for terminally ill recovery he had enthusiastically responded. When she said she wanted to be injected with their hybrid autologous stem cell rescue, he had answered her directly and told her that she had not yet donated her marrow. Cleo, having read the literature, responded that she would try their most novel approach to her brain cancer disease. When she reiterated the donation he decided he could help.

Upon arrival, Cleo was accommodated and received the next day an injection of stem cells generated from an embryo they called "Elysium". The trial took into account her one-month life expectancy. Edward remained with her the whole time. He had been caring, thoughtful and there when she had fallen into utter despair. Startlingly, within two weeks the cancerous tissue in her brain had shrunk. The remission was not common. While she was receiving the last injection a man was led into the room who was a detective. Edward had looked up with an unsurprised look on his face. Nothing seemed to matter anymore. He had found his love. The world was, as usual insane. His life would be ruined. As Cleo lay in bed in remission the detective read them their rights and then arrested them for grand larceny of the Blue Tavernier Diamond. They had picked up everybody else save for E.L. who had somehow disappeared. Too weak to be incarcerated, Cleo was kept in hospital until the doctors claimed, in amazement, that she had had a full recovery.

The next week she was brought to a superior court in San Francisco, the case moved from LA for reasons of sensationalism. There, in full health, Cleo met Jack, Cherry, and Frank. Frank looked casual. Cherry was shaking. And Mark had begun to mumble. They all took their seats in the front row while the State Prosecution delivered the case on the other side of the aisle.

The courtroom was cold. Cherry could recall the court he had been privy to on a hallucinatory day not too long ago. Yet, here, unlike in his vision, everybody was moving. The defense had been offered to them by The State. A small man with an ugly red tie told them to get together and pray.

The jury entered and declared itself to the Judge. It was a monotone group, a usual looking jury made up of men and woman of what Cleo thought was regular State existence. Their faces looked relaxed.

The room fell quiet when Cleo arose for her statement. She did not feel she had anything to hide. She related the wish she had made and the help she had gotten to steal the Blue Tavernier. She named all in on the robbery, save for E.L.. Every once in a while she looked at the jury and the judge with clear eyes. The jury listened closely. She found that when she had looked at them to begin they were stern, but as she related her story their faces had softened and some even smiled. She noticed this same thing when Cherry, Mark, Jack, Frank, and Edward took the stand. They seemed to be nodding their heads in agreement with the robbery, a strange effect that none of the convicted could quite say was a normal Larceny charge demeanor.

When Cleo was called up for a final statement the court stilled. The final question asked by the defense was simple. "Why," the attorney asked, "did you commit this crime?" Cleo looked out into the courtroom from her brown eyes, brown as the seed of coal in the diamond. "Would you," she said, "Kill a living fetus in the womb? Would you leave your daughter bereft in this world, without a mother to support her, without a family to care for her, without anything?" The State Prosecution did not respond. The courtroom was silent. After a brief deliberation by the jurors they returned to the courtroom and read the verdict. "We the jury find the defendants not guilty of the crime of Grand Larceny. We the jury find the defendant guilty of Familial Compassion under extreme circumstances. In consideration the defendant acted as any person would act to...save a life. Not guilty."

Cleo felt a deep twinge go through her muscles. The State had lost its first case of "Familial Compassion". Were things turning around? She looked at her daughter. She looked into her deeply. She could see her eyes in hers. She could not take her eyes off the innocence she had bared, and the innocence conceived in the darkest hour of a man's life, in the most horrible place, now growing inside her. Cleo let her gaze trace her daughter's smile. Her hair. Her hands. Her love. Through them she could see a future worthy of her trial. And in that instant Cleo knew the exact, the most exact reason why anybody would do what she did, and there was absolutely no compromise.

As the doors opened into the busy street, they were confronted by a drove of cameras and people. One of the cameras pressed into Cleo's face and then lowered. Cleo beheld the face of E.L. He looked at her with a shocked countenance.

"What the hell are you doing here?" Edward said, startled.

"I dosed them. The whole lot."

"What the hell do you mean? We got off."

"I dosed the whole fucking jury," he said, trembling. He pulled them aside. "I've got a van over here. Come with me."

They hurried after E.L. and hopped into the van on the side of the courthouse.

Frank, Jack, Mark, Cherry, Edward, Cleo, and E.L. crammed in.

"What do you mean you dosed them?" said Edward sharply.

"I fucking put High Grade Purity in the jury's coffee."

"Shit!" said Cleo. The others looked with ambiguity in their eyes.

"Where did you get it?" asked Edward.

"Emotional Library pick," he said.

E.L. started the van. It revved. "Number one steal. Absolutely the purest grade you can get."

"Shit, E.L." said Frank. "That means they were really empathic."

"Oh, yeah, really really empathic. The whole lot of them, dosed to grade 10 purity understanding of life." E.L. accelerated away.

"What the fuck are we going to do now...they're going to know know!" yelled Mark.

"Oh no, they'll get over it, they'll come down cranky and wondering and will want more. Can't go back now. Can't change a ruling in Superior Court. You are all off Scott free."

"What you got to do," said Frank turning to Edward. "You got to go to your New York Psychiatry Conference and you got to relay your paper."

"Yeah," said Mark and E.L., "you gotta just lay it on low and tell them exactly what you are thinking."

Edward closed his eyes. They had gotten off of grand larceny for the famous Tavernier Diamond on High Grade Purity, and now they wanted him to pitch himself up against the behemoth of psychiatry.

"What the hell do you want me to do!" he yelled.

They looked at Edward with wide, innocent eyes.

"Kick ass," said Frank. "I know your paper isn't some crème puff for the status quo. I know it's got some vibe."

"It's not your goddamn paper!" yelled Edward.

Cleo reached over and placed her hand on his. They had been under a lot of pressure. When her hand touched his his muscles trembled. "We've been through a lot. I am carrying your baby. We have robbed a bank. We have dosed a jury. As your significant social interest I think you should now jack the program."

Edward could feel her warmth flowing through her hand to him. "It's not just about that...it's an important paper on the fundamental differences between medicine and privacy." Edward sighed a big sigh.

"Don't stop," said E.L., "just keep going, we're obviously

doing the right thing."

"Alright," Edward, sighed. "E.L. Take us to the airport. New York is where the convention is at." He looked at his watch. "Two days. We'll get a hotel. We'll settle ourselves and then I'll give the thing."

AIRPORT

They had become streamline. Frank wore black glasses that accented his greasy black hair and wolf-like features. Cherry had put on his favorite color and was trying to persuade Mark that he shouldn't be afraid. E.L. was thief groomed, a loose fitting jacket flapping behind him in the LAX Terminal wind. Edward held Cleo's hand and Jack followed with the bags.

They checked in without breakdown and made their way to the entry of the plane. But Mark was having a bad time. He could remember his last trial, the Warner flight where he had barely maintained himself. At security he kept apologizing to the security. It wasn't his fault, he said. He iterated that he understood that the machine was sensitive, that it might be alive. The security looked at them suspiciously, but there was not incident.

But Mark Nichols's mind wanted to get off the plane, exit the surreal, stop The Matrix that slurried in his projections, push the pause button in the machine of society, blank out the terror of the ride, to become or be calm in something other than the trip that kept happening. What he did know was that they had a mission and at least this presented him with purpose. However he was a weathered schizophrenic and knew that at any moment he could crash like a hard drive filled with too much information, and this he did not want. For this reason Mark did not want be left alone. They soared over the United States, over the Mid West Wall like a great bird.

And then they touched down. Like a spinning top launched out of the hands of a child, the group stepped off the airplane and spun through the airport, which Mark thought was a large pin-ball machine leading to a hole that could swallow him if he didn't bump the right way, or fit into a slot, or use the levers right. And the levers in his imagination—were they being controlled by God or the Devil? In the past, in his extreme adaptation to his visions and voices and all the transmissions, he had, like the rest of them, become a number of famous people. The host identities echoed: Jesus Christ Clone, Saint Laura Clock, Jack Special, Adolf Hitler, and Floral Handly. He had even become a computer and thought he was being turned on every day when his eyes opened. A wetware with a pixel face and a bio body. Meds had helped him ooze back into Markness, Nicholness, diminished identity of no one, of cog, of a spoke in the wheel. Indeed, they had counter-clocked his do-pamine so it would not deplete or gush over. Would be in time. And in this cushioned drug world his body shook like a vibrator inside the whore that he knew the consuming world was. Pleasur-ably high. Terribly high. Deep penetration of the sublime trash of warp speed perception. Spin.

Nevertheless, a mission was forming, he knew, and had been forming ever since the acquittal. Cherry had somehow picked up from Mark his agitation. Edward was becoming worried. His patients often felt off each other, like in the Tower episode, little pips and peeps that were contagious. Frank knew that the program that infiltrated their sacred space that he was going to re-write could be handled if you just got into your flow. Edward. Ed-ward Wells, their psychiatrist, perhaps, he mused, even his other self, needed to be saved. What he considered to be the now very focused importance in their lives.

They weebled through the airport, bouncing off other people, energy crackling in Cherry and Mark's now manic selves, relief barely coming through the post plane trip, voices telling them... yes Mark, no Mark, Wouldn't you want to be a Cherry, too, Eat at Jack's, GO GO Franky boy, step on a flower and you got the power, E.L....Spin.

Edward knew that the best bet of finding the Psychiatry Conference would lead them to a hospital, the leviathan institution that had once housed Frank and Mark at one psychotic juncture in their pasts, their fear, their outside, their contortions, their souls. Edward knew that his patients would have to be as calm as possible—what they actually were not most of the time—the horror of life on the inside of their flesh casings. He knew that once there he would, with Cleo, plant the deepest seed in the most important way. He fathomed that answer would come, like every other transmission that his patients picked up, to the truth. And that the answer would present itself in the form of action.

"You going to town?" a Brooklyn voice yelled from a cab.

Yes, Mark thought, I am going to town. He was incredible relieved. "Two town. Toto town. Oz because," yelled Cherry. "Going to town," thought Cleo. They slipped into the back seat the way Edward imagined his patients popped medicine and the taxi rocketed off, the Lego landscape of JFK blending into a circuit board full of circuits and wires and gray.

"Goddamn beautiful day. I like the smog. It's like a blanket that makes the city city." The cabby took a deep hit off a Camel and puffed it into mushroom shapes on the windshield.

Mark listened to the man and agreed.

"It is beautiful," Frank said. "It makes sunsets more red and the air more textured."

"It is authentic," said Cherry.

"Perhaps even organic," said Jack.

"Organic smog," E.L. said.

Mark rolled down the window and inhaled and felt like a dragon just after torching a town. The smell of...electricity, pain, waste, exhaust, relief and actuality, all mixed together. Nothing could be more significant than the real trash of a city. A city that was born Dutch and grew up fighting, from transmutation to transmutation. A city that screamed like a celebration in the veins of lost angels on heroin every night. A city that could become virgin in the snow, washed by pure white and ice, blanketing the mania, freezing the din. Mark realized he was in the best place. The city was dirtier and harsher even than his imagination.

The cabby kept talking. "You're from Cali aren't you? I love that place. Full of aura and that Cali stuff. And the girls! Shit, what I wouldn't do to catch a snatch there. Go down. Load a muffin. Hide the hotdog. Bun the oven. Shoot the shit. Purloin some poontang. Plug the drain. Porn storm. Slip and slide and fuck, man, you're from Cali, right?"

Cherry did not answer after riding all of those visions.

"Yes," Frank said. "California is a sexy State. A big geographical cock on the West Coast." He had seen it. Heard the stories. It vibrated. It did have aura.

"And you know what, guys, I bet if you go to Hollywood you'll be clipping the lawns of every famous babe in that sweet mansioned tinsel town. I mean, all those lonely, emaciated blondes and the movies. Have you seen remake of Talk to Her? That scene, guy, where the man shrinks and crawls right up inside that giant cunt...again. What a dream! Hey, get the hell out of my way you Butt Cake! But I mean really, it's the best. What a prophetic film, for men."

Mark could see the cabby's brain cells. They were like amoebas over a flame, oozing and popping every once in a while and then fusing. He imagined the brain as a piece of fruit hung from a building, the Empire State, and the Japanese tourists taking pictures of the inside of a cabby's brain. An abstract art exhibit of a working sponge. The perfect chow mein noodle.

"Hey, and Cali has got a new Gov. A Terminator 7. What the hell! I mean next they'll have Max Headroom or Snoopy. Imagine the sixth largest economy in the world run by Max or Snoopy. It would be crazy. You're not potz though. I can tell. Nobody who is potz gets in my car. I'd know. My sister was potz. Tried to jump off the Brooklyn Bridge and snagged on the railing. Snagged by a dress, no less. She hung there for an hour. Now she's a poet and writes about stuff like that. She's stellar. Newyoriqueno beat chick. I'd know if you were off your rocker. It's professional insider outsider information in my family. Get the fuck out of my way, you goddamn tourist idiot!"

Edward felt relieved. He liked it when people talked about things he knew about. He liked it when people were open and he liked the cabby because he represented a transmission without static. He was pure.

The car hurtled toward Bellevue Hospital. The Wish Foundation was behind him. The robbery was behind them. He knew it had taken all their courage to think of this. But, he knew each of them wanted to see a limit, a limit that they had been pressing for the mere fact that creativity was a vital that must live. And what was Edward outside of their sessions? All that stuff that he had so often analyzed into existence, an existence where harbors manifested everywhere yet none had yet been anchored in.

THE HARBOR DOCUMENT

The conference room had stilled. A podium graced the stage. Doctors, professionals, purveyors of medicine, industry figures, lobbyists, and others sat in the dim light of the hall. Upon the entrance of the speaker the audience rose and clapped. Edward assembled himself and his papers on the podium and then looked into the faces. He paused, his hesitation revealing a shaking hand.

"Ladies and gentlemen," he said. "Ladies and gentlemen, I have looked at my life through my own eyes and through the eyes of others in search, like most of you, for the best place to anchor myself. I have looked at this as a harbor, of the sort not much different than what you might find in any port city, anchoring boats behind sand bars, jetties, stones laid to protect from nature's forces." He faltered. "Nature's forces which, in the often inexplicable course of events, human and other, beat us down, destroy, cause terror, and trammel life without pity. This is what mentally ill people feel; that they are caught up with, torn apart by, subjugated to, and leveled with force beyond their control. Hence "docking" to counter the "fritzkrieg" of social and natural phenomena. Indeed, a counter-fritzkrieg in the undulation of neural toning may be found outside the medicine, medicine that is supposed to make you well but unfortunately often only exacerbates the problem of "being" in this world. There are numerous instances of harbor that I have found, mostly in practical, everyday places such as rest rooms, memories, words, friends, sex, and…" Edward paused… "what I have not been able to possess until now…love. Indeed, the greatest harbor of all, one would think is material, but the fact remains that the immaterial, what one might think of as this unique feeling called love, is perhaps the greatest change and sanctuary which chemical medication cannot bring about.

The drugs speak a different language, their time-zone shifty as a fly having a smashing time at life's window, dopamine vocabulary parachute high, the float-down syllables' ticking slur. Whitewashed, yesterday is a canvas ready for its make-up brush. Did you see it? Did you plan this? Somewhere neural time says don't rush; the world is a flip-flop game of blur. Condensed, the minutes one can almost touch play hopscotch until they explode. You thought you had a key to your pain but are locked out, feel, don't know, know too much, know it all, plummet now, an unchained sun into ocean. Was it that we broke when the world showed us the refined meaninglessness of all jobs? Was it that disbelief became so true that we fell into the city's gears? It is challenging to live in three thoughts at once. A moment cracks and gravity hits the tongue that tries to hold love. And no snow falls softly in heart until it makes pure our words, the cold proof full of multiple meanings, as all crystals are unique in shape: "real acts," "real ax," "relax." The echoes distill themselves…thank goodness hell's on holiday, beats like a dream upon this reality's door."

The audience clapped.

Ed looked out the window, his eyes paused in the sunlight like the place in between the stammer of Mark that gave strange eloquence to the world. He really could not believe everything that had happened since his initial Harbor findings. The privacy of the rest room. The solutions contrary to medicine in docking where no flux could unwind reality. He couldn't quite believe that he had worked with a group of patients against The State as they evolved from minute quirks to host identities, to his office where he counseled them or followed them into the various strata of mental dissolution. Neither could he truly believe that his patients had come up with a solution of voices born from a genetic code mixed with radio transmissions that was beautiful enough to cause him to fall out himself. Was it necessary dissolution? And then all the museums, his chaos in the deluge of ass that had stricken him, his rise from psychotic trauma, and the most recent hallucination that had been "seen" by the authorities.

He paused again and wiped his brow and looked dead on into the industry. The State faces looked back in what seemed a cold distance he could not name. His hand was shaking. He looked into the lobbyist eyes, the drug manufacturers, the program men, the chemical company now looking at him. He looked deeply at these doctors of conscience. What had they been doing this entire time? What were the pills really made of that supposedly corrected innocent men? How far had they gone? He looked down into his sheaf of papers. He hadn't really expected of himself to get the answer right. After all, he was just one man, one man in billions who had been infected with the material. Then, moved by some deep desire to answer the most crucial and fundamental part of the problem he read.

"Behind the cigarette, the simple state spiraling twitchy with reflections of Jews, snake eyes slick amok the diamond of history, the turn now Normandy's, is a sentence... 'My dear invaders, you see I am the news rapt with audience purity, the word soaks in the assault on shoreline, I, as always, roar in laughter at your thought that you will see me through. Nothing sticks to the eyelash of truth, that power will sink to the depths of my root and clear me. I am...after all, the music that everybody fell for.' In the pith of his cocked tongue he feels... 'They say that the Allies will pour through the front lines in sincere form, like Marks in a gypsy's hand, but they cannot pay me to death. I sweat only the multiplicity of bad puns in my writers, bunkered up here like a box from Egypt. Time evens me up with my medicine so I don't lose the whole. My plans (you see it here) sculpt sure the contour of vision. And I am not the absence, but the entirety of time, like brother Rommel in the desert, our footprint of lion, Sphinx-poised, eternal, occult-sweet, reflecting in cross. My cyanide and my Luger, the cocked sure feeling of multiple deaths abstract, I, Goebbels! Architect of the German Uber Stadt! Ever vain of Reich power, exist! Outside the reports are sporadic. My wife sits with her legs spread, picking sex blood from her hair. My gun is precariously balanced in a bible. I remember my vows and infinity blessings. This will not end, I muse, with one war. This the beginning.'"

Edward looked up to the people shifting in their seats. They did not know where he was going. He would read them their mirror, he thought, read them into their own horror.

"Hitler's forty-six offspring do not know who they are. One death nurse for each whelp. They tend the tyrants in forty-six different countries. The nurses are trained to teach each magic trick. The lies are sure to claw open at a certain point and swear down the root of the next century, real as every wonky surreal. Pop! And these worm empty out, like seeds a-fire, meaning a-pulse in slurry death of previous assaults, plumbing memory for the secret loops all powerful with fake architecture. Spool out and within the spawn law absurd! Then, like truth, but not, they take their seats afire with life act of hell. It took Hitler one thousand nights of copulation to get his boys. Goebbels did it in a straight forty-six. Himmler was barren and killed his tricks. Rommel was greedy and had seventy. Himmler struggled with gay issues. But in the end a solid Aryan pack of two hundred and eight demons to continue the race. This means two hundred and eight death nurses, all of which tick hide in the social skin, screwed in for fuck all time with their kid fit to enter institutions for profit. Each would, of course, teach the child occult matters of high Reich way. The boys would think in church of all the good they could do. God will grant us our life!...

as he does always. Then into business and politics. Who would know the cryptic tease in their heads? Mini Fuhrers who would plant every act, their reflective learning of horror... two hundred and eight chances to subvert the major nations! For what? For the black queens. The vision of the future. For death song."

Edward could not help himself. He saw a few people leave. He continued with the assault.

"Hope was the lack of art that was not Hitler's strong point. The Allies have painted the Mulberry Harbors red! Parachuters everywhere, like lemmings. In war silence he gazes upon his stock, the multiple couplings with other women to preserve the race funny, his Uber plan punctured like molar rot. The air in the room is dank. The chocolate lined up for the children. The maps burned. The last Jew ready to prophesy in the fires. 'I feel sad that I will not meet Churchill in the commons, or on the moors with a gun. We could have ended it that way—proper as the decimation of my million souls. I will listen to radio and look at reports. The entire channel full with those pasty white Roast Beef! I am the champion of the new world! My melancholy is poetry! My spirit is the ash of Jew graves! How will I look with a bullet bursting through my temple, blood and bone red splattered into the wall? Beckman beautiful...Picasso smart. I want to be filmed. I want it to last forever on an American reel! Put it in the eyes of all those heathen children! I want it to roast in the frontal lobe of Roosevelt until his wheelchair roll is battery powered. It is silent. The room is perfect. I have gotten a belly from all those nice meats. I am looking in the mirror... All I wanted was to be an artist. Now death, the finest art project of all!...Ja I could have painted the world with my blood.'"

He could not believe himself, the most ultimate delusion pumping through him to the truth. What was the truth? Creativity would, in its struggle for survival, manifest in all shapes and forms, like an animal adapting to a wilderness, no matter the cost.

"I am up the ass of Hitler for a botched job. Always upp the ass of the Fuhrer. It wasn't my fault. We didn't prophesy with the body's right. I told him to read the crows feet we cut up In Mussolini Olive Oil, not blood. I like my soldiers. The tanks are exciting when they explode. Luftwaffe are fantastic for children. When we were shut out by MacArthur I was on the turret looking at the ass of an Egyptian girl. Ja. I could have won. I hated Hitler, his gold horde, the genetic engineering, the way he felt maps, his stoicism, the risk he took going into France. I hated him because when I fucked him upp the ass he extracted my cock and said it was a lizard. We never got on after that. Now in this bunker and my Luger isn't even greased. I'm going out fighting. Blow a hole in my head, ha. I'll run right into this Doughboy fantasy on my ruin. We will bleed together. I, Rommel of the desert, once bitten vamp, Hitler bugger, boy leader. I will suck my final cock and then blast a hole in the Special Forces front man so we go together. It will be like my ejaculation into the cumquat turdhind of Hitler. I will absorb the bullet. It will be in my memory of Poland, the first betrayal in the theater. I will be naked, Teutonic, and real.

Lattarice Aroshel glint lights with the direct mark, pulls into the channel of the General's thought figuring into 'once bitten vamp', and then curls on the curvature of 'Hitler', skipping to 'absorb' and at 'bullet' plunges 'I will' in her turn of storm "In my memory" to steel (in-to 'ki-ss') open 'theater' shifts, flash art I call edge to the throat... 'naked' in the 'Teutonic Real'...slices the chords of breath from his words... I, Lattarice Aroshel of storm, demand your soul! The room quivers and History fixes the depth of the blade in Rommel, forever."

In stride, Edward shivered out the insanity, his voice rising to fine pitch.

"Looking into the twilight, Himmler's cross glints as if a film in tide-pool, where his mind reruns again and again, Jesus-hooked and impossible as escape. He pitches. 'I, hung up in this bunker, the scent of Hitler's tense return, Goering's map sweat, Goebbels' radio to communicate the disaster...sink. I feel like a leaf looping in the air, dizzy as the yessing 'Zero Zoo' infatuation dame school! Turn this around? GI unstrung on beach. I, the essence of a pool. Beautiful, beautiful. The Roast Beef cracking our safe... Will the bullet really be silver? Silver as will really bullets be? Return the times I have communed with vamps, Ja my pulse sweet, blood sucking vamps. A religion of indubitable emptiness. My allegiance to the vein... And nobody will know, my stalking around the Paris palaces in my briefs howling like a wolf. We must play. There is no other way to relieve the stress. All that fighting and then what... who could deny a taste of our occult matters? When the Royal Marines break down the door my candles will be lit, my sacrificed lamb drunk, my Luger barrel hot with my self-made endnote that I have named 'Genie'. Bang! And then what? Do I Believe in God? Really? I have only succumbed to the cock of my Fuhrer. What after? Snake charming? They will put my body in a museum and the children may see my tattoo, 'Skin Flick'. But God...if he does exist, I will kill him and start a franchise in Heaven. Himmler folds his ego and in the crease is surged out of flux by reflection. 'I am...I,' Yet Farina pulses blue in her music, turns him to face and her edge sleek light plunges answer... Whispering deep desert words she settles the edge of Fremen promise in a turn like a tide. Off sung his throat screams silently blue, cutting the dream of war with particular care... Himmler slumps to this absolute truth: justice will answer all horror exact...we are the song of our illness, unbound and pure in our fate."

The literature and delivery were mixing. He looked up and into the eyes of the industry and could see their reflection of his words, could see his words pounding like a heart against their dubious realities. Edward shivered and noticed his voice began to change.

"I used to play a violin but now I play machine gun. What poetry there is in the pen of a bullet! I have lined up the chefs against the stove. The only witness will be the meat. We are negotiating for seconds... How funny it all is...the war...the deaths. If only Churchill knew my most intimate thoughts. He would see me in a pram with a lollipop bomb. I would see his jowls puff smoke from his tobacco chops. We could have been friends, bunkmates and cricket hitters. Now just these destitute cooks...they burned the sausage and overcooked the potatoes. If I am going to go the whole fucking staff will, too. Negotiating for seconds... Ha, the fools! In ten minutes the door will crack. Churchill and I, we could have tossed the rugby ball back and forth. I will tell him how to lay mines with champagne, he would discuss Carthage and Rome. Can a mind summon one's fate? If I imagine Churchill as a cook will I truly kill the Minister? Fucking cooks, they have got ten seconds off me. Churchill in my head like a Shepherd's Pie. I cannot shake him... I am shaking. His cheeks puff one last cloud over me: 'Eichmann, Eichmann! Do you see my field revolver? I am pointing the muzzle at your German Cross. I am a real dream with a bullet! If you think trigger you will click your heels and enter Heaven.' Fuck Churchill. But he's right; the trigger is God, a bi-polar swinging Deity for all. 'Eichmann, did you know that the imagination designs destiny!' God damn you Churchill, I'm going to pop your fat cheeks so your cigar penetrates your brain! 'There you Kraut muttering mad man...look at my thought...' Eichmann drops to the ground, a puppet show bow, crumpled into Winston's idea of lead."

A bit of spittle oozed from Edward's mouth. He sucked it in and continued, eyes wide.

"I am loaded like pistons in the push. Ja... I protect the liberties of the Reich...Ja... free German. Free Uber Stadt. Free Kraut. I am loaded like my cards are loaded: Ace Liquor, fine whisky, cure-all champion champagne to fuck up the ebullience of assault. Stout British Sten to Pop Tart the beef. I am loaded on Gaverte Strategy number Mein Kampf. God damn tippling Luger fuck! I will spill out only most savory bullet throw-up. Swine Roast Beef. Let them come and I will suck back the last bottle of blitz barrel one thousand and two and pop them English with my load. Load? Yes... was ist dis wonder chill of ignorance...? 'I am loaded' Slinkwell a-tunes 'liberties of the Reich' 'Number Mein Kampf' 'savory' 'blitz' 'caves' in 'my massacre' 'buffing the spume' curves deep into the 'fat cow chugger' 'bullet beast', and into the marks, like... 'Howitzer cock'... bursting over the seamen! They will eat my muzzle blaze, bullet beast that she is. I am more loaded than the boats that cave my massacre into zipping cream puff points in my Howitzer cock buffing the spume in squirrels on these heathen. There, I said it. My hand is on the...hiccup...trigger...hiccup...the Blam! Hiccup, God save the Fuhrer. God save the hiccup, blam! Fucking

Doughboy! Bastards. I will stutter their blood across the walls and sing...BLAM!"

Edward realized his hand made the shape of a gun pointing at the audience. He fired indiscriminately

"Ludwig fucking Beethoven...we've got him. Wolfgang fucking Mozart...Wilhelm fucking Richard Wagner... Johann Fucking Bach...Goddamn Friedrich fucking Baumfeld...Jean fucking Berger...Johannes fucking Brahms, and the beginning of the English Language...and still we can't hold a goddamn beachhead! Ah, the turntable of life! Circular geists are storming my signs. The needle is the fog light. Play back the crystal nodes of my dreams. Scratch in the vinyl the sound for the times. I turn and empty. I empty and turn. Surrounded by life! War life!' The needle skips and the gap in the composers opens up the whole....through the mist the note of a blade. Aroshel Lattarice turns on the pitch of her edge. 'Pour oil on all of them Britich Roast Beefs! Grind them into shoreline mud! Bulldoze their history in their eyes with German Uber Stadt!" In the contour of the language Aroshel, figuring, illumines 'pour' and slips into 'shoreline', flutters on 'history in their eyes', and then plunges into 'Stadt'... 'But it is no use my Fuhrer. They have broken the bunker door! They are storming down the hall! You must... escape or die!' Click. Blam! 'Enough with you, servant. This is my glory. I am going to the devil...' Rivulets of voice, Aroshel falls into 'use', interpreting 'broken', turns to 'door', fulfilling 'storming down', curves into 'must'... 'I will sit at my seat with my bible and then, when they turn the knob, I will pull the trigger and blow infamy into their line. Bastard English! They will not trouble my last minute with pansy actions. Let them see my moment as the lofty rampart gaze into their lack. Churning into 'infamy', to 'see my moment', the blade 'lofty' 'into their lack' sings... 'All Royal Marines into my divorce from their clutch-hungry teetotalling hands. There. The Flight of the Valkyries. I will add my crescendo. Less than a minute. Ten, nine, eight, seven...one click! NO! A jammed bullet! The knob! I am fucked!"

When Edward looked up again he knew to whom he was reading, the entire apparatus he had hated for years. The State looked back at him with almost blank stares. He smiled and resumed, wicked feelings surging through body.

"The fog—such a British bard—hugs the coast. Seamen come up the beach in furtive waves. I am looking down the barrel of a Howitzer, my dear, waiting to put a puncture into the prow of the cordite fire-spitting ships. My eye, if you must know, was donated by a black wraith. 'You'll see God more than once a day, Sir!' I, however, cannot see a thing! I will tend to the witchdoctor later for my gaze. In the crack of the bunker, I, Goering. more famous than the Spam advertisements on tongues! If it is the crack of my skull that tends the gun, I will fire it with my neurons and feel the Serotonin elate the harbor. Suddenly shrieking from the air...a new radio instrument to destroy our field? We are nameless the fog holds. Feeling into 'witchdoctor', I 'crack the bunker' slips to 'famous', curl back 'on tongues', deeps into 'skull that tends the gun' 'fire' felt, whips back 'neurons', and dives into 'Serotonin' 'ships' 'my dear' 'waiting' 'my eye' and turns Goering illuminated by a cigarette... A black shadow shrieks in with blade.... 'The harbor' floods, 'suddenly shrieking', opens 'from the air' into 'radio instrument', trues the 'field' and 'we are nameless' in depth. The smile on Goering's neck slits. Blood hot the shrill cry gurgles. But there are always last thoughts for tyrants.... 'All I felt was the curvature of my sex...and then blackness darker than my idea of love.' The pulse in the darkness slumps the body down. The clink of the Iron Cross on cement. Vacant eyes curl back the pitch honesty of fate."

And for the finale, Hitler, who Edward knew was the very node of the problem, most likely gazing back at him in the audience, the very man who had designed the entire system, blitzed from his mouth.

"In a memory loop, Hitler intuits the feel and the shot in his brain matter blitzed red on the wall...watches his thought ricochet back into brain and out the other side...ricochet off his silver coffee cup and back through his eye...off ricochet to his bone and punch in a brilliant splurt ricochet of brain... ricochet off the Luger handle and burst through (of his right ventricle)...ricochet off the hilt of his sword and blow out the cerebral cortex...ricochet sword out and into his German Cross and blow out his right eye...I, Aroshel Lattarice, the 'hilt' and 'bone' of truth my 'cup', at the 'handle' 'burst' out 'into his German Cross' 'horror' 'broken' and 'blitz' 'liver' off the back 'Language Center', 'his right eye' of 'monocle' and 'mirror', his ricochet of 'spirit' un-arted and void, ricochet off the box of maps and ricochet off on through his jaw...ricochet off his molar blow on off life and explode against his sinuses...filling off ricochet out and off the mirror frame and plummet ricochet back through his coccyx...blow out his hip and back ricochet off the pile of pocket change and reenter his ricochet left eyeball...blow out the Language Center and left ricochet off the monocle chain...back into ricochet and through his stomach...tear out the other side and ricochet out off the back of his gilt chair ricochet slam into his liver and bust out his colon...slam! Ricochet off the door handle and blitz in to ricochet his bloody crotch in blood blow...out the tip of his cock his lodge and death bunker of fate, lodge forever eternal, lodge deep in his Language Center splintering out voices...deep. Ah, mein Fuhrer...the horror..."

The audience was dead silent. Edward gazed into the verbal destruction. Then he stuttered, and resumed his crescendo. "I..." he began... "I am not sure really if very many people in this world are in love judging from the way the world works. Indeed, I do not know if there are more people in love than the number of rest rooms in the world to relieve us of our waste. But what we waste is not only valuable time, but ourselves, doing whatever we do, living however we live, thinking however we think, if we do not instantly and vitally recognize, even with all the technically inclined medicines, our natural love."

Edward paused.

"I have failed my paper actually. Failed it for the mere reason that I have looked in all the wrong places. Toilets do not love you. Memories do not love you. Sex will never love you. Museums will not love you. Your patients, if they love you, must only tell you that you are ill by analysis that sits coldly across from them with all the psychological intention of a piece of ice. Money will not love you. Big ornate skyscrapers will not love you. The game will not love you. Cash will not love you. Your car will not love you. Sleep will not love you. Exercise will not love you. Your lawyer will not love you. The president will not love you. And...drugs will not love you." Edward paused and then resumed. "Can we love ourselves with synthetic medicines, on chemicals so strong our fortitude is compromised by the mere act of our bodies fighting not the disease but the remedy? I am on some kick-ass meds now and I have not been in love for over ten years. I am forty years old. I am tired. I am strung out. I am lost. I am incapable of saying to someone the right words to have them understand that I want to love them. I am delivering this paper pretty much because I hate you all. And in the medical transformation of my self I am successful in this in the synthetic sense. But I do not love. And this, ladies and gentlemen, is what I found in my Harbor Document. I am not, as probably you are not, in love with this world, with myself, with all the problems, with the shit that keeps ruining the higher values of life. I am only in hate with The State. I am not in love with it because it is all fake. It is all a bunch of lies. It is all made up of phony men in offices who have lost themselves so they make everything wrong for every body else. I am, indeed, only in quiet hate with it, and this, friends, is the thing that I love. That I can hate a system that is wrong and know, simply, despite all this shit, that my hate is right."

Edward looked at the audience and then left the stage. No person clapped. The silence was deafening. He went back into the lounge with a feeling inside that was closer to love than he had ever been. Holding his bunch of papers he sighed. He had read his Harbor Paper with complete disdain, like some discarded understanding that even if you do all these things you still won't get it right if you do not love. He closed his eyes.

I have poured jazz on the air and it is playing a record round like orbits, is suckling a mute to the nothing here, is liking the lick of its honey ripe, is I mean pouring like water jaunts, is getting the room going to know, it is giving itself up as if fruit, is peeling off the back of the sky, is you should really hear when it is slipping the nonchalant move of a day, is laughing in a way you can never laugh, is one universe spinning out of some brass, is a tempt of truth that shucks its truth so you are a Peterman with hands on the pith of how music could "sweet the sky tender", is a place to live in when you've got none, is the booming now tempered to a ride of steel on a tongue that wants to sing, is reincarnation just after the big bang, is our hope slinking in my cat.

Edward sighed and rose from the table. He walked to the phone. In his mind E.L. had stolen him from himself, Frank had rewritten his reality, Cherry had stopped the courts where reason was so impossibly displayed, Mark shivered in his stutter like a madman making music riff the right way, and, coming up to the phone, the psych ward's number in his hand. There was one thing that he had forgotten. What was this one thing? He pressed the numbers with a hand that did not shake and then waited.

STATE PSYCHIATRY BOARD

The door slid open with a crisp electronic lisp. Edward walked in. The overhead fan rocked slowly above a spartan room. He could make out in the phosphorescent light three figures sitting behind a committee table. The only visible object upon the table were monitors that he presumed were for sentient array scans. Some office cabinets lined the wall.

"Please be seated, Dr. Wells."

The ambient light changed in the room from dim to clear. Edward made out the faces of three people, one of whom he recognized was Mrs. Falk. She motioned him to sit in the swivel chair in front of the table.

"You know why you are here," Mrs. Falk said.

"Yes."

Edward felt a lightness in his stomach and head unlike the last times.

Mrs. Falk looked at a dossier and then slapped it closed. She was an efficient creature, like an ant. He watched her face and saw through her to a little girl. It was perhaps like one of his patients' hallucinations. The girl was a prodigy, smart, ruled by etiquette, lonely, vengeful, and sad. He looked at her jaw twitch and in the twitch he saw a billion highly calculated decisions, some perfect, some faulty, but meticulously careful about her reality. She blinked her eyes once as if she was a camera taking a picture of him. He wondered what she saw in that picture. He wondered if the lens was moved by a neural message that was in some other world where only mechanistic structures live.

"Your case has been reviewed." She leaned back in her chair. Her hands fidgeted with a Mont Blanc. "You will be going to the Marx Asylum in California. You will be interned there for a review of one year...and seeing how the review goes you will either be given social care or," she paused and the pen fell onto the table, "or you shall remain there as a patient until you are professionally fit to leave."

Edward felt the lightness of his body lifting above her to a great height. He could see the circuitry of wires in her head like some nest made by a crow, dark and brooding and distant and sad, and so smart she chose her own death rather than live.

"But we want to know some things first." She turned to her cohorts sitting next to her. One man brought his hands up upon the table.

"We want to know for the record what made you go over the edge." He paused as if concerned. "We want to know how you have come to this position today." He smiled and then sat back in his reclining chair.

Edward observed the man from a great distance. He thought to himself that insanity has no great distance. Insanity is up close and fractured and shifty and without objectivity. He saw the man as what he thought the man was. A button pushing, anal retentive, fearful, bureaucratic, boss pleasing synthetic loving emptiness.

"You want to know what I did to go over the edge?"

Edward felt himself as if he was an animal, deep and running in some great field. He felt the strength of his muscles, the fresh air of a hunt, the vitality of life and death and the truth of his soul. "You want to know my feelings?"

The man leaned forward. "Ah, yes. Your feelings...what were your feelings, let's start there."

Edward smiled. He had done what he wanted to do. The committee had not. The committee had done what The State told them to do. Edward swiveled back in his chair. "I'll tell you everything," he said, "every damn thing..."

"Good," said the man in a syrupy voice.

Mrs. Falk nodded and the other man shifted in his seat.

"I, as experimental status C3 psychiatrist, under the authority vested in me by the State Psychological Board did three things."

The room was silent.

"I let my patients act freely. I discovered how to love. And I discovered the truth."

Edward gazed at the psych aficionados. He watched them try in their minds to fit some puzzle together like in the tests. He watched them attempt to grasp emotion that they did not have. He could perceive that they did not know what he was about to unleash upon them.

"Good," said the man.

Mrs. Falk interrupted. "We know you let your patients act freely, we know that you broke regulations, we know that you robbed a bank for what you called 'natal charity', we know that your experimental chit was picked up with so much hate in it that you could very well be a hotspot in a war. We know all of this. We know that you encouraged your patients to hallucinate at will under placebo anywhere authority seemed to be watching. We know that you blatantly snubbed our warnings and our care to keep you on the reservation. We know, indeed, how you sleep at night, what you eat, who you talk to, where you go for privacy in that imbecilic bathroom, we know that you are a hallucinatory wreck when it comes to medicine, and we know your vital signs going into the bank." Mrs. Falk's authority had made her flustered. It was as if she wanted to be Edward, switch personalities and adopt his sense of liberation. She clawed with her black nails upon his dossier.

"What we don't know is how you found love." She stopped and smoothed her skirt out. She was trying to control her voice. "We don't know how you found love or what you think the truth is. Could you please tell us what these two findings are before you are taken away?" Her lips pursed up in haughty and even jealous curiosity.

Edward looked right through her and into the unfeeling core of her soul. She had never really found love herself. She probably didn't even know what the truth was about anything outside of her curt design of behavioral science. He could see in her a writhing worm that someone had spilt salt on, writhing in its segments upon hot cement in a merciless hot sun.

"I found love by trust, Gloria," Edward said....Mrs. Falk's eyes squinted..."and after I found trust and love, I found truth."

The room was splittingly silent. All three leaned in on the desk to hear.

"What is the truth, Gloria?" said Edward. He watched her comb back her black bob into a pony tale and put it up in a band. He could see her fingers trying to control her body.

Edward smiled. They had missed this part of the Empathy Exam, missed in the reports, the surveillance, the sensory security, the engineering, the tests, the behavioral analysis. Missed the reality completely.

He waited until a minute had passed, looked up at the fan and then leveled his gaze upon the three. "The truth is, Gloria, that you are using other human emotion to discern reality, the same way you were enhanced by Dr. Bessingham."

Gloria's eyes slit. "What do you mean?"

"I mean you are taking, illegally, human emotion to make crucial decisions about the state of your subjects and of The State itself."

Both men looked quickly at Mrs. Falk. She paused in mid

space and then settled.

"We are not on any emotional residue, we could not run The State fairly if we were on the Library Archives."

"I see," said Edward. "Well my friend has a check with the signature of the Head of State for Human Affairs, one Dr. Bessingham, who you committed adultery with, in the amount of some ten million dollars for an assortment, a Circuitry Pack of emotions from every high grade source available to man."

Gloria looked at him coldly. "This is outrageous! None of our committee is on any emotional library selections. Dr. Bessingham was a friend." Her eyes were wide.

"Well I've got a check with one signature the same as your Dr. Bessingham in my possession. And not only that, I just happen to know a person who writes your exams who says you are addicts, addicts of love, hate, disgust, fear, anger, happiness, joy..." Edward paused, "do you even know what the truth is? Your own truth?"

Gloria turned to the men. "Close it up," she said. "Close this down!"

Edward pulled a cassette out of his pocket. He pushed the stop button. Gloria looked at it startled.

"You're on tape here, Gloria, for lying while on high grade truth, purity, happiness and whatever else. I've got a check that is so hard copy a judge would have a difficult time proving its falsity, and a man by the name of Jeremy Smith, an exam creator, has informed me that a majority of your medicines are chemically negligent. Can you imagine, Gloria, what would happen if The State discovered its Empathy Exams to be fake? Do you know what would happen to your entire C1 programming if the hallucinations were actually real? Every hallucination a false face lift?" Edward turned in his chair.

Gloria gazed on him with searing eyes.

"Now what are you going to do, Gloria? Are you going to put me in the funny farm with your other reject studies or are you going to let me finish my experiments."

"What other experiments could you possibly have going?" said Gloria. Her face had turned pale.

Edward looked long and hard at her. He could see her crawling up from some dark place to try and breath fresh air, choking on her confusion like someone who has been under water for too long. He could see her in some backroom sucking like a vampire the truth and happiness of the world she needed to properly track her psych cases. He could see her in her used emotional state spinning in hate, fear, disgust, and tints of joy and love trying to understand the human states of trust and truth.

"Freedom, Gloria, is an experiment. I'll take that for starters and then I'll see you in court for substance abuse, adultery, and misuse of other people's emotions while lying in a committee board session." He took one last look of her pathetic form sitting like a china doll in her dead space. And then Edward rose and turned and walked out and into the lobby where he sat down and wiped his brow and picked up the phone.

At that moment the door down the hall opened. When he looked up he saw a woman. The woman looked at him and he at her. The sudden feeling inside him communicated his gaze into him, deep and direct as if he were the feeling of this view. There, before him, was Cleo with a young child. Cleo looked at him and smiled. He dropped the phone. His heart beat quickly as he rose.

"I am not sure if I am seeing correctly," he said,

"Nice job, Ed," Cleo said.

He gazed at her as if all the gravity were raining on him nothing. In his mind he could feel only one word. Love. Indubitable love beating effusively from his heart.

Edward dropped his papers on the ground and reached out a hand with a quarter in it. Cleo opened her hand. He looked at it as if in another time and remembered Jack's words, "Love can you come and pick me up." He paused, waiting for the communication from a phone that went everywhere save for into himself, his hand open, the silver circle glistening in the fake light of the room.

"Here," Cleo said, taking from her purse a CD that glistened in its plastic form in her hand.

"What is it?" Edward asked.

"Frank's, it's Frank's earliest steal."

"From the Operation A Program?" Edward said in utter disbelief.

"Yes. It is Wagner's *Die Walküre*. He told me to give it to you, said you would know what it meant."

Edward took the CD in his hand. It felt like some sliver of very light light. "Impossible...that was a hallucination," he said. Then he recalled what Jeremy Smith had told him. The medicinal changes at a minute level to offset the whole program. "So it is real? It has been real this whole time?"

"Yes," said Cleo.

A mammoth shiver coursed through his body and everything suddenly crashed in him into an echo.

"After I ran to Sergeant Aremac and assessed the wound, I did not witness the woman. All I could see was Sergeant Aremac who, in the moments in which I administered CPR, was failing to breathe. I continued administering CPR until Sergeant Aremac's pulse stopped. I looked at his closed eyes. He was my partner. He was...When I looked up nobody was in Borders. When I looked for the woman downstairs all I saw was the Thirty-Eight, which was Sergeant Aremac's weapon. When I realized that Sergeant Aremac was dead and there was nothing else I could do I walked outside with the weapons you now see before you. As you can see, all the weapons have been discharged. This is all I know."

AUG 15

Patrick Denton Mackay is the author of eleven volumes of poetry, two novels, and three CDs of spoken word. His work has been published in numerous magazines in the United States, and in *Ambit* in The United Kingdom. He has also published book reviews and articles in *Rattle E Reviews*, and in the *Santa Barbara News Press*. Recently, Mackay won Honorable Mention in the New Fiction Contest in *Glimmer Train*, and was chosen "Best of the Decade" in *The Hawaii Pacific Review*. Please reference, under his name, Amazon Books for titles.